# THE MISOGYNIST

**PIERS PAUL READ** was born in Buckinghamshire and studied History at Cambridge University. His books include the novel *Monk Dawson*, for which he won a Hawthornden Prize and a Somerset Maugham Award, and *A Married Man* which was dramatised for television in 1984 with Anthony Hopkins in the title role. A work of non-fiction, *Alive: The Story of the Andes Survivors*, documented the story of the 1972 crash of Uruguayan Air Force Flight 571 and was adapted into the 1993 film *Alive*. In 1988 he was awarded a James Tait Black Memorial Prize for his novel, *A Season in the West*. Piers Paul Read lives in London.

# THE MISOGYNIST

## PIERS PAUL READ

BLOOMSBURY

LONDON · BERLIN · NEW YORK · SYDNEY

First published in Great Britain 2010
This paperback edition published 2011

Bloomsbury Publishing Plc
36 Soho Square
London W1D 3QY

www.bloomsbury.com

Bloomsbury Publishing, London, New York, Berlin and Sydney

A CIP catalogue record for this book is available from the British Library

ISBN 978 1 4088 0989 1

10 9 8 7 6 5 4 3 2 1

Typeset by Hewer Text UK Ltd, Edinburgh
Printed in Great Britain by Clays Ltd, St Ives plc

# PART ONE

# I

JOMIER BROODS. HE broods about the present. He broods about the past. He types his gloomy thoughts on to his computer screen – a digital journal. At one time his journal was handwritten in notebooks with canvas covers. Now, when he has nothing more to say about the present, he returns to the past, copying the entries from the old notebooks on to the hard disk of his computer. There remain ten years still to go but one day the transcribed entries will link up with the new digital entries and his entire life will be contained in a single document. It will join digital inventories of his letters, books, CDs, DVDs, furniture and *objets d'art*. Everything there is to know about Jomier will be contained on a single CD, or a memory stick the size of his thumb.

Jomier does not envisage publication, despite the felicitous alliteration in the title: *The Journals of Geoffrey Jomier*. The project is to fill the empty days of his retirement; to create order out of disorder; and perhaps reach some understanding about what went wrong. Were his journals to be published, others might benefit from his experience and avoid making the same mistakes; but Jomier does not care enough about others to expose himself in print. To risk rejection. To admit to the banality of taking up writing in retirement. Jomier has half a dozen friends who are writing books. It is a rite of passage for men of his age. But no one wants to publish books by old men because no one wants to read them. Not, at any rate, if they are white and middle class and live in London. They want books by Asians and Africans. Or by women. By women, for women. Chick lit. Aga sagas. Women are inexhaustibly interested in themselves. Men are more wary of letting an author into their head.

There is an article in the morning paper: 'When Can Grown Men Cry?' It is by a woman, in the section that caters for women. Jomier does not read it but thinks back to the three occasions when he has wept as a grown man – his father's death, his mother's death, and when he discovered that Tilly was sleeping with Max. He sometimes rereads the entries in his journal that describe these events. Or he goes back further in his life to read the letters that Tilly wrote when she loved him. After the divorce, when she no longer loved him, they would communicate by fax. The faxes are in the box with the letters, but have faded into blank yellow scrolls. This will not affect the integrity of Jomier's archive: the faxes are mostly matter-of-fact statements about the comings and goings of the children which are recorded in his appointment diaries. Jomier has kept all his appointment diaries as well as his letters, journals and printouts of significant emails. They are in an Office World cardboard box.

In other Office World boxes are the letters from other women whom Jomier has loved or thought that he loved; women who loved him or thought they loved him. Or pretended they loved him. Jomier remains tormented by the idea of love. He still yearns to love and be loved by a woman and despises himself for this yearning. Why will not his psyche face the facts? *Si jeunesse savait, si vieillesse pouvait*. Every morning mocking emails break through his spam filter on to the screen of his computer to offer drugs that will restore his potency, enlarge his penis, drive women wild. Why him? How do they know? Was his penis too small – too short or too thin? Was that what Max had over him? He had asked Tilly. A bigger penis? A better technique? A more mature ejaculation? She would not answer. '*C'est privé.*' She was English and so talked about sex in French. *Frottage. Soixante-neuf. Ooh la la!*

When Jomier was young, in the years between the loss of his virginity and going steady with Tilly, he would attempt to have sex with any girl he fancied. It was less easy then than it is now. Girls were afraid they would get pregnant. The pill had been invented but doctors would not prescribe it for unmarried women. Married women could get Dutch caps and IUDs – intrauterine devices – from their doctors. French letters could be bought from seedy barbers' shops but Jomier, like most of his friends, was too embarrassed to ask. It was up to the girl to take precautions. And there was abortion – illegal, but discreetly available for those who could pay.

Trawling through his archive, Jomier compiles a list of women he has desired, women he has propositioned, and women with whom he went to bed. He calculates that around 63 per cent of the women he propositioned said yes and 37 per cent said no. But these statistics are misleading. Eighty per cent of the 63 per cent who said yes did so either before he was married or after he had divorced. After his divorce, his success rate was high but the sample was small. The second largest category consists of those women whom he fancied while he was married but did not proposition.

Because he was married. Or because they were married. He would like to have slept with them, and perhaps they would liked to have slept with him, but neither wanted to jeopardise their own or the other's marriage. And the unmarried women on the whole did not want to waste emotional resources on a man who clearly would never leave his wife.

It has also to be said – by Jomier, as he studies his list – that there is no one whom he wishes he was married to now. This is why Jomier is so exasperated by his yearning for a woman's love. It is generic. Invariably the specific disappoints. From behind, in the street, a tall swaying figure, long fair hair – the promise of love. He walks past and looks back. A face. Dull, arrogant, stupid, common, vain. The face of a person. Jomier is not looking for another person. Persons have moods, needs, appetites, aspirations, irritating habits. Jomier's ideal is blank beauty – eyes, nose, mouth, ears, chin that express no personality; no character; no thoughts or feelings. Such women do exist – models on billboards or actresses on the screen. Other men search for women without qualities. Jomier is not alone.

Every now and then, Jomier sees such a blank beauty in the street. She scowls. Women take great trouble to be noticed. They think about eyeshadow and shampoo and tights and skirts and tops. But they want to be noticed only by good-looking young men. Or by other women. They are angry if these fail to notice them, but they are also angry if they are noticed by older men. Men like Jomier. Hence the scowl. Pretty girls – the blank beauties – scowl because they are so often noticed by the wrong people. Jomier can read the thought behind the scowl. 'Fuck off!' 'Leave me alone!' 'Piss off, grandad!' Jomier accepts that his glance is, in a sense, an invasion of privacy. Professors at American colleges are told not to make eye contact with their students. Seminarians are taught 'custody of the eyes'. Jomier is not a seminarian or an American professor, so he looks, admires and suffers to think that he will never hold that girl in his arms.

These anguished passions are less frequent now than they were before. This is not because Jomier is older and wiser but because he has moved from Kensington to Hammersmith, a borough where there are fewer attractive women. Jomier ascribes this to natural selection. Rich and successful men live in Kensington and they choose beautiful women as their brides. Pretty girls know this. They flock to London to find rich husbands. It used to be said that the most beautiful women in England lived in Nottingham. No longer. The pretty girls from Nottingham have gone to London to work in the City. They are there to attract and breed with young bankers or hedge-funders. Their plain sisters remain behind in Nottingham, or Manchester or Stoke. Or they are already in London but live outside the pale, south of the river or, like Jomier, west of Shepherd's Bush, that bucolically named transport hub with its litter-strewn triangle of tired grass and queues of *misérables* waiting for buses – asylum seekers from the White City estates, schizophrenics from the halfway houses, the homeless from the bed and breakfast hotels, the long-term unemployed, the chronically sick, the clinically depressed, wearing dirty jeans and synthetic anoraks or hooded tracksuit tops, eking out their disability benefit or jobseeker's allowance, living off TFC chicken ('Tantalising Fried Chicken') or doner kebabs – dour, defeated, a few white – some Poles and Slovaks and Lithuanians here to make a quick buck before they retire to a wooden chalet on the Masurian Lakes – but mostly black – Ethiopians, Nigerians, Zimbabweans, Somalis, Egyptians, the detritus from the blighted continent of Africa who will never go home.

Jomier studies them from the top of the 94 bus. They file into the Shepherd's Bush market to buy mangos and bananas. Arabs sell falafels, Parsees kebabs, from plywood stalls. The shops on the north side of Shepherd's Bush Green could be in Delhi or Accra. Who needs to travel to the Third World when it is here in London – the Bangladeshis in Brick Lane, the sheikhs in Mayfair, the Turks in Haringey, Hasidic Jews in Tottenham, and a mix-and-match here in Hammersmith, fifty different nationalities milling around in the street with no apparent purpose? Fire practice at the Tower of Babel!

Jomier's eye on the upper deck of the 94 bus is on the level of the windows above the shops. Plants grow in rotting sills and clogged gutters. He can alight here to go underground to catch a Central Line train but prefers to stay on the bus for another three stops to the station at Holland Park. He passes from the Third World into the First. On Holland Park Avenue, a butcher's shop displays its cuts like jewellery in the window of Cartier's; a French patisserie glitters with Tiffany-like confections; a bookshop offers novels up for literary prizes; a brightly lit chemist's sells expensive elixirs for eternal youth; and there is a coffee shop where long-legged young women in designer jeans and preppy young men in chinos sit reading the *Herald Tribune* or *Prospect* or *Foreign Affairs*.

Jomier alights at Holland Park Tube station. There is a risk that in the lift going down to the Central Line Jomier will meet a former neighbour and have to make cheery conversation. At one time he might have run into Tilly or the children. Not now. Tilly lives with Max on the other side of Campden Hill. The children are grown up and gone. And Tilly never takes public transport. She either drives herself in her Prius or summons a minicab from Addison Lee.

*       *       *

Jomier moved to Hammersmith after his divorce. And because of his divorce. It was a 'no-fault' divorce. The Family Court had no interest whatsoever in adultery, the breaking of vows. It required only for one party, Tilly, to decide that the marriage had 'irretrievably broken down'. The vehicle was a write-off. It could be disposed of as scrap. The function of the Family Court was not to dispense justice but ensure the well-being of the children. The mother was their default carer; the father the default provider. The children's way of life and standard of living must change as little as possible. The Family Court ruled that the house in Blenheim Crescent should be sold and the proceeds divided – one-third to Jomier, two-thirds to Tilly. Jomier was to continue to pay the mortgage on Tilly's new house on Princedale Road and a monthly sum for each child until they reached the age of eighteen. His disposable income was suddenly a quarter of what it had been before.

Jomier's one-third share of the proceeds of the sale of his house in Notting Hill has enabled him to buy a terraced cottage in one of the streets between the Goldhawk and Uxbridge Roads west of Shepherd's Bush. It had been built for a Victorian artisan. There is the usual double room on the ground floor running from front to back, and a small kitchen on the extension built into the garden. There are three bedrooms. The first has a wide bed; the second two bunk beds in which the children slept when they came to stay. Now they are too old for the bunk beds and they never come to stay. They have their own houses and, even when young, they preferred the comfort of their mother's home in Kensington. Jomier knows that he should get rid of the bunk beds but does not.

The third bedroom is Jomier's study, with his desk, his filing cabinets, his reference books, his computer. Jomier's study is very tidy: everything has its place. So too the living room where the books and CDs are arranged neatly on shelves. Jomier has a Brazilian cleaner but she has little to do but wash and iron his clothes. The house is spick and span. So too the garden. No weed survives for more than a day after rising from the earth towards the sun. A leaf from his apple tree no sooner falls to the ground than it is put in a bag made of white flimsy biodegradable plastic stamped with the logo of the Hammersmith & Fulham Council. There are also orange bags for paper, plastic, bottles and tins – detritus that can be recycled – and black bags for real rubbish – vegetable peelings, broken light bulbs, soiled tissues, fish-skins. Jomier has his doubts about whether the contents of the orange bags are really recycled; he has been told that the black, orange and white bags all end up in the same landfill, or are dropped into the North Sea from the same barge. Even if this were proved to be true, Jomier would still sift and sort his rubbish. It satisfies his love of order. It gives him something to do.

Much that goes into the orange bag is junk mail. Among the cards from minicab companies and flyers from take-away Indian restaurants, there are thick glossy magazines with page upon page advertising houses for sale. Jomier's spirits rise when he sees a house similar to his offered for sale at twice the sum he paid for it; but they sink when he sees that houses in Notting Hill comparable to the one he lived in with Tilly going for ten times more. If they had remained married, Jomier would be a property millionaire.

Tilly is now married to Max and lives with him in a large house on Phillimore Gardens. Max's first wife, Jane, has returned to live in New York with her two children,

Hayden and Chuck. The house on Princedale Road that Tilly bought after the divorce is let to an American banker. The rent is her pin money. Or perhaps she is building up a fund – a safety net – in case she and Max split up. Or perhaps she plans to use it to pay her grandchildren's school fees. Jomier does not know about Tilly's finances. She and Max live in a different world. The disposable income of Tilly's Filipina housekeeper is larger than Jomier's. When they were married Tilly showed no interest in where money came from or where it went. She always assumed it would be there. She took it for granted that providence would provide her with the means to lead the English upper-middle-class life to which she was accustomed. Jomier succeeded Tilly's father as the agent of providence and whenever he failed to provide she became annoyed. She was not extravagant. She was not frugal. She spent money reasonably and thought it unreasonable if Jomier complained that she spent too much. The early years of their married life were punctuated by quarrels about money.

The divorce made her astute. At the time there was no talk of her marrying Max. Max had a wife already – Jane. Jane was American and was also rich. As rich as Max. During the bust-up, Jomier used to meet Jane for lunch to talk about Max and Tilly. At first Jomier looked forward to these lunches: there was much to discuss. Jomier was obsessed with his suffering. He was an Ancient Mariner. His friends had grown bored. Jane was an interested party. And then Jane too grew bored. Or perhaps she had never been particularly interested in what had gone wrong. Jane had always been hard to read. All those holidays they had taken *à quatre*; the trips to the movies; the dinners in one another's houses; the weekends in the country; the children's birthdays.

Why had they become friends? What was the trade? For Max and Jane, recently relocated from New York, the Jomiers were a couple who knew the ropes in London – who could advise them on where to buy a house, where to shop, where to eat out, where to send their children to school. For Jomier and Tilly, the Stutzels brought a touch of cosmopolitan glamour into their life: Max, a child of globalisation – a home on the shores of Lac Léman, the International School in Geneva, a degree in Economics from Stanford University, an MBA from Harvard Business School; Jane, a stylish East Coast Wasp, raised in Connecticut, a family house on Cape Cod. She was out of an ad in the *New Yorker* – clipped, slim, casually elegant – a little too tall, perhaps, so those of median height saw more of her nostrils than her nose. She had a degree in English Literature from Radcliffe but, for reasons no doubt rooted in her childhood, lacked confidence in her own opinions. She deferred to Max on the big issues, and relied on Tilly to teach her the subtleties of British upper-middle-class life – to steer her away from the crude esteem for titles and landed estates that is sometimes found in expatriate Americans; to interpret English irony and self-deprecation; to distinguish between the culture of north and west London, and warn her – in the nick of time – against living in Islington. Tilly helped Jane find a house in Kensington and pulled a few strings to get Chuck and Hayden into Norland Place.

The vexed question of what to do with young children at weekends in London brought the Jomiers and the Stutzels together. They would have Sunday lunch in one another's houses, then take the children to the playground in Kensington Gardens or Holland Park. Or they would go to Ladbroke Square Gardens: Tilly had a key and was a member of the tennis club – both privileges that money could not buy. In summer they would have picnics on the large lawns behind the high railings that kept poor people out, and Max and Tilly would play singles at tennis while Jomier and Jane stayed with the children.

Sometimes, if there was a third party to watch the children, they would play doubles. Jomier disliked ball games and had to be cajoled on to the court to partner Jane. Max was a better player than Jomier. Tilly was a better player than Jane. The balance made for uncertain outcomes when the Jomiers played the Stutzels which in one sense was welcome; but Jomier felt unmanned by his dependence upon Tilly to take the points. Max was competitive: a triumphant gleam came into his eye when he thwacked the tennis ball at Jomier. Jomier understood that testosterone-fuelled competitiveness was a necessary quality for a successful banker, but he did not see why a languid barrister should have to play the same game.

Off the court, Jomier did better: he was a trained advocate and felt he had as good a mind and a wider experience of life than the focused, driven Max. The focused can be blinkered: the driven look neither to left nor right. Jomier enjoyed arguing, and Max could never get the better of him in an argument about this or that; but sometimes, when Jomier's polemic was at its peak and victory seemed certain, Max would turn to Tilly, saying: 'What do you think?' Max knew quite well that Tilly had no opinion at all on the Israeli incursions into Southern Lebanon or the kidnapping of Aldo Moro; but by putting the question to Tilly he managed to suggest that the British habit of excluding women from discussions on serious matters was at best backward, at worst impolite. Jomier was denied his triumph. Game, set and match to Max.

\*     \*     \*

Or did Max put the question to flatter Tilly? Was she already in his sights? Was his Cary Grant charm a form of flirtation? Had he been coming on to Tilly from the start? It had not occurred to Jomier that Tilly might be attracted to Max because he was not attracted to Jane. While Max and Tilly had giggled in a cloud of pheromones on the facing banquette in a restaurant – or at a Cycladic beach bar, or the loggia of an Italian villa – Jomier and Jane had remained antiseptically friendly and polite. Jane exuded no pheromones when he was with her. Or, he now suspected, when she was with anyone else. Was it a gene she had inherited from Puritan ancestors, or another unresolved complex from her childhood? She was neat and dry with skinny legs and puny breasts. Clearly, she had had sex with Max, but did she enjoy it? Too messy? Too untidy? Too uncontrolled? She would never have admitted, even to herself, that she did not like sex – a heresy since the 1960s – and no doubt there were mini orgasms, little hiccups, little yelps – well down on the Richter scale from Tilly's cries and groans and seismic buckling.

For how long had Jane known about Max's affair with Tilly? Had she turned a blind eye because she was happy to get him off her back? Or off her front? His face out of her pudendum? His cock out of her mouth? Like Jomier and Tilly, Max and Jane had no doubt followed all the recipes in *The Joy of Sex*. Jomier, having raised in his own mind an image of Max making love with Jane, could not prevent himself imagining Max making love to Tilly – his face in *her* pudendum, his cock in *her* mouth. A day does not pass without Jomier seeing in his mind's eye Tilly and Max in the Strand Palace Hotel; and, when Jane was away and the Filipina off-duty, on the sofa in the children's nursery chez Max. Jane had no such visions. She had no imagination.

It became clear, during those lunches, that she could live with the cheating but dreaded the untidiness of a divorce. If Max had gone on fucking Tilly discreetly, would she have let it run ad infinitum? Jomier had put it to her. She had been evasive. Had she known? She had had her suspicions. Had she said anything to Max? No. Why hadn't she told Jomier? He would have made a fuss.

A second hypothesis – a variation on the first. Jane was aware of her frigidity and felt that she owed it to Max to let him have sex with Tilly. Max was a Swiss-Prussian *Übermensch* on his father's side of the family, but with swarthy, hairy, hot-blooded genes from his mother's Lebanese grandmother and Alexandrian Greek grandfather. Max made no secret of his strong appetites. He drooled openly at girls with big busts. 'Nice cantaloupes.' It was a running joke that Jomier had never found amusing. Tilly had told Jomier that he was a prude.

Tilly had large breasts. She was sweet and juicy like a cantaloupe melon. Jomier thought that he had always shown a due appreciation of her sexiness but not, perhaps, the enthusiasm shown by Max. He was, perhaps, a prude. He felt, like Montaigne, that a woman should discard modesty when she took off her clothes and resume it when she put them on again. Tilly thought so too. They had that in common. She did not like to talk openly about sex. Even in French. Yet she laughed at Max's lubricious jokes. She loved his immodesty. His lack of inhibitions. Clearly she had longed to shed her inhibitions, discard her modesty, take off her clothes.

Edmond de Goncourt: 'the duplicity of woman's soul, of her prodigious gift, her consummate genius for mendacity'. On the death of his beloved housekeeper, Edmond

15

had discovered that she had been stealing his money. What had Tilly stolen from Jomier? His home. His family. Much of his money. And trust. More than trust: confidence in perception. Tilly had never stopped sleeping with Jomier even when, as Jomier later discovered, she was sleeping with Max. She had never pretended to have headaches or stomach aches and only occasionally said that she was not in the mood. She never suggested sex. But she never declined. She complied. Submitted. Acquiesced. Why not? Jomier had assumed that this was the way she was. Jomier had done his best to make sure that she enjoyed it. He had studied the recipes in *The Joy of Sex*. Now Jomier spends hours, days, months looking back over his diaries, rereading letters, emails, faded faxes, looking for clues that should have told him when Tilly had started sleeping with Max. There are none. There is no entry that notes an expression of dissatisfaction or a change of behaviour, in or out of bed. A genius for mendacity. She should have been a spy. Jomier feels particularly foolish because as a barrister he thought he could judge whether or not a witness was telling the truth. But Tilly was never a witness; nor was she the accused. In the early days of their marriage, Jomier had occasionally complained when she flirted with other men. She had smiled. A Desdemona. His jealousy was absurd.

The self-fulfilling prophecy? Had his jealousy driven her into the arms of Max? Given her the idea? Made her suspect that *he* was unfaithful? Which he was, once. A pupil at his chambers. Sandra. Twenty-five years old. Flawless teeth, clear eyes, silken skin, glossy hair. Bright. Determined to learn. About the law. About life. A weekend at a country-house hotel — supposedly a seminar on racial awareness for would-be judges — gluttonous dinners, a glossy body, dyspeptic sex, faked affection, alien odours, insomnia;

dull walks in national parks and visits to National Trust gardens; more gluttony, more force-fed textbook sex; the drive back to London; silence; insincere farewell kisses; lying joy; never again. Then home. 'How was it?' 'Terrible. Political correctness gone mad . . .' Deceit. Guilt. Pretence. A role that men play so badly and women so well.

## 2

JOMIER HAS TWO children. A son and a daughter. Jomier's son Henry is now thirty-seven. He works in the City and by Jomier's standards is a rich man. Henry does not think he is rich because so many of his friends are richer still. Henry pays interest on a mortgage of half a million pounds. This represents 70 per cent of the value of the purchase price of his house in Queen's Park. The house is now worth twice the amount he paid for it but this brings little comfort to Henry whose friends' houses in Notting Hill have tripled, even quadrupled in value. Henry is a partner in an investment bank. He hopes one day to earn enough money to buy a house in Notting Hill. And a cottage in Dorset. But he must also pay the salary of a nanny and fees at private schools. Jomier fears that the high-flying Henry may, like his father and grandfather before him, never quite reach the sun. The Jomier gene: mediocrity triggered in middle age.

Henry's wife is called Sandra. This embarrasses Jomier because it reminds him of the other Sandra who in most ways is identical to the Sandra who is married to his son. She is a corporate lawyer and goes off to an office in Holborn every morning, catching a Bakerloo Line train at Queen's Park. Their two children are left in the charge of Tracey, the

Australian nanny, and Alena, the Slovakian au pair. Jomier's five-year-old granddaughter Samantha speaks English with a bizarre accent — half Danube basin, half Great Barrier Reef.

Henry Jomier is a good son. He treats his father politely but thinks he is a loser. Henry has friends whose fathers are also barristers but all are either High Court judges or QCs. Jomier applied three times to the Lord Chancellor's Office to be made a QC and all three of his applications were rejected. Henry tells his father that if he had been black or Asian or female his application would have succeeded. Yet Henry's friends' fathers who are High Court judges or QCs are not black or Asian or female but plummy members of the English upper class. What Henry means is that if Jomier had been black or Asian or female his mediocrity might have been overlooked. Jomier does not have a first-class mind. The Lord Chancellor knows it. Jomier knows it. Henry knows it. His father is a loser but you cannot divorce a father so you make the best of it. And Henry does make the best of it. He rings his father every now and then to make sure he is OK. He asks him to Sunday lunch every month or six weeks. There are no other guests. Just the children. Tilly and Max are asked to dinner parties by Henry and Sandra. Henry feels more at ease with his mother. They share the same values. And Max is a figure in the City. Henry's friends are impressed.

Jomier feels a pang of anguish when he thinks of his daughter Louisa. She lives in Argentina. It is as if she is dead. She is married to an Anglo-Argentinian with an apartment in Buenos Aires and an *estancia* in Corrientes. Jomier loathes his son-in-law Jaime as much as he loves his daughter: the opposing emotions are in perfect equilibrium.

Jaime is called Jimmy by his mother and father, his five siblings, twenty-three cousins and his Argentinian friends. The Anglo-Saxon diminutive is to remind the world that he has Anglo-Saxon blood in his veins. But there is not much: Jomier estimates that it is no more than a quarter. He is three-quarters Argentinian, which means mostly Italian since 60 per cent of the immigrants to Argentina came from Italy, shedding everything fine as they crossed the Atlantic – their culture, their cuisine – retaining only their *mafiosi* vendettas and taste for posturing dictators – Mussolini, Perón.

Jimmy is tall. That, perhaps, comes from his Anglo-Saxon genes; or perhaps just a diet of flat meat. He is also thick-set and strong. When he greets Jomier he slaps him on the back. A heavy blow lands on Jomier's shoulder blade; a sing-song greeting is bellowed in his ear. There are many things that Jomier dislikes about his son-in-law: his crass materialism, his snobbery, his contempt for the poor, for losers (like Jomier); but most of all Jomier hates his Chiquita-banana accent. And the venom has spread to anything South American – salsa, the tango, *One Hundred Years of Solitude*, Che Guevara.

How? How, how, how could his beloved Louisa, the creature he loved more than anyone else in the world – a precious child, an intelligent adolescent, a beautiful young woman (universally acknowledged) who went from Godolphin and Latymer to Bristol University, leaving with a 2:1 degree in History – have married this *bufón*, Jaime Miller de Ramirez? She had travelled in her gap year to South America, then had returned to Buenos Aires to teach English as a Foreign Language. Good, Jomier had thought. She should see something of the world before settling down with a nice young journalist or lawyer in London. But fate had decreed otherwise. She had introductions to families in BA. She had met and married Jimmy. Married him in the parish church of St Edward the Confessor in Appleton, Hampshire, with a reception in the Old Rectory, Tilly's childhood home. Louisa had walked down the aisle of the church on Jomier's arm. Jomier had wondered at his ability to hide his misery and smile. At the reception, genteel delight: a good match. Ten thousand acres of pampas. Jollity. Celebration. Jimmy's *compañeros* from Argentina hoping to get lucky with Louisa's spinster friends. Old friends of the grandparents in morning coats and dowdy dresses. Friends of the middle-aged Jomiers. Louisa's stepfather, Max, and adoptive siblings, Chuck and Hayden. But no Jane.

Was that why she had fallen for Jimmy? A man like Max? Tall, rich, foreign, strong. Was the *macho* Jimmy chosen because he was as unlike the unsexed, hoodwinked papa as it was possible for a man to be? Consciously? Semi-consciously? Unconsciously? Or had Jomier nothing to do with Louisa's choice in love? Pheromones. The tanned and muscular *estanciero* versus the pallid bankers and lawyers back home. Jomier does not like thinking of his daughter in bed with Jimmy. He had always had a problem with her boyfriends – in her adolescence anxious about late nights, sleepovers, weekends away. Sooner or later, he had known, she would lose her virginity; sooner rather than later; to a boy at Latymer; a boy at St Paul's; a boy at Bristol. He knew it would happen. Tilly hoped it would happen. She wanted her daughter to have the adventures she wished she had had at the same age. Go for it! Had Louisa sensed her mother's urging her to have sex? Had they discussed it? Girl talk? Discussions hidden from Jomier – like all fathers genetically programmed to protect his daughter from sexual predators; young men who want sex without commitment – a redundant and so ridiculous instinct thanks to the liberation of women and the invention of the pill?

## 3

JOMIER LIVES ALONE but does not lack contact with other human beings. He talks to someone almost every day – mostly on the telephone, and often people at the end of help lines, the human interface between huge corporations and their customers. Because Jomier is methodical and keeps precise accounts, he notices the *slippage* that takes place across the board – small increases in direct debits, discounts forgotten, interest unpaid, surreptitious charges, computer errors – always, Jomier notices, in favour of the provider. He spends much time listening to recorded voices, pressing buttons on his telephone, waiting to reach an operator, repeating yet again his name, his date of birth, his postcode, the first line of his address; grappling with security codes and passwords and account numbers prior to stating his case to a woman in Scotland or a man in Mumbai. The sums in themselves are not large: often the cost of the call – the numbers that begin 08 or 09 – cuts into any refund or recompense that Jomier may negotiate. Were Jomier still working as a barrister, it would not have been cost-effective for him to spend so much time talking to the utility companies and service providers. But he is now retired. His time has no pecuniary value whereas the utility companies are paying the wages of the woman in Scotland or the man in Mumbai. He is costing them more than they are recouping from him.

Jomier also talks to government agencies – in particular his local council. Jomier's house was built on low-lying land and after heavy falls of rain the sewers back up and effluent rises through the drain in Jomier's garden. Jomier telephones the council to complain: he is referred to Thames Water. He telephones Thames Water, who refer him back to the council. It seems that no one is responsible and nothing can be done but build a new super-sewer to run along the bottom of the Thames towards the North Sea. It will not be completed in Jomier's lifetime. It may not solve the problem. And it may become redundant before it is built because of global warming. Jomier has found on a government website a map of the flood plains around London. If the world warms as predicted and the sea level rises, most of Hammersmith will be under water. Jomier's house will be submerged in a lake of effluent. He will form part of the human detritus – boat people sailing for the shores of Holland Park.

There are times when Jomier meets other human beings face-to-face. There is his doctor, his dentist, the barber and the postman. Inevitably his conversations with the doctor and the dentist are brief – with the doctor because he has a ten-minute slot in which to discuss deafness, cancer scares, prostate problems, vague aches and pains; with the dentist because his mouth is wide open and he cannot speak. The postman is friendly: Jomier likes postmen in general – humble loners – and this one in particular, who signs for things when he is out. But they meet only rarely – when Jomier is in and signs for a missive himself, or if Jomier happens to be coming or going when the postman is doing his rounds. They do not have much in common. Jomier listens to him talking about sport with an expression of feigned interest. He dare not admit that he has no interest in the kicking or hitting or carrying of large, small, round or spheroid-shaped balls. Jomier is afraid that were the postman to know this, he would decide that Jomier was a patronising git and dump important letters in a Hammersmith & Fulham refuse bin.

This leaves the barber, a Turkish Cypriot. Jomier does not like his hair to grow long and so spends half an hour each month with Nazim. Before the divorce, Jomier would have his hair washed and cut at Trumper's in Mayfair. Thirty-five pounds would buy him a shampoo, a trim and the deference due to an English gentleman by a man who knew his place. His father had his hair cut at Trumper's, so too many of the great and the good. But after the divorce Trumper's was beyond his reach. Geographically. Financially. At Nazim's barber's shop off the Askew Road his hair is cut and washed for a third of the price; and instead of deference he has half an hour of Nazim on the state of the world, which Jomier in his reduced circumstances prefers.

Before he retired Jomier met other people in the course of his working day – the clerk at his chambers, his fellow barristers, court officials, solicitors, clients. Work forces us to interact with others. The retired have to make arrangements. They form book clubs. They give dinner parties. They have to pick up the telephone or send an email to suggest lunch.

Jomier never picks up his telephone or sends an email to suggest lunch but he is telephoned and emailed by others. Jomier is in demand among the *salonnières* of Hammersmith, Kensington, even as far afield as Islington. This is not because Jomier is popular but because he is an unattached man. There is a shortage of unattached men among Londoners of a certain age. The women who give dinner parties are liberated but nonetheless like to have an equal number of men and women around their table. Jomier would be happy to sit with the other male guests at one end of the table but this is not allowed. He must sit between two women. Nor are the male guests permitted, as they once did in certain circles, to remain behind after dinner while the women withdraw to the withdrawing room. Now people rarely get up from table until it is time to go home. Jomier is trapped between two women for two or three hours – one on his left, the other on his right.

Jomier is perfect for the role of the extra man. Like most barristers, he has been trained to go on talking long after there is nothing more to be said. He is thus a good conversationalist. He is presentable. Even handsome. He has no ponderous belly and a good head of hair. He drinks moderately and does not have the red blotchy face of those who down a 75-centilitre bottle of wine every day. Nor does Jomier smoke. He used to smoke but kicked the habit while still married to Tilly. Tilly too had smoked before she married but quit when she was pregnant with Henry. Jomier quit some time later, not for reasons of health – his health, Tilly's health or the health of his children – but because he no longer enjoyed inhaling smoke from a cigarette. He remembers the feeling of concentrated tranquillity that it had once induced in him but little by little it ceased to have that effect. It was the same with reading. With travel. With sex. He remembers enjoying what he no longer enjoys. When Humphrey Bogart lights up on-screen Jomier feels a pang of acute nostalgia. So too when he kisses Ingrid Bergman or Lauren Bacall.

Though Jomier is in demand among the ladies of west London it is not because of his wit or charm. Women are happy to be placed next to him because they know that the conversation will never flag, but they sense that Jomier's sociability is insincere. He asks questions about their lives or discusses films they had both seen as if he is reciting lines from a script – a script in which he is not playing a leading role, nor even a supporting role, but is simply 'a man making conversation' from central casting.

Jomier has no dress sense. He wears off-the-peg suits to drinks parties; pale blue shirts; dull ties. Jomier knows what is meant by 'smart casual' – the linen jacket or dark blue suit; the white shirt, open at the neck. Before the break-up, Tilly had given him ties from Harrods or shirts from Gieves & Hawkes as Christmas and birthday presents. Now, the supply cut off, Jomier has reverted to the status quo ante. He buys his clothes from Marks & Spencer and wears a tie. He does not like a naked neck – in men or in women: the skin between chin and breastbone is the first to wither with age. No amount of Botox can get rid of those turkey wrinkles. But Jomier does not wear a tie to conceal these signs of ageing. He wears it, he tells himself, to stop draughts going down his chest. If this makes him seem fogeyish – so be it. Jomier is not vain. He avoids looking at himself in the mirror. He does not like what he sees. His face. This since the Fall. Since the bust-up. Since he learned about Tilly and Max. The mirror had lied. It had not shown the horns growing out of his head. The Narcissus-smile of self-admiration was the smile of a sucker. A fool.

Jomier prefers cocktail parties to dinner parties – drinks to supper. At a drinks party he is not trapped between two women but can hop from person to person like a bee going from flower to flower, taking about as much time as a bee takes to pick up the pollen before moving on. At a drinks party Jomier can talk to men as easily as to women, and in five minutes of conversation everything worth saying has been said. He does not have to eat heavy, indigestible food at ten at night, but can be home in time to eat a sandwich in front of his wide-screen Panasonic television.

There are disadvantages even to drinks parties. As often as not, a number of the other guests are men and women Jomier has known for many years. He has known them but never felt inclined to get to know them better. That ten minutes of conversation back in the 1970s was even then enough to inform Jomier that he and his interlocutor would never be friends. Year after year Jomier comes face-to-face with these same acquaintances of yesteryear. Jomier and Tilly had had them to dinner but had never been asked back. Or *vice versa*. 'We must ask the Platitudes to dinner . . .' An intention never fulfilled. Social guilt gradually fading. Then once again face-to-face with the Platitudes. You know. They know. No shared sense of humour. No sexual attraction. No social ambition – the mixes that might have gone into a mortar to bind the Jomiers and the Platitudes together. They will run into one another again. And again. And again. See you in Purgatory: but they are in Purgatory – the drinks party. Words lost in the hubbub. Gusts of foul breath. But at least this is not a dinner party. They are not in Hell.

# 4

NARRATIVE. THERE IS no narrative in Jomier's life. A life like a story has a beginning, a middle and an end, and Jomier has now reached those last chapters that drive biographers to their wits' end. Nothing happens. There is nothing to say. The last lap between retirement and death can last a year, ten years, fifteen years, twenty years – the elastic of life stretched by new drugs, medical techniques, robotics, diagnostic machines.

There *had* been a story. Jacques Jomier, a French Protestant, had moved to London in the seventeenth century after the Revocation of the Edict of Nantes. He was a bookbinder. He set up shop in Soho. He had a wife who was also a Protestant and also French. With her he begat a Jomier who begat another Jomier who begat another Jomier. These later Jomiers married women from the indigenous population and with each begetting the Frenchness was thinned by British blood, and the Calvinism by easier-going Anglicanism, until there was nothing French about the Jomiers but their name, and nothing Calvinist but the occasional feeling that Jomier has upon waking in the morning that the whole human race is damned.

As a child Jomier had been in two minds about his ancestry. It made him different – even special – but meant that he was called a Frog at school where the pupils were addressed by their family names. A public school. It was common for public-school boys to pick on anything distinctive as a pretext for teasing and bullying. Red hair. A big nose. A spotty complexion. A French name. The teachers *in loco parentis* looked on and approved. Ragging, like beating, bullying and brutal sports, formed character. It was part of the 'ethos' of the public school. It transformed cringing wimps into leaders of men.

Jomier's mother and father had made 'sacrifices' so that their only child should receive a private education. Jomier *père* had been a civil servant. A high-flyer in the Home Office who in the event did not fly quite as high as had been expected. They lived in Sussex. He would take the train each day from Haywards Heath to Victoria and return in the evening. At the weekend he would play golf. Jomier's mother did not work. She was pre-Betty Friedan. Pre-Germaine Greer. There was some 'family money' which for a time filled the gap between income and expenditure. Jomier *père* only looked cursorily at his bank statements or letters from his broker. He assumed that providence would provide the means for him to lead the life that his father had led before him. He made some economies after the war: he sacked the cook and in the evening ate what his wife had gleaned from Mrs Beeton. But other expenses were non-negotiable. Membership of the Garrick. Glyndebourne. A Humber. School fees. They were covered by his salary from the Home Office and, after his retirement, his inflation-proof Civil Service pension. When he died, Jomier's mother moved into a flat in Holland Park to be near to her son. Then to an old people's home. Then to a hospital. Then to a coffin. Then to a grave.

\* \* \*

Had they been worth it? The school fees? Would Jomier have won a place at Oxford if he had not been taught by good teachers in small classes? Would he have made the right kind of friends? Would he have got a place in chambers in the Inns of Court? Would he have met Tilly? Would he have fallen in love with Tilly? Would Tilly have fallen in love with him? No. If Jomier's education had been paid for by the state rather than by his father, he would be a different person. He knows this. His father and mother had known it. In England a private education is the peg hammered into the rock face that prevents a free fall into the abyss of social indistinction. It is what differentiates *hoi aristoi* from *hoi polloi*; the patrician from the plebeian; *les gens biens* from the *canaille*; the gentleman from the common man.

Jomier marvels at the ability of the English to say one thing and do another; to talk of equality of opportunity while preserving a system under which, generation after generation, the dregs stay at the bottom and froth rises to the top. The English. Jomier is as English as most of the English but from his Huguenot gene comes a certain detachment. From time to time the Frog jumps on to the leaf of a water lily to study its habitat – the pond. How open English society seems to be. How welcoming to people throughout the world. Most of the billionaires in Britain are foreigners – Indians, Arabs, Russians, Iraqi Jews. Elegant squares in Belgravia remain empty and silent because the non-domiciled millionaires are elsewhere. Deep pits are dug into the ground in Knightsbridge and Chelsea, and cranes reach to the sky, as blocks of sumptuous apartments are built by sovereign funds for sheikhs and oligarchs. Feudal titles are bestowed upon immigrants – Sir Joshua and Lady Zion, Lord and Lady Japati, Baroness El-Aksa, Nazir Bookerbanana, OM.

Does Jomier resent this? Yes and no. At times he feels aggrieved that the English have been expelled from those elegant Georgian and Regency streets and squares where Sir Pitt Crawley once walked with Becky Sharp; that the only English to remain are the collaborators with the colonists, the acolytes of Mammon, leeches fat with money-blood that they have sucked from the system in the City; that the auction houses and shops and department stores patronised by his parents and grandparents – Christie's, Sotheby's, Harrods, Harvey Nichols, Fortnum & Mason, Paxton & Whitfield, Berry Brothers, Lobbs – now charge prices that only the bankers and hedge-funders and sheikhs and oligarchs can afford – the tradesmen meeting an enquiry from an indigenous Englishman with the mix of a smirk and apologetic smile: 'If you ask the price you cannot afford it' and 'What do you expect?'; Go to Tesco, Primark, Sainsbury's, Marks & Spencer. Like a Navajo Indian, Jomier has been ejected from his ancestral lands in St James's to live in a reservation under the flight path of jumbos, Airbuses and Boeings bringing the oligarchs from Moscow, the sheikhs from the Gulf, the oil barons from Caracas, the bankers from Zurich and New York.

Outside London and Islamic city states such as Bradford and Leicester, there is still an England familiar to the English – pubs, parish churches, village greens. In hamlets in Hampshire Jane Austen's England thrives. There may be more squires than yokels, more manor houses than peasants' cottages; and what cottages there are belong to weekending stockbrokers and advertising copywriters – the descendants of the peasants now packed into little Persimmon homes, each with a Georgian portico; but here all can pretend that they live in a country with an English culture and an English history, not a polyglot global growth vortex that sucks in immigrants to build larger airports with more runways to receive more immigrants to work in supermarkets and schools and hospitals to cater for immigrants or the children of immigrants. Only 20 per cent of children attending primary schools in London are born in Britain. When Jomier keeps his hospital appointments surly West Indian women at the reception desk tell him to wait with the Ethiopian, Iranian, Malaysian patients to be seen by an Iraqi or Indian or Sri Lankan or Nigerian doctor. The only specialist Jomier has come across with a white skin was Czech. Her assistant was also white: a German. The male nurse was Albanian.

Is Jomier a racist? He reads the newspapers. He watches television. He knows that there is a thought police out there looking for racists among white middle-class Englishmen like Jomier. It is the first of the Seven Sins of the Secular State. These are:

Racism
Misogyny
Homophobia
Elitism
Smoking
Obesity
Religious belief

Jomier is innocent of faith and fatness, and he no longer smokes. But the others? Can one be a racist without knowing it, like the carrier of a disease? What is a racist? How is racism to be defined? Is it a mere awareness of the race or nationality of others? A preference for one race or nationality over another? Jomier likes the courteous Indians or Pakistanis who sit behind the counter in the newsagents and sub-post offices across London and dislikes the West Indian youths who saunter around in flash trainers and baggy trousers and drop chocolate wrappers and pizza boxes in the street. But Jomier's prejudices have nothing to do with the hue of human skin. He dislikes the blarney-bullshitting Irish and, most of all, the sullen, sarcastic, shaven-headed, white-van-driving *Sun*-reading indigenous Estuary English.

Jomier's prejudices, he decides, are not based on race but on characteristics that transcend race. Jomier likes people who are intelligent, articulate, curious, amusing, cultivated, considerate, kind. He likes people who share his sense of humour and catch his ironies; people who are oblique, unassertive, cynical, disillusioned. 'Vanity of vanities, all is vanity . . .'

'Vanity of vanities, all is vanity . . .' The words of Qoheleth, son of David, King of Jerusalem, three hundred years before Christ. Jomier is familiar with the Bible: he reads the copy he won as a prize when a child to cull absurdities, monstrosities, contradictions to use in arguments with his Christian friend Theodor Tate. Qoheleth alias King Solomon asked God for wisdom rather than riches and so was given not just wisdom but also riches and a thousand wives. 'Much wisdom, much grief,' wrote Qoheleth. 'The more knowledge, the more sorrow.' And the wives? Qoheleth says nothing about love though he, King Solomon, was himself a child of love – the offspring of his father King David's adulterous passion for Bathsheba. 'It happened towards the evening when David had risen from his couch and was strolling on the palace roof, that he saw from the roof a woman bathing; the woman was very beautiful.' David made enquiries about this woman and was told, 'Why, that is Bathsheba, Eliam's daughter, the wife of Uriah the Hittite.' Uriah the Hittite. Jomier the Huguenot. It happened towards the evening that Max was sipping ouzo at a beach bar in Crete when he saw Tilly hitch up her bikini top that had slipped while swimming in the sea. Max has no need to make enquiries about the woman with beautiful breasts. He knows that she is Tilly, daughter of Roddy Gardner, wife of Jomier the Huguenot, his friend. 'Then David sent messengers and had her brought. She came to him, and he slept with her.' Then Max made a telephone call and she came to him, and he slept with her.

Uriah the Hittite was sent to war with a message to Joab, David's general: 'Station Uriah in the thick of the fight and then fall back so that he may be struck down and die.' And Joab did as he was told. Joab, then besieging the town, put Uriah on the front line. The men of the town sallied out; the army suffered casualties, and Uriah the Hittite was killed. And when Bathsheba heard that Uriah her husband was dead, she mourned for her husband. And when the mourning was past, David sent for her and fetched her to his house and she became his wife.

Jomier the Huguenot was not a soldier. He could not be sent to war. He was not killed. He was merely deceived. *Cocu*. Life left in his body. Death to his self-esteem. Better to have died a hero like Uriah.

'But the thing that David had done displeased the Lord.' Jomier often wished that he could believe that Max would get his comeuppance in the world to come. 'Vengeance is mine, says the Lord. I will repay.' But Jomier does not believe. He notes, too, that it was David who displeased the Lord, not Bathsheba. Even God is duped by women. Bathsheba surely knew that David could see her naked in her bath. Why else would she take it on the roof in full view of the palace? So too the hitching up of Tilly's bikini top was for the benefit of the hairy alpha-male Max – the connoisseur of cantaloupe melons. Uriah the Hittite – Uriah the poor provider – versus David the Lord's Anointed, legendary slayer of Goliath – cool, courageous, rich. *Nolo contendere*.

Jomier keeps his thoughts about Bathsheba to himself. He expresses them in his journal which is now password-protected, though he knows that it would be easily bypassed were his computer ever to be seized by the thought police. Failing to find paedophile downloads, they would extract evidence of misogyny, that second of the Seven Deadly Sins.

Is Jomier a misogynist? Or a gynophile – a lover of women? Both. Both to extremes. Jomier's earliest memories are of a preoccupation with the female of his species: an *emotional* preoccupation – a tenderness for Belinda, a girl with a squint at his nursery school; and a *physical* preoccupation. An early memory – being surprised by his mother as he examined the private parts of Sally, the girl next door. In the garden. A summer's day. Rebuke. A smack. He did not understand what he had done wrong. Was it not natural to be curious about the physical differences between the sexes, shrouded by navy-blue knickers, hidden between closed legs? His mother had been evasive. One opening, perhaps, but not the other. She did not specify which was permitted, which forbidden. Nor had Jomier had time to establish that there were two. He was to learn about that later in life – from books and further research.

Sally had been quite happy to be the object of Jomier's researches. So had other Sallys since. Such as Tilly. Tilly 1. In thinking about Tilly, Jomier distinguishes between Tilly 1 and Tilly 2 – Tilly 1 being the Tilly he loved and courted and married and who was happy, like Sally, to be the object of his attentions; and Tilly 2, the sly Tilly who never rejected or deflected his attentions but had her mind on other things – on Max and when she would next see him and how much she would rather she was having sex with him. Most of Jomier's current thoughts are about Tilly 2 and they are ugly – prima facie evidence of misogyny. But there are times when they give way to memories of Tilly 1 – a different person, a girl young and fresh and loving whose face lit up when she saw him and laughed at the silliest of his jokes. They had met at a party and started talking and became so engrossed in their conversation that others in the circle had drifted away. What was the topic? Forgotten. The first kiss? On the Thames Embankment after a concert at the Festival Hall. He had issued the invitation. She had accepted. Both keen to be thought cultured. Later revelations: they both preferred movies. Hollywood pap at the Kensington Odeon: the smell of popcorn as they came in from the autumn urban mist. Or French mysteries at the Gate cinema in Notting Hill. Or any old film at that old music hall, the Coronet – with supper afterwards at the Ark or Costa's Grill.

Jomier feels sad when he thinks of Tilly 1. He mourns. He grieves. He thinks back to the first time they made love and remembers only that he remembered nothing: there was no 'other' to observe. 'This at last is bone of my bones, and flesh of my flesh!' Adam's cry when he was presented with Eve. Jomier's inward exclamation when he had first made love with Tilly. Tilly 1.

Jomier is not a Jew but he sees elemental truths in Jewish myth. God creates Adam but decides 'that it is not good that man should be alone' and so creates Eve as a helpmate and companion. Adam is delighted. But Eve is discontented:

from the start, woman runs true to form. She likes the look of the one thing they may not eat in the Garden of Eden. The Forbidden Fruit. Fuck that! She plucks it, takes a bite, then inveigles Adam to do the same. The result? The end of innocence. 'They saw that they were naked.' He looks with revulsion at her pubic hair and slimy vulva; she, with the same disgust, at his dangling penis and swaying scrotum. Yuk. They cover up with loincloths made from fig leaves. The birth of shame. God notices this screening of their private parts. 'Who told you were naked? Have you been eating of the tree I forbade you to eat?' Now comes the blame game. 'It was the woman you put with me,' says Adam. 'She gave me the fruit, and I ate it.' And Eve: 'The serpent tempted me and I ate.' The serpent!

Their excuses do not wash. God kicks Adam and Eve out of the Garden of Eden, but before they go, he 'makes clothes out of skins for the man and his wife'. The start of the rag trade. The birth of fashion. Now, a million years later, the skins are silk and satin. Diaphanous *lingerie* with lace edging to at once entice and veil the shame. Bras, corsets, stockings, garters, camiknickers. Jomier knows them all only too well. He has unveiled and unbuttoned and unhooked and pulled down to uncover the soft and the spongy, the puckered and the hirsute, the slippery and the engorged. Jomier has observed and mentally dissected but never again has he known the primordial innocence of those early years with Tilly 1 – when they did not know that they were naked and remembered nothing of their acts of love.

## 5

BETTER NOT TO think back. Better to forget fickle human passions from the past and concentrate on the solid reliable loves of the present – his car, his television, his computer. Jomier likes technology. He admires the skill and audacity of scientists and engineers – the Channel Tunnel, the Millau Viaduct, the mobile telephone, the Oyster card, the DSG automatic transmission on his Volkswagen Golf. He feels physically strengthened by the torque of his car's turbo-diesel engine and mentally empowered by the software on his computer. Each is more than a mere convenience. Jomier rarely drives anywhere because the roads are clogged with traffic; and he is aware that he spends too much of his waking life creating spreadsheets and entering names and numbers into databases; but he is proud of the end result. With only two or three keystrokes he can discover how much money he spent in August 1998 on groceries, petrol, gifts, books, wine, telephone (landline) or telephone (mobile); or how many people he knows who live in W11 (Notting Hill), how many in W6 (Hammersmith), how many he has classed as friends, how many as acquaintances and how many are dead.

When someone dies, Jomier enters 'dead' next to their name on his FileMaker Pro database. At first he typed the initials RIP for 'rest in peace' or rather, given Jomier's views on mortality, 'rot in perpetuity'; but, because the search engine is not case-sensitive, it meant that Johnny Ripley and Sue Ripon come up as deceased when they are not. Or so Jomier supposes. 'Dead' serves Jomier's purpose: he has no friends or acquaintances whose names contain the consecutive letters d-e-a-d. He considers entering 'lost touch' by the names of Johnny Ripley (a fellow student at Oxford) and Sue Ripon (a girl he briefly dated before he met Tilly), and by the names of those friends and acquaintances he has not seen for a number of years. But as he flicks through the database, he realises that there are too many. Easier to write 'still in touch' or 'current', but Jomier does not do this. There are too few.

Thirteen of Jomier's friends are dead. Three killed themselves. Two died of drink. Six had cancer. One had a weak heart. Another a rare wasting illness. The three suicides were all young women. Statistically, more young men than young women now take their own lives. But this is now. That was then – the 1960s. Two of Jomier's suicidal girlfriends had fallen in love with 'unsuitable' men. One of the swains was Welsh, the other a Pakistani. The third girl was married to an oaf. She had three children. She saw no way out. Jomier wishes he could return to those times and talk them out of it. But what would he say? That they were under a misapprehension that life was meant to be happy? That they set too great a store on human relationships? That if they could only hang on for a few more decades they would find other consolations – a Volkswagen Golf, a mobile phone, a computer, a thirty-two-inch flat-screen TV.

Of Jomier's six friends who had cancer, four smoked – chain-smoked – one cigarette after another. The health apparatchiks are right: a large ingestion of alcohol and nicotine leads to an early death. But their admonitions are issued on a presumed preference for longevity. They do not consider that there might be some who, just as Achilles opted for a life that was short and glorious, might choose a life that is short and fun.

Only four of Jomier's friends have died 'through no fault of their own'. In one, his heart stopped. Two – moderate drinkers, non-smokers – died of cancer all the same. One succumbed to an obscure genetic disease. *Schicksal*. Fate. Jomier assumes that he too will die of cancer. Like father, like son. But cancer of what? Cancer where? Jomier waits to see where it will strike. He feels his body for lumps and pesters his doctor. He does not want to be told, as his father was told by *his* doctor, that if only he had come earlier . . . But what is a symptom? Subcutaneous nodules. A change in bowel habits. Festering moles. How is one to know whether blood in the faeces means haemorrhoids or a tumour in the bowels? Is back pain the symptom of a strained ligament or bone cancer? How is one to tell which ache or pain is par for the course, and which the beginning of the end? Jomier takes no risks. He has had barium scans and swallows, cameras up his rectum and down his throat. Jomier is not a hypochondriac. Nor is he afraid of death. But he believes his body merits the same attention as his Volkswagen Golf.

Dead friends. How easily they pass out of one's life. How soon the waters close over them. How quickly 'life goes on'. If Jomier thinks of them, it is because of his journal. Their deaths merit entries and comments – about them, about death, about Jomier's feelings about death. The feelings are not profound. They are mostly 'better him than me'. If Jomier could save the life of one of his friends by accepting permanent toothache without analgesic, he would not do it. This is what he thinks when he visits his dying friends. He dislikes the silly, sombre expressions that people feel they must put on their faces at funerals. He likes it when, after a couple of drinks at the wake, the mask slips. Jomier does not feel sadness at the time. He feels it later, but the sadness is at his loss, not theirs. They are dead. Their suffering is over. Jomier must go on living with fewer and fewer friends.

Most of Jomier's remaining friends go back to his youth. Jomier has made few in later life. It is as if friendship requires that we go through things together – schooldays, gap years, college, choosing careers, chasing girls, getting married, having children. A shared purpose in later life does not suffice. The friend from his youth who Jomier misses most is the one who died from an obscure genetic disease. Marco – Mark Davenport. They met in Paris in their year out – both attending a course on French Language and Civilisation laid on for foreigners at the Sorbonne. They hung out together in the Latin Quarter. They hung out together when they got back to London. They hunted as a pair. Marco asked every girl he met to go to bed with him on the grounds that one in ten would say yes. He also had affairs with older women. 'After the age of fifty, they always say yes.' He did not mind slack stomachs, sagging bosoms and dry, wrinkled skin. 'They're fantastic. Their desperation makes them wild. Girls are dull. Who wants to ride a horse that hasn't been broken in?'

Jomier did not follow his friend's example. He was too fastidious. His curiosity had its limits. Nor could he be as cavalier as Marco. 'You must always sleep with a woman at least twice. Once is insulting.' Marco moved in without promises and moved on without recrimination. With Marco there were no false expectations: a woman always knew where she stood. He wanted sex, not love. So, it appeared, did some women. But Jomier wanted love. He knew the feeling of animal exultation followed a one-night stand, but then came the backwash – shame – a feeling unknown to Marco. Shame not at the sin – Jomier did not see sex as a sin – but shame at the post-coital repugnance – as powerful as the desire he had felt the night before. 'This is not flesh of my flesh or bone of my bone.' He never wanted to see Daphne or Daisy or Susie again.

Jomier always had, in his mind's eye, a girl who would love him and him alone. He would not be one among others – a bloke to tether once the body clock reached five to menopause and it was time to settle down. She would be dignified, modest, chaste – her body held in reserve for a lifelong love. Even as Jomier snogged and groped and shagged, this imaginary maiden stood in a niche in his psyche, smiling sadly down at his heaving buttocks, like the statue of the Virgin Mary at Lourdes.

Jomier had found her. The imaginary maiden had come to life. Tilly. Tilly 1. Marco had liked her. Tilly had liked Marco. She found him amusing. Marco and his escapades. But now that Jomier was one half of a couple, he could no longer hunt with Marco or even talk about the chase. A line had been drawn. So what had they talked about? Jomier toggles back through his digitalised journals. Politics. Theatre. Food. Travel. Books. Even here they followed different paths. Jomier read Graham Greene, Iris Murdoch, Anthony Powell and Angus Wilson; Marco read Henry Miller, William Burroughs, Allen Ginsberg, Jean Genet, Lawrence Ferlinghetti. Jomier read the *Spectator*; Marco the *Evergreen Review*. Every summer, Jomier and Tilly spent two weeks with other married friends in a rented villa in France or Italy while Marco set off to some part of the world he had never seen – Patagonia, the Atlas Mountains, Lake Van, Damascus, Kashmir. He slept on mud-packed floors in Cambodia and ate guinea pig in Peru. For six months he lived in New York, fighting Norman Mailer in a loft over a woman and going to bed with a man. 'It was vile,' he wrote to Jomier, 'but you have to try everything once.'

Marco was gaunt and prematurely bald. He spoke with a lisp and a faint French accent. The accent was an affectation: he had a foreign mother but she was Austrian, not French, and his education and upbringing had been in England. His rich parents paid him an allowance and the rent of his flat in Chelsea. He was a dilettante, working on and off in the art world, charming old masters out of old ladies – rewards, perhaps, for the sexual ecstasy that they thought they would never know again. Through his mother, a Frycht, he had an entrée into the grandest families in Europe. Christie's and Sotheby's vied for his services as a consultant.

Jomier's recollection is that his friendship with Marco ended with Marco's death but, rereading his diaries, he sees that some years before he became ill Marco had imperceptibly passed out of his life. He had returned from New York with a passion for tennis acquired when staying with rich Americans on Long Island. Jomier preferred not to play tennis: he only did so when needed by Tilly for a game of doubles. Now Tilly had a partner in Marco to play with her friends at the Campden Hill Tennis Club or on the courts in Ladbroke Square Gardens.

There was an entry which described Marco coming to Sunday lunch. Tilly had asked one of her single girlfriends. Marco showed no interest. His expression throughout suggested that he wished he was elsewhere. Marco was Henry's godfather; he had held him at the font. But now

Henry was eighteen months old – a tiny Caligula who threw tantrums if he did not get his way. Shrieks. The smell of cabbage and damp nappies. A needy spinster. After lunch, Marco declined to join them on a walk in Holland Park. He took his leave.

Soon after Marco went back to live in New York. It was there that he went down with some rare and fatal illness. He had been flown to a clinic in Austria close to the schloss of his grandparents, Graf and Gräfin von Frycht. It was there that he died. Seeing the back of his friend scuttling away up Holland Park Avenue turned out to have been Jomier's last view of Marco. There was a memorial service at the Church of the Holy Redeemer in Chelsea and a reception afterwards at his parents' house in Chester Square. No one seemed to know exactly what had killed Marco: there seemed some embarrassment, even shame. These were the early days of Aids. Jomier wondered whether Marco had found his homosexual experience less vile than he had said; or whether he felt that his quest for experience had led him to try it again with other men – perhaps plunging into the Mineshaft to have anonymous gay sex.

A year or so later, Jomier met a young Austrian at a dinner party in Pimlico. Initial probing conversation revealed that they had Marco in common. Jomier was his friend. The Austrian was his cousin. He told Jomier that Marco had died from a rare hereditary blood disease – a galloping anaemia – passed through the Frycht gene. It had been misdiagnosed in New York: it had been thought to be Aids. In Austria the disorder, Frycht's anaemia, was better known but, by the time Marco had been flown there for treatment, it was too late. Complications had set in. Removal of his spleen. Blood transfusions. All in vain. The young Austrian sighed. Only Frychts were susceptible to the disease. It was

45

a hereditary disability like the Habsburgs' protruding jaw. He sighed again. *Noblesse oblige*. Clearly, he thought it was a risk worth running – a fair exchange for the blue blood.

'So it wasn't Aids after all,' Jomier had told Tilly on their way home from Pimlico. Tilly: 'Whoever thought it was?'

It had never occurred to Jomier until the memorial service at the Church of the Holy Redeemer in Chelsea that Marco had been a Roman Catholic. When Jomier came to think about it, with an aristocratic Austrian mother, he could hardly have been anything else. When Jomier came to think about it further, he realised that it explained a lot. A Catholic takes risks because he is confident that his sins will be forgiven. Sin for a Protestant betrays that he is not one of the elect. Jomier does not think of himself as a Protestant but he has a Huguenot gene. Or a gene that had inclined Jomier the bookbinder to be a Huguenot. Better than a hereditary disease, perhaps. Did Marco know that he was doomed? Was that why he lived so furiously? Never settled down? Like Achilles – a short and glorious life; rather than one that was long and inglorious – like Jomier's.

# 6

DID MARCO REPENT? Did he receive absolution? Has he now passed through Purgatory into a rococo paradise filled with Habsburgs, Schwarzenbergs and Frychts? Jomier knows about Heaven and Hell and Purgatory from his Catholic friend, Theodor Tate. Theo is quite unlike Marco Davenport. He goes to Mass every Sunday at the Brompton Oratory wearing twill trousers, a tweed jacket, brown brogue shoes, sometimes a waistcoat, always a tie. He is a Knight of Malta and a member of the Athenaeum: he and Jomier meet there for lunch from time to time. Jomier puts on a suit and travels up to Piccadilly. Jomier enjoys these outings. He likes London clubs such as Brooks's, White's, the Travellers, the Athenaeum – the grand rooms with pillars and porticos; the leather armchairs; the atmosphere of male exclusivity; the unctuous staff. Like his father, he had been a member of the Garrick. After the divorce he could no longer afford the subscription.

Theo can afford the subscription: the fogey runs a hedge fund and, by Jomier's standards, is rich. He has no children. He has no wife. Jomier cannot decide whether Theo is single because he is not attracted to women, or because women are not attracted to him. Or both. Theo is tall, bald, with bulging short-sighted eyes. He talks precisely and thinks precisely: hence his success at managing a hedge fund. Is Theo gay? A repressed homosexual? Or a repressed hetero-sexual? Or nothing at all? Does he feel no urge to remove the clothes of a beautiful woman, nibble her nipples, plunge his penis into her entrails? Or has that shrewdness which anticipates the rise or fall in the price of copper, nickel and oil also made him realise that a wife, like a car, depreciates sharply and brings a poor return?

Jomier suspects that, were Theo to unleash his libido, he would like to caress the naked bodies of slim young men. But Theo is no more likely to unleash his libido than he is to wear an open-necked shirt. The tourniquet is tight. Like the priests at the Oratory, Theo condemns all forms of 'disordered' sex. This includes masturbation and the use of contraceptives. He tells Jomier that, just as there are natural laws that govern inanimate matter, so there are natural laws that govern human behaviour. Newton arrives at the law of gravity from the fact that an apple falls to the ground. Aquinas deduces that a man's penis was created by God to inseminate the female of his species. The exchange of pleasure that creates a bond between the copulating couple is a secondary end. It is wrong to thwart God's intentions, particularly his primary intentions. Moreover, were it to be admitted in principle that sex was a good thing in itself, it would open up a Pandora's box. Why confine it to marriage? Why not have sex before marriage, outside marriage? Men with men? Women with women? Why not cottaging, sheep-shagging, or sex with consenting gorillas?

Jomier and Theo had rooms on the same staircase in their first year at Oxford. They had exchanged visits. Jomier had served cheap wine, Theo sherry out of a decanter. They had argued about religion. They still argue about religion. The position of neither has changed. Theo would like to convert

Jomier and Jomier to convert Theo. But convert him to what? Jomier is aware that his agnosticism is a spongy alternative to Theo's clear-cut Christian beliefs; but he feels he is in tune with the zeitgeist whereas Theo is not. He watches Theo eat liver and bacon in the dining room of the Athenaeum and tries to judge what in his friend is genuine conviction and what pose. Is Theo's medieval morality adopted to match his fogeyish attire? Is Theo a reincarnation of G. K. Chesterton? Or Hilaire Belloc? Theo admires both writers though he is embarrassed by some of the things Belloc said about the Jews. Jomier tells Theo that his views are anachronistic; Theo retorts, quoting Chesterton, that the great advantage of Catholicism is that it saves a man from being a child of his time. He reminds Jomier of their contemporaries at Oxford who were Existentialists, Logical Positivists, Deconstructionists, Marxists, Maoists, Marcusards, Laingites, Reichians, Deridans and quotes St Paul: 'The more they called themselves philosophers, the more stupid they grew.' Jomier thinks back to the philosophical fashions that have come and gone in his lifetime and finds it hard to disagree.

Jomier has never felt the need of a philosophy – least of all a philosophy of life. He is, after all, a lawyer and there are now no principles behind the law beyond Rabelais' *'Fay ce que vouldras'* – 'Do as you please so long as what you do doesn't prevent me from doing what I please'. Theo would like our laws to be based upon Christian principles as they were in the Middle Ages. He tells Jomier that the rot started with the Enlightenment – with Voltaire, Hume, Rousseau and co. – and spread slowly but inexorably via Marx and Freud and Bertrand Russell and H. G. Wells to a point in the 1960s when finally the whole tree was rotten and came crashing down.

Jomier disagrees. There has always been a consistent principle behind the law – the interests of the legislators which by and large matched those of the rich. Nabobs were ennobled. Poachers were hanged. Adultery does more harm to society than poaching or shoplifting but when it became a favoured pastime of the powerful it ceased to be a crime.

Jomier recalls that enticement was a crime until the 1970s: a man could be prosecuted for suborning another man's wife. Should it still be a crime? Jomier thinks of Max and says yes. And adultery? Jomier thinks of the weekend with Sandra and thinks no. Theodor remains non-committal. When it comes to enticement and adultery, Theodor knows that Jomier has an axe to grind. He knows about Sandra and Tilly and Max. Theodor could write a doctoral thesis on Jomier's lovelife since his was the shoulder Jomier cried on at the time. Theodor listens but does not condemn. He is like a priest in the confessional. Jomier often wonders why he is not a priest. He has put the question to Theodor. 'I'm not up to it.' What does he mean? That he has some secret vice? That he is too fond of Mammon – of adding zeros to the digits in his hedge-fund account? He presses Theodor. Theodor gives a laugh instead of an answer. Jomier presses him further. '*Dominus non sum dignus* . . .' 'Lord, I am not worthy.' Theodor often drops phrases in liturgical Latin, or illustrates a point with a Latin quip. *Mea culpa, mens rea, nota bene*: Latin – the language for priests and pedants and lawyers and fogeys just as German is the language for highbrows and French the language for sex.

# 7

IT IS HALF-TERM. Jomier is telephoned by his son Henry to ask for help with Jomier's three-year-old grandson Ned. Tracey, the Australian nanny, is to take Samantha to a play-date in Knightsbridge and Alena, the Slovakian au pair, has to go to her language course in Ealing.

'What about your mother?' asks Jomier.

'She can't. She has things to do.' Jomier, Henry knows, does not have things to do.

Jomier has no change for a parking meter. He walks along Askew Road, litter swirling around his ankles, past the halt and the lame, the second-hand furniture emporium and dusty vegetable racks outside the Pakistani stores, to the Co-op – the neon-lit supermarket that, like a mission station in the upper Congo, caters for the tastes of the middle class. Jomier buys a packet of Kettle Chips to get change from a £20 note. He returns to his Volkswagen Golf and drives to Queen's Park. Tracey meets him at the door – tall, bouncy, the quintessence of physical fitness. Her skin is still tanned from the beaches of Queensland and the pores cleansed by regular sweaty sex with her boyfriend, Jeff. Jomier has seen a lot of Tracey over the past two years. He sees more of her than do Henry and Sandra. Tracey lives out. She arrives from Earls Court at eight thirty in the morning when Henry has already left for his office and Sandra is about to leave for hers. She leaves the house ten hours later when either Henry or Sandra returns. It is a long day for Tracey. Jomier admires her stamina. She is good with the children. But she is not their mother. She is paid to care for the children. Weekly. In cash.

Samantha kisses her grandfather with a brush of her lips on his cheek. She has her mother's drive. Her mind is on the play-date with her friend Alexa. Ned stamps his feet up and down – a little war dance reserved for Grandpa. Jomier takes him by the hand. They walk towards the playground in Queen's Park. Ned stops in doorways and runs up garden paths. Jomier waits. The objective is not to get to the playground but to look after the child. At the sound of a siren Ned shouts 'Am'ulance!' He is not good at pronouncing his *b*s but he is bright as a button, the star pupil at Top Totts, his nursery school – a future shoo-in for Westminster Junior School or Colet Court, those first rungs on the ladder to worldly success.

At the playground, Jomier sits on a bench watching the mothers and nannies and au pairs pushing their charges on the swings. There are sometimes one or two out-of-work fathers among them but today Jomier is the only man. The young women look at him uneasily: is he Ned's father or grandfather? Jomier has friends who have children the same age as Ned – ensnared by determined young women with unresolved father complexes.

Over time Jomier has made some playground friends. There are nannies and au pairs who know Ned from his nursery school. Some know Tracey; some Alena; some both. The Australians and New Zealanders are friendly: they tell Jomier about their folks back home. The East European au pairs engage with Jomier to practise their conversational English.

A rare mother, Tessa, is a friend of Henry and Sandra. She knows Jomier from Ned's birthday parties which she has attended with her four-year-old daughter Tatty (Tatiana). Tessa is happy to talk to Jomier. It makes a change from chatting to her Estonian au pair. Tessa is lean and thin, her long legs tightly clad in designer jeans. She is in her late thirties or early forties – attractive but without the bloom of youth. Tessa has an Eton and Oxford husband who makes bucketfuls of money. They have spent a million pounds on a house and another half a million doing it up. She has a child; an au pair; a Prius – yet she is, Jomier senses, discontented. She wonders if, by not working, she has disappointed her parents who spent so much money on her education. Is she wasting her university degree?

Jomier tries to reassure her. A child surely benefits from the presence of its mother. But is he confident of the truth of what he says? Is a child any better off with a mother who worries about not working than with a mother who works and worries about not looking after her child? Pushing swings, hovering around climbing frames, waiting at the bottom of slides – this is dull stuff. If one turns one's mind to other things – if one takes one's eye off the ball and thinks about Virginia Woolf or a Jamie Oliver recipe – then Ivo or Hermione might slip and fall onto bouncy tarmac or bed of wood chippings.

Was it a mistake to educate women? Jomier remembers the buffoon in Stendhal's *De L'Amour*: 'If women are educated they will no longer be content to look after their children.' Stendhal makes him the mouthpiece of reaction but is there not something in what he says? Jomier's friend Theo tells Jomier that women should be educated to make them suitable wives for educated men. But that is not the way women see it. They want to be educated to be able to live independently from men. They are empowered by their university degrees. This is why Tessa, the mother in the playground, is uneasy. What was the point of a degree in Politics and Economics from Oxford if it was not to pursue a career? But then what is the point of a nine-to-five job in a boring office when she has more than enough money as it is? She wants Jomier to solve this riddle. He is old and so may be wise.

Jomier prevaricates. He has to think about what he thinks on the question and then decide how many of these thoughts should be expressed to Tessa. He feels he has had the worst of both worlds: a wife who earned nothing, then left him and took him to the cleaners. If Tilly had had a career – a lawyer, a teacher – that had given her a standing in the world as something more than Mrs Jomier, would she have felt less impelled to have sex with Max? Or would she have found some Lothario in the workplace? A partner in the directors' dining room? The personal trainer in the corporate gym?

Jomier likes Tessa. He feels sympathy over her dilemma. 'I have a friend,' he says, 'who thinks women should be educated to make them good wives for educated men.'

Tessa scowls. 'That's medieval,' she says.

'He would take that as a compliment,' says Jomier.

'You have strange friends,' says Tessa.

'We go back a long way,' says Jomier.

'Even so,' says Tessa.

Jomier asks Tessa about the role models in her childhood. Tessa's mother did not work and was neurotic and so was left by Tessa's father, a professor of Spanish, who took early retirement and went to live with one of his students in Madrid. Tessa does not visit her father. She remains angry with him for deserting the home. Jomier senses that she looks to him, at that moment, to play his role. Jomier, thinking of his own daughter Louisa, far away on the pampas, accessible only on the telephone or via Skype, tries to rise to Tessa's expectations but he is afraid to talk. He does not want to infect her with his pessimism, his cynicism, his disillusion. Jomier feels sorry for Tessa just as he feels sorry for Henry and Louisa, and for all those whose adult condition has been blighted by the distress of their parents' separation. Jomier is against divorce. It enables women to take men to the cleaners and causes children to suffer in ways they do not understand. It lays a time bomb in the child's unconscious mind which is only detonated in later life – self-obsession, self-doubt, depression, the doomed sense that what happened to their parents will inevitably happen to them.

'It seems to me,' says Jomier at last, 'that children need stability, continuity, firmness and overwhelming love. The first thing, then, is for you and Hugh to stick together . . .'

Tessa shrugs and smiles as if to say 'take that as given'.

'But when it comes to caring for the children . . .' Jomier hesitates. Does he know what he thinks? 'Nannies and au pairs are fine so far as they go but they are like Gurkhas or prostitutes. They are doing the job for money.'

Tessa listens: so far she seems to like what she hears.

'You might well find a job that was challenging and fulfilling. You might rise to be the CEO of ICI or the Director General of the BBC or even editor of *Vogue*. But there will always be others who could do the job as well as you. There is no one else who can be Tatty's mother.'

Tessa looks uncertain. ICI and the BBC, perhaps, but editor of *Vogue*?

Jomier reads her thoughts but does not want to get bogged down with detail. 'We live in an age . . .' he goes on – but then falters. He wants to attack feminism that has freed women to be wage slaves, neglect their children and let men off the leash. He knows it will not work. Simone de Beauvoir, Germaine Greer, Virginia Woolf, Betty Friedan, Sylvia Plath – these are the saints in the pantheon of the modern woman. Tessa may have a degree from Oxford in Politics and Economics but she is a child of her time. Anti-feminism is a symptom of misogyny and misogyny is one of the Seven Deadly Sins.

Tessa fills the silence created by Jomier's hesitation, telling Jomier that she is ashamed of her dissatisfaction because she knows that her life is not bad as lives go. Jomier listens and commiserates and does not think less of her for the whinging leitmotif. Even if a life is free of major aggravations – cancer, poverty, a drunken husband, a sick child – there are plenty of minor ones about which to complain – stepping on dog shit, a broken-down gas boiler, a parking ticket. Women are genetically programmed to complain after generations of being dependent upon men. From the Stone Age to the 1950s, a wife depended upon her husband to get things done – hence the instinct to manipulate by mood. Sulks are the stick: sweet smiles are the carrot. If you want sex, put me in the mood for sex – a pearl necklace, a candlelit dinner, a weekend in Paris – first class on Eurostar, a suite at the Ritz; or, among the financially challenged, a suite of a different kind – a three-piece suite in cream leather from Leather World, or a week on the Costa del Sol, or new shelves in the lounge – SEX bartered for DIY.

Women, Jomier realises, have yet to adapt to their own liberation. Perhaps they never will. Jomier's mistake when it came to Tilly 1 was to treat her as a liberated woman. Her opinions on this and that – sex outside marriage, the Vietnam War – were 'progressive' because progressive views, like Biba dresses, were then in fashion. But she did not want her feminist views to be taken at face value. She did not want to be consulted about what they could or could not afford; she did not want to think about the means to the end. She had been born into a certain position in English society and expected Jomier to maintain it. She hated being treated by Jomier as a *compañera* – a comrade-wife who went to cheap restaurants to save money; she wanted to be a kept woman who felt sexy eating pâté de foie gras and drinking champagne.

'Idiot!' Jomier is not thinking of Tilly. He is thinking of himself. Tessa's stream of consciousness is momentarily arrested: Jomier has said the word out loud.

'Oh, I wouldn't call him that,' says Tessa.

Who is she talking about? Jomier has not been listening. He tries to pick up the thread of what she is saying.

'I think the proposal probably wasn't much good. That's the trouble these days. You have to do as much research for the proposal as you do for the book . . .'

Jomier remembers. Tessa is a writer. Or she was a writer before she married. What had she written? Chick lit? A biography of her great-aunt? He cannot remember. It does not seem to matter. Tessa burbles on. Jomier wants to look at his watch, to see if the time has come to take Ned home. He is afraid that Tessa will take this as a sign that he is not interested in what she is saying. He waits for a natural break; or for some act of God. Rain. Or Ned falling off the climbing frame.

Feminism. Jomier has a theory that he would like to put to Tessa. Feminism is a form of flirtation. The female of the species is genetically programmed to provoke the male of the species to assert its strength. Only thus can the female discover at whom to squirt her pheromones and direct her come-hither looks. In the past there were wars to sort out the men from the boys but after two world wars they no longer serve this purpose. They cost too many lives – the baby was thrown out with the bathwater. There was no sifting in the trenches: the strong died with the weak. No heroes returned. Technology – the Maxim gun, the cluster bomb, the tactical nuclear weapon. Valour is redundant.

Test men in other ways. In an era when the survival of the fittest depends upon brains rather than brawn, provoke men to assert their prowess with absurd theories about the oppression of women. Tell men whose forefathers fought and laboured to provide for and protect their wives and children that they were tyrants in the home. Bring forward Sartre's highbrow doxy, Simone de Beauvoir, to ascribe the mediocrity of women to their disdainful treatment by men. Praise Betty Friedan for holding that women are better off without husbands, and Germaine Greer's view that children flourish without fathers. The female of the species knows this is nonsense. In her viscera she is looking for a mate who will fertilise her and provide for both her and the ensuing offspring but thinks her feminist bravura will eliminate the wimps; that, like a Stone Age hunk with his club, the real man will grab her and fuck her and tell her to shut up.

But he does not. The real man does not rise to the challenge. He does not swat the feminist absurdities like pesky flies. Why not? Because the feminist hypothesis suits him just fine. By all means liberate women! Free them to work. Let them pay their own way and have sex at will. Abolish all those pejorative terms – tart, bolter, slag, slapper, whore, *demi-mondaine* – and with them cad, bounder, blackguard, roué, scoundrel, rake, libertine. The male of the species who until now had to pay for sex – either in cash to a prostitute or with a joint account to a wife – now calls the feminist's bluff and enjoys sex without strings. No longer need he deploy the subterfuge of a Vicomte de Valmont to seduce today's Cécile. Her virginity is an embarrassment. *She* seduces *him*.

At the back of her mind there is an endgame – commitment, marriage, children – but before that stretch two decades of mix & match, test drives, sea, sun and sex. Lord Halifax's *Advice to a Daughter* gathers dust on the shelves: the norms for today's young woman come from *Friends*, *Frasier* and *Sex and the City*. She emulates the heroines of Hollywood movies who bestow their 'final favours' on the first date. Thanks to the pill, she no longer worries about getting pregnant; and thanks to the zeitgeist, about being thought loose. Her only concerns: Is he wearing a condom? Will he find me 'good in bed'?

Jomier thinks about these things and feels an emotion he cannot define. Does he approve or disapprove of modern morals? He debates the question with his alter ego – Dr Jekyll *in conversazione* with Mr Hyde. But which is which? In Stevenson's story, Mr Hyde is the dark side of Dr Jekyll – passionate and angry rather than sensible and scientific. But today's sensible and scientific Dr Jekyll would read the *Guardian* and favour sex as a recreation from the earliest age; while it is the irrational Mr Hyde with his primitive superstitions who bundles sex with marriage, procreation and unromantic love.

Ned wants to pee. Jomier is grateful for this alert. Ned's potty training is not as established as his mother would have the world believe. Tracey, the nanny, has told Jomier that he can count on a four-minute interval between Ned's announcement of a call of nature and his answer to that call.

The timing has been proved to be imprecise. There have been accidents. Jomier is sympathetic towards his grandson. Soon he too will be incontinent and have accidents too.

Jomier and Ned take their leave of Tessa and Tatty. They stop off at the public lavatory by the entrance to the playground. Ned pees. Then the dawdling walk home. Jomier hands Ned over to Alena, the au pair, who has prepared tea for Ned and Samantha – penne with peas and snippets of ham. She offers Jomier a cup of tea. Jomier would like a cup of tea but making conversation in broken English with Alena is too high a price to pay. He politely declines. He stoops to kiss his grandson, says 'bye-bye' in a babyish voice, and leaves.

# 8

JOMIER IS INVITED to dinner by Ruth to meet her friend Judith. Jomier has known Ruth for many years. There was almost something between them. Almost. But not quite. She is not a former lover but a might-have-been. An also-ran. That is a sufficient basis for lifelong friendship: women never forget the men who have fancied them. The friendship went into abeyance when Jomier married Tilly because Tilly could not stand Ruth. She went reluctantly to Ruth's dinner parties but never asked Ruth back. Ruth was gushy, blowsy, not in their league. The friendship revived when Jomier was cut loose from Tilly and became that rare commodity, an unattached man. Ruth is a matchmaker. She introduces Jomier to her single friends and her single friends to Jomier. Ruth herself is divorced but has tethered a presentable lover. He is tall and languid and was once an important person in the BBC. He does not have much money but, at Ruth's stage in life, one takes what one can get. No one knows what he does now and no one likes to ask.

Ruth is a natural evangelist. She is determined that her friends should succeed where she has succeeded and enjoy what she enjoys. Jomier finds this tiresome. Ruth tells him that he *must* read this novel or go to that play or see such-and-such an exhibition. Jomier dislikes reading novels. It is an invasion of his privacy to have an author enter his mind and manipulate his imagination. He also blames the novel for flattering women. Nineteenth-century novelists knew which side their bread was buttered: their books were bought by women and they portray lovely, clever, witty, charming heroines and spin elaborate narratives around what *au fond* is their quest for insemination.

Jomier also dislikes the theatre. As actors prance around on a stage, it strikes him that they are having more fun than he is: why, then, is *he* paying *them*? The dramas are banal. Playwrights titillate the bourgeois audience with obscenity and left-wing views. Rich solicitors and brokers from Hampstead get a frisson from the leftist agitprop; their wives from the 'fucks' and 'shits' and simulated sex onstage.

Why does such mediocrity thrive? *Raison d'état*. The state has spent many millions on building theatres and theatres must have plays. Actors must have something to act, directors something to direct, critics something to criticise, the inhabitants of Hampstead and Islington something to discuss with their friends. It is the same with the visual arts. Great galleries have been built. Something must be placed on the podia or hung on the walls. Millions file through former power stations or warehouses to gawp at the totems of modernity that they have been told are high art. Who will dare say that the Emperor is naked when the art-world apparatchiks insist that he is fully clothed? So thinks Jomier who once loved to look at a painting by Manet or Vermeer. But now even the old masters do not draw him from his home. Why travel up west on the crowded Underground to be jostled by the crowd of culture pilgrims, and peer over their shoulders to catch a glimpse of some sculpture or painting? Will Jomier lie on his deathbed racked with regret that he has never seen the *Mona Lisa* or the *Venus de Milo*? No. When Jomier hears the word 'culture', he reaches for his TV remote.

Jomier does not express these thoughts to Ruth. No one, not even Jomier, wants to be thought uncultured. He assures Ruth that he will go to see the Gormleys at the Royal Academy or the Freuds at the Tate; and, when caught out at missing a show at Dulwich or Whitechapel, he hits his forehead with the palm of his hand to show his exasperation at his own forgetfulness. Or he lies. Yes, no sooner had he read Dorment's review in the *Telegraph* than he went straight to Cork Street! Yes, he was *enormously* excited at the Frieze Art Fair. Or he turns the tables. How *could* Ruth have driven to the Dordogne without stopping off to see the tapestries at Angers? Or from Rome to Naples and miss the amazing murals in the crypt of the cathedral at Anagni?

As with art, so with women. Ruth tells Jomier that he is sure to like Judith. Jomier has heard this before and has never known Ruth's predictions fulfilled. By 'like' Ruth does not mean a temperamental affinity; she means sexual desire. Jomier recognises that some women in late-middle age are more intelligent than others, some more amusing than others, some more elegant than others, but as a genus they are unlikely to inspire desire. Nature dictates that men will be attracted only to pre-menopausal women. In Africa, Arabia or the Mediterranean littoral, older women shroud themselves in black. Even younger women, once they are married, wear veils and shawls and loose-fitting garments to cover their bodies which, if they remain delectable, are for the delectation of their husbands alone. If, after giving birth to children, they are no longer delectable they are best hidden from public view, leaving their menfolk free to play backgammon, puff at hookahs and sip sweet mint tea.

Not so the women of the West. They eschew such primitive customs. They wear décolleté dresses and spend billions of pounds on elixirs and unguents to retard or reverse the depredations of nature. Wax strips off the unwanted hairs and tights flatten ripples of cellulite and veil scaly skin. Bright-coloured skirts and tops distract the eye from the wrinkled flesh and bleary eyes. Artful coiffeurs and coiffeuses wash and dye and tint and streak what is left of a once glorious head of hair. And what does Western man do but play the game – pretend to notice and admire and chatter and flirt; pretend to respond to the fluttering of eyelashes, heavy with caked mascara; pretend to be open to possibilities when he would rather be chatting up their daughters or be back at home watching TV.

But TV offers no respite from the aphrodisiacal imperative. It is not a backgammon board containing dice and counters and geometric shapes but a glass window through which Jomier sees gangsters and pundits and attractive women. Every soap, every drama, cries out: *cherchez la femme*. Jomier does not watch porn: he does not want sex. He watches film noirs where the good guy gets the girl. They fall in love. Jomier wants to love. To be loved. To cherish. To be cherished. He wants a Veronica Lake to fall in his arms. The urge to mate has left his loins but remains lodged in his brain. But Jomier is a retired barrister, not a taciturn private eye. He does not bear the scars and bruises from punch-ups with thugs and toughs on his body; he bears the scars and bruises on his psyche from the punch-up of life. Veronica Lake would sniff out a loser and move on to a Max.

Ruth does not give up. She has introduced Jomier to Pamela, Annabel and Taffeta. Now Judith. Jomier arrives before Judith. He talks to Ralph, Ruth's languid lover who was once someone important in the BBC. It is June. Ralph talks about Wimbledon. Jomier has no interest in tennis but listens all the same. Ralph asks Jomier why Serbia produces champions when Britain does not. Jomier talks about the legacy of state sponsorship under Communism but his mind is elsewhere. It is on Ruth's bust and bottom which extend in equal proportion to front and rear. Jomier notes the unusual equilibrium. There are women with large busts and women with large bottoms but rarely do they balance one another so well. It is unusual to see, outside Africa, a woman's bottom as muscular as it is large. Jomier wonders if Ruth has African blood.

'Do you remember Boris Becker?' A direct question from Ralph distracts Jomier from his train of thought.

'Wasn't he the blond German who won Wimbledon in . . .?'

Ralph: '1985. And 1986.'

Becker, Jomier recalls, had a black wife who bore him two children. Ruth's ancestors were slave traders from Bristol. Could one of them have fathered a child by an African and passed it off as his heir? Is there a touch of the tar brush in her past? A big-bottomed African gene introduced by one of the slave traders in Bristol? Or were they sugar merchants? Or perhaps both. The triangular trade. Trinkets from Bristol to Africa, slaves from Africa to America, sugar back to Bristol.

Ralph: 'But he lost in 1987.'

Enter Judith. Jomier notes at once that Judith is physically unlike her friend Ruth. She is tall and has no protruding bust or bottom. Jomier notes too that Judith seems familiar. This puts him on his guard. There have been embarrassments in the past. Jomier has put questions to a woman over dinner which she had answered over dinner a year before. He had forgotten. She had not. And Ruth? Has she forgotten that she has already introduced him to Judith? Jomier thinks not. If he has met Judith, it was not at one of Ruth's dinner parties. It was further back in the past.

Jomier does not talk to Judith as they stand awaiting the call to dinner. He knows he will be placed next to her at the scrubbed pine table in Ruth's basement kitchen and wishes to hold in reserve what little he might have to say. Ruth has briefed him. Judith is not a widow. She is divorced. This encourages Jomier. He prefers divorcees to widows. Widows are sentimental about their dead husbands. With death all the sharp edges are rubbed off. A special bovine look comes into their eyes as they reminisce about their happy years with Edward or Humphrey or James. Safely reduced to ashes in an urn, Edward and Humphrey and James are not there to contradict them. Dead men tell no tales. Only a few friends who knew the couple well wonder at the rewriting of history.

Divorcees are more entertaining. They are bitter. There are only rough edges. Johnny, Simon, Tim or Harry were weak, two-timing, alcoholic, stingy, absent. Jomier listens with attention because this is no doubt how Tilly talks about him. Weak, yes. Two-timing, yes. Alcoholic, no. Stingy, yes. Absent, no. Bad in bed? The undersized penis? The premature ejaculation? Or adequately equipped but sexually neglectful? Saturday nights spent reading Herodotus. Or watching CNN.

Will Judith be different? A non-embittered divorcee? Ruth ushers her guests down the stairs to her basement kitchen. It is not large but she has crammed in an Aga, a dresser, an upright piano with a sofa in the bay. The view from the bay window is of the door to the coal-hole beneath the pavement. The other window looks out on to a paved gully with steps leading up to the garden. The dresser displays Victorian plates and saucers.

Jomier is placed between Ruth and Judith. This is to prevent him from talking to any of the other women among the guests. Jomier knows what is expected of him and turns to Judith. Again the sense that he has met her before. He asks: 'Who do you think will win Wimbledon?'

Judith laughs. 'You *have* changed.'

Jomier is caught off guard. She remembers. He does not.

'Changed?'

'You used to say that sport was for idiots.'

'I did?'

'Don't you remember?'

'When?'

'A long time ago.'

'Where?'

'At your parents' house. I came over with the Hardings for lunch.'

The Hardings. Neighbours in Sussex. Suddenly Jomier remembers. The pretty girl, a school friend of Lucy Harding. Cheerful. Friendly.

'We played croquet. You said that humanity's obsession with hitting and kicking balls was only explicable in theological terms.'

'Theological terms?'

'Yes. Games were the Devil's distractions.'

'*Divertissements*.' Jomier remembers. He had been reading Pascal.

'You had been reading Pascal. Anything to take our minds off death and eternity.'

'How pretentious.'

'Not at all. I was impressed. Particularly because you went on playing croquet in a most vicious way, knocking me into the bushes.'

'I knocked you into the bushes?'

Judith blushes. 'My ball.'

A sheet of light-sensitive paper immersed in a chemical solution in the darkroom: slowly the patches of dark and light take shape. Jomier remembers that hot day in June; a lunch al fresco; the Hardings – Mr and Mrs Harding, Fred their son, Lucy their daughter, and Lucy's friend Judith. The image is like a Seurat or a Manet in his imagination – *déjeuner sur la terrasse chez les Jomiers* – with this utterly beautiful girl whose eyes had twinkled with merriment as he aired his sophomoric theories about ball games, male rivalry and man's potential destiny outside space and time.

'You married young.'

'You remember?' Judith holds an oval plate to enable Jomier to help himself to a slice of kipper pâté – that stand-by hors d'oeuvre of the 1970s. Has Ruth organised the evening as a trip down memory lane?

'I remember because . . .' He now holds the oval dish for Judith: a glaze covers the brightly painted clay. 'I remember because I wrote to you.'

Judith looks puzzled.

'But you never received the letter.' Jomier feels around for memories in the sludge at the bottom of his life. 'I wanted to ask you out . . .'

Judith waits; a slice of toast holding a smear of kipper pâté is suspended in mid-air.

'But you lived in Suffolk.'

'Norfolk.'

'I thought we might meet in London.'

Judith takes a bite from her piece of toast; munches; listens.

'But I had to get your address from Lucy.'

'Wouldn't she give it to you?'

'It took time to summon up the courage to ask her.'

'Courage? Why?'

'It was a declaration of intent.'

'To Lucy?'

'And through Lucy to the world.'

'Was the world that interested?'

'One thought so . . . at the time. I had to have a pretext.'

'For writing to me?'

'Yes.'

'Wasn't it to ask me out?'

'Yes. But I didn't want Lucy to know that.'

'Why not?'

'I felt that she might want me to ask *her* out.'

Judith shrugged as if to say that this was a poor excuse.

'And she would gossip.'

Again, a shrug.

'We were very timid about dating.'

'Who?'

'Young men from public schools.'

'*Some* young men from public schools.'

'Clearly not . . .' Jomier could not remember the name of her husband.

'Beresford.'

'Anyway, I told Lucy that a friend was giving a party in London and didn't know any girls; that I'd put her on his list and thought that you might like to be asked.'

'So she gave you my address in Norfolk.'

'Yes.'

'Was there a party?'

'No.'

'But you had my address . . .'

'I had your address and I was about to write the letter but I put it off.'

'Why?'

'The summer holidays. I went to Greece.'

'Why not write before you left?'

'To make a date for September? It seemed too far off.'

'So you went off to Greece . . .'

'And when I got home I wrote the letter.'

'Asking me out?'

'Yes. I suggested that we meet up in London to have supper or go to a film. I wrote the letter at night, before I went to bed. I meant to post it the next morning.'

'And?'

'The next day I read *The Times* at breakfast.'

'Ah. *The Times*.'

'The Court Circular. Births, deaths, marriages and engagements. Your engagement. To Beresford. You had been taken off the shelf.'

'So you never sent the letter?'

'I tore it up.'

'A pity.'

'Why?'

'You might have been a reason *not* to marry Beresford.'

'I was still very young.'

Judith nodded. 'Beresford was older.'

'How much older?'

'Ten years.'

'Thirty. A grown man.'

'Yes. And you were?'

'Twenty-one.'

'Too young to marry.'

Yes. I had had little . . . experience.'

Judith smiles. 'You were not part of the sexual revolution?'

'Later. When I went to live in London.'

'Sowing your wild oats?'

'You might call it that.'

'Though that phrase,' says Judith, taking Jomier's empty plate, placing it on hers, then passing both to Ruth, 'dates from long before the 1960s.'

'From the nineteenth century?'

'The eighteenth. So one can't blame Freud or D. H. Lawrence or Havelock Ellis for the breakdown of traditional morality because the sowing of wild oats went on long before Freud or Lawrence or Havelock Ellis – indeed, one might say it is a constant of human nature.'

'Among young men.'

'Yes. Among young men. The *real* change that took place in the 1960s – I mean what was *radical* and *quite different* from anything that had taken place before in human history – was precisely the fact that, thanks to the pill, girls could, and *did*, scatter *their* wild oats without having to worry about getting pregnant –'

'Or social stigma.'

'Or social stigma. Because, while it was always thought that social stigma was a by-product of Christian morality, it was in fact a *social* construct. Bastard children had to be paid for by the parish.'

'But you –' Jomier begins.

'I was born three years too soon.'

'No wild oats?'

'A few snogs and fumbles.'

'Necking.'

Judith laughs. 'Yes, necking. And then marriage.'

'Which didn't last.'

'No. But it might have lasted if I'd married ten years later.'

'After more than a few snogs and fumbles.'

Judith nods, then looks over her shoulder to see if she should help Ruth serve up the chicken-and-mushroom fricassee from the Aga. She rises, goes to the Aga but is sent straight back to her seat. 'Where were we?' she asks Jomier.

'Sex.'

Judith sighs. 'Yes, sex. Sex before marriage. A good thing or a bad thing?'

'A good thing, surely.'

'Well, *I* think so because if I'd married later my marriage might have lasted . . .'

'To Beresford?'

'To whoever. But because I married at the age of twenty, without having sown any wild oats whatsoever, there came a moment when I was bogged down with the children and bored by Beresford and I thought to myself – *Am I really going to die only ever having slept with one man?* And there was this very attractive *other* man and we'd have lunch together and the time came when we either *did* it or we *didn't* do it and we did do it, and Beresford found out and it broke him. Poor Beresford. He wasn't cut out to be a *mari complaisant.*'

'What happened to the other man?'

Judith laughs. 'He got scared and ran off.'

'He left you?'

'He had a wife.'

'Did you think that he would leave his wife?'

'I hadn't really thought it through.'

'And since?'

Judith does not answer his question but continues with her train of thought. 'But are women really better off? My daughter Ophelia has led the life of a liberated woman – a career, relationships, a six-month marriage, divorce, bla-bla-bla – and now she's thirty-eight with no boyfriend, mixing with exes and rejects, and the prospect of a nuclear family looking increasingly remote.'

'And Beresford?'

'Oh, Beresford's fine. He's made a pile of money in the City, and married again – a mousy, calculating, demure risk analyst – who as soon as she had secured Beresford stopped work and now spends her time doing up their houses in Chelsea and Gloucestershire and the South of France.'

'While you . . .'

'I get by in Wandsworth.'

Jomier is attracted to Judith. Her breezy 'fallen woman' line does not irritate him; he does not react adversely, as he usually does, to this woman of 'a certain age', though the neckline of her dress shows that her breasts, while still smooth and soft, no longer run on in a continuous curve from her breastbone but have sunk in their foundations. The eyeshadow, the artificial curls of her tinted hair – all the artifices of the post-menopausal woman – do not trigger the usual indifference. It is as if Jomier has removed his varifocal rimless glasses and sees Judith through an astigmatic haze that softens the image, airbrushing away the wrinkles around her eyes and mouth, the small bleb on her lower lip. Using the tools of an inner Adobe Photoshop, the memory of the twenty-year-old Judith is superimposed upon the reality of the same woman forty years on. Jomier is thinking: this woman is intelligent, amusing, sincere. If she had married me instead of Beresford . . . If I had married her instead of Tilly . . .

And might it be possible, all these years later, Jomier asks himself, to pick up where we left off?

'Perhaps we should pick up where we left off,' Jomier says to Judith. By now they have done with the chicken fricassee and are eating rhubarb fool.

Judith smiles – a nice, friendly, youthful smile. 'You mean . . .'

'I'll rewrite the letter and ask you out.'

'Or an email?'

'What is the address?' Jomier is about to reach for the small notebook and ballpoint pen in the inner pocket of his jacket but suddenly feels the same awkwardness that he had felt forty years before. He does not want to be seen writing down Judith's email address by the other guests.

'grant.j76@absmail.com.'

Jomier repeats what she has said. 'I'll remember it.'

Judith looks at him sceptically. She has understood. Again Jomier fails to feel the irritation he habitually feels when a woman reads his thoughts. 'If you forget, you can always ask Ruth.'

'Of course.'

'Unless . . .'

'What?'

'You might be embarrassed as you were with Lucy?'

'At my age?' Jomier gives an unconvincing laugh.

'I'll give you my card before we go.'

'Your card?'

'A business card.'

'You have a business?'

'I teach yoga.'

A yoga teacher. A potter. A garden designer. A psycho-therapist. An instructor in the Alexander technique. These are the occupations of women of a certain age. A yoga teacher will at least have a supple body. She will know the routines of the *Kama Sutra*. When they stand at the end of dinner, and for a moment Judith looks away, Jomier stands back to assess her figure but her dress is long and loose. It covers her like muslin over a cheese. All that is exposed is her face, her hands and what can been seen through the window of her décolletage – the loose skin under her chin, the tight skin over her breastbone, the soft, tanned, freckled, chamois leathery base of her breasts. And her eyes? Jomier cannot remember their colour. And now she is looking away.

It is eleven o'clock. The guests would like to go home but if they leave now Ruth would consider that her evening was a flop. It is another half-hour before the party breaks up. Jomier takes his leave. As he enters the narrow hall, Judith comes down the stairs. 'Here.' She hands him her card. Jomier smiles at her but she is already past him. Jomier leaves the house. He stops, takes out his wallet, puts the card in one of the slots designed for credit cards. He gets into his Volkswagen Golf and returns home.

## 9

JOMIER SLEEPS BADLY. Jomier always sleeps badly after drinking more than one glass of wine. Jomier knows this and would like to drink less or nothing at all but cannot endure a dinner party without a drink. The immediate effect of the first drink is to undermine his resolve not to have a second. Alcohol enters his bloodstream. He becomes eloquent. He laughs as if amused. He flirts. He responds to flirtation. He makes foolish suggestions: 'I'll rewrite the letter and ask you out.' 'What about an email?' Six hours later, at five in the morning, he lies wide awake. What had possessed him? He has made a commitment. He has raised expectations.

In the morning, as he eats his breakfast, the exasperation at his own folly persists. Here before him are the elements of perfect happiness – the morning newspaper, a cup of coffee, a slice of toast, an empty day – nothing to do but transcribe the past from his handwritten notebooks and enter the present into his digital journal – his blog. His toilette out of the way – shaving, defecating, vitamin pills, making his bed and taking a short walk around the block – Jomier goes to his desk, switches on his computer and loads Microsoft Word. He opens the document 'Journal – current'. He writes an account of what he did yesterday – Ruth's dinner party, Judith, the kipper pâté. He then opens the document 'Journals 1950–1970' and searches for 'Judith' but the search item is not found. He tries 'Lucy' and up comes Lucy Harding, the neighbours' daughter. It is 1958. He reads and remembers. A teenage party. The Harding parents away. Dancing to music from a gramophone – the early days of LPs. The lights go out. Couples sidle to sofas or fall on the carpeted floor. Kissing. Fumbling. Heavy-petting. Lucy leads him into her father's study – his den. They tumble onto the leather sofa. He slides his hand down the front of her dress and, with the index finger of his right hand, fiddles with a nipple. 'A crystallised cherry on a plate of junket.' That dates it. No one eats junket now.

Jomier scrolls down with the wheel on his mouse. Another party where he manages to put two fingers beneath the elastic of Lucy's knickers and feel moist, squidgy, bristly flesh. They go no further: he is still only sixteen, Lucy fifteen, and other couples are necking and petting in the same room. The holidays end. Jomier and Lucy go back to school and, when Jomier presses 'Find Next', the cursor leaps forward six years to 'The Hardings come to lunch. Lucy brings a friend.' Some months later: 'Get the address of Lucy's friend'; then 'Back from Greece. Write to Lucy's friend'; then finally, her name. 'Jydith engaged to Beresford Grant. Tear up the letter.'

Jomier corrects the spelling of the name of Judith, searches again for 'Jydith' to see if the same typo occurs elsewhere and, after a search lasting a microsecond, is informed that the item was not found. He reads on. He seems to have been unaffected by the engagement to Beresford Grant of Jydith-Judith. There are more fish in the sea than ever came out of it. Is that the expression? Jomier has a careless memory – for sayings, proverbs, lyrics, hymns. It had irritated Tilly.

Other fish. More crystallised cherries on junket, on jelly, on blancmange. Jomier is both the participant and detached observer. 'C. When she is sexually excited she puffs like a pair of bellows.' Who was C.? Catherine? Or Clare? The Clare who had turned down Marco? 'A foreigner. And almost certainly queer.'

Did Jomier only write in his journal about his encounters with girls? If, instead of leaping through his life in microseconds with the search facility, Jomier scrolls down the pages of 'Journals 1950–1970' he sees that there are long, and now tedious, passages about politics. Jomier and Marco decide to right the wrongs that prevail in the world. They have a one-word solution. Revolution! They are both Communists – not party members but fellow-travellers. Marx: 'Our aim is not to understand the world but to change it!' Jomier and Marco see themselves as Left Bank left-wing intellectuals with Gauloises dangling out of their mouths – Sartre, Camus, Aragon. But both are cautious. At the great demonstration against the war in Vietnam outside the American Embassy, they stand at the back of the crowd, ready to retreat to Claridge's. Jomier cannot serve the proletariat as a lawyer with a conviction for a breach of the peace. And Marco dislikes physical proximity with the masses: throughout the fracas in Grosvenor Square he covers his nose with a handkerchief soaked in eau de cologne.

Jomier is now more embarrassed by his socialistic past than his fingering of young women's private parts. Marx, Lenin, Mao, Castro were his heroes. Even Stalin! Without the industrialisation of the Soviet Union in the 1920s, he explains in his journal, there would have been no T-54 tanks to defeat the Germans on the Kursk salient. Hitler would have been victorious. An Auschwitz-Birkenau would have been built in England's green and pleasant land.

Jomier reads on. The Russians were right to crush the Hungarians in 1956. And the Czechs in 1968. Without Soviet hegemony in Eastern Europe, all the old *casus belli* would be revived. The Sudetenland. The Danzig corridor. It was the only way to kill off German revanchism once and for all.

Jomier keeps reading his journal of 1968, not to find references to the historical Judith but to keep the twenty-first-century Judith out of his mind. But she cannot be ignored. There is her card next to his keyboard on his desk. Judith Grant. Yoga teacher. grant.j76@absmail.com. He closes both his journals and opens Outlook Express. He clicks 'addresses' and enters her details. There are no other Judiths. Now as soon as he writes the letters j u d his computer will know who he means. grant.j76. A digital label for a woman of flesh and blood. Days pass. Jomier postpones sending an email to Judith. He has it in mind. He means to do so. He writes 'email Judith' on his list of 'things to do'. There are other items on the list. Putting things on the list is the first step towards doing what Jomier knows he must do. He waits patiently for the time to be right: for the day, the hour, the minute when he will feel up to making the call, writing the email, reading the book. Other things are postponed which do not even make it to the list: articles in periodicals which look interesting and will be read in due course – the *New Yorker,* the *TLS, Prospect,* the *New York Review of Books.* Jomier is minded to return to them but is deterred by the dense mass of words in those columns of print. How much easier to switch on the radio or the television. Particularly the television. Jomier likes to watch films – not just the black-and-white film noirs but Hollywood blockbusters in which Bruce Willis, Arnold Schwarzenegger or Steven Seagal triumph over evil incarnate in Lee Van Cleef, Robert

Shaw or Alan Rickman. He has seen them all before – the sequels and prequels, the *Die Hards, Terminators, Under Sieges* – but thanks to his age he only remembers the plot when he reaches the last reel.

Jomier avoids the main channels at prime time with their inane quiz shows and documentaries about menstruation or obese Siamese twins; nor does he watch afternoon made-for-TV Hollywood movies about the travails of lesbian mothers with autistic sons interspersed with ads to appeal to the retired or the unemployed – conservatories, double glazing, incontinence pads, personal loans. He also hates romantic films with happy endings; or erotic films with misty, tasteful takes of heaving buttocks, groaning and grunting on the soundtrack, which make him think of Tilly with Max but also that it would be good to be hugged and caressed by a warm woman. Judith. Should he try for one last throw of the dice?

Ten days after Ruth's dinner party Jomier sends Judith an email suggesting that they meet up to go to a movie. She accepts. 'I'd love to.' They agree on a film – French, enigmatic, thrillerish but not a thriller, starring Daniel Auteuil rather than Jean-Claude Van Damme. It is showing in Chelsea – midway between Wandsworth and Hammersmith. Jomier buys the tickets and waits for Judith in the foyer. She arrives – controlled, calm; dressed stylishly but not dressed-up; a little folksy; low-heeled shoes. She smiles. He smiles. They go in.

Jomier finds it hard to understand the film. Is it intentionally obscure? Or is he slow on the uptake? He is distracted by thoughts about her low-heeled shoes. Does she wear them because she is tall? She is no taller than Jomier but, with higher heels, would tower over smaller men. Height is an under-acknowledged factor in sexual attraction. Women like men to be taller than they are. A small man does not trigger the impulse to reproduce. There are no glandular secretions, however handsome the shrimp, unless he is a world-historical genius like Napoleon or a successful actor like Daniel Auteuil. Are the low heels to increase Judith's chances? To reduce the height of potential lovers by two or three centimetres and so enlarge the pool? Would Judith have accepted Jomier's invitation to go to the movies if he had been 5´4" rather than 6´1"? Would he have asked her if she had been 6´1" and he 5´4"? Does the historical conundrum posed by Pascal about the shape of Cleopatra's nose apply to the feelings of two English divorcees sitting in a cinema on the King's Road?

On-screen Daniel Auteuil is having sex with a beautiful girl. She murmurs. She gasps. She is acting. Can a frigid actress simulate orgasms? Or a virgin? Or must she draw on her own experience? Can the husband of an actress ever know if his wife's response to his caresses is sincere? Or any husband? Jomier thinks back to Tilly. Was she pretending? Or was she thinking of Max?

The film ends. They come out on to the King's Road. It is dark but still warm. People sit at tables on the pavement. They might be in Rome. Judith tells Jomier that she liked the film. Jomier is glad of her forthright opinion. He has no view about the film but, being a barrister, argues against the position she has taken, saying that the director's intentions were obscure. Gently, tentatively, she suggests pointers in the plot that Jomier has missed.

They eat at Pizza Express. Judith asks for a tomato and mozzarella salad with dough balls; Jomier an American Hot, a side salad; they share a bottle of house wine. They continue to talk about the film. Jomier attacks the hypocrisy of 'art house' films which purport to be superior to Hollywood blockbusters but invariably rely for their appeal on a pretty actress at some point in the drama removing her clothes.

'Do you object to that?' asks Judith in the gentle tone of a psychotherapist.

'It makes one complicit in voyeurism.'

'And voyeurism . . .' She hesitates.

'What?'

'Is wrong?'

'It's demeaning.'

Judith smiles. 'You are puritanical . . .'

'My ancestors were Huguenots.'

'But you're not a Calvinist?'

'Far from it.'

'Then what is wrong with enjoying the spectacle of Emmanuelle Béart's naked body?'

'Was it Emmanuelle Béart?'

'No. I meant only . . . Let's say Brigitte Bardot.'

'Because it provokes desires that it cannot fulfil.'

'The fulfilment comes afterwards when all those young couples go back to their flats and make love.'

'Not all moviegoers have lovers.'

'That's true. But the celibate moviegoer, as you say, must know what to expect and can therefore stay away.'

'Or . . .'

She knows what he means. Masturbation. The love that dare not speak its name.

The waiter brings the bottle of wine. Jomier fills their two glasses. He proposes a toast. 'To old friends.' Jomier clinks his glass against hers. She repeats what he has said. 'To old friends.'

\*　　\*　　\*

The mozzarella, the sliced tomatoes, the dough balls, the American Hot pizza are all eaten; the bottle of wine is drunk. Jomier asks for the bill. When it arrives, Judith takes a purse out of her bag, meaning to pay. Jomier will not allow it.

'But you paid for the tickets –'

'It's a generational thing. I would feel emasculated . . .'

She smiles and gives in. Jomier wonders how a man can be emasculated when his cojones were long since removed – by Max the surgeon, Tilly the nurse. Yet he used the word. Why does he still feel that on a date the man should pay for the woman? A faulty signal to the brain like a twinge in the toe of an amputated leg? Or a necessary first step in the ritual of courtship – an assertion of strength, an implicit promise to provide for and cherish and protect?

Jomier walks Judith to her car – an old Peugot 305. She turns. 'That was lovely.' They kiss – not mouth to mouth but pursed lips on cheeks. A last look under the eyelashes and a smile that says: 'I am sure we will progress from cheeks to mouth but we must take things slowly – step by step, date by date. This may be the last throw of the dice.'

## 10

NED IS FOUR. Jomier is invited to his grandson's birthday party and feels he must attend. He would rather stay away, and supposes that Henry and Sandra would be relieved if he came up with some convincing reason for declining their invitation, but such an excuse is beyond anyone's invention. What pressing engagement could Jomier have at four o'clock on a Sunday afternoon? It would seem odd if he did not go – and Henry is embarrassed by any manifestation of oddity. He also knows that Ned would like him to be there. Jomier is loved by Ned. Ned's face lights up when he sees Jomier. Samantha's too. Samantha also loves Jomier but she does not relate to him in the same way as Ned. Both Samantha and Ned are acutely aware of gender. Both flirt with good-looking members of the opposite sex. They are aware of the difference between a mother and a father. Samantha's role model is her mother. Ned's role model is his father; but Jomier is a secondary, auxiliary role model. The long dull hours spent by the swings and see-saws in the playground bring a return. Trust. Familiarity. Love.

Jomier would rather stay away from his grandchildren's birthday parties because Tilly also attends. Tilly not only attends but helps with the preparation. Nominally Sandra is in charge but Sandra has other things on her mind

– management buyouts, corporate takeovers, private-equity finance. When a misplaced comma in a contract can mean catastrophe, it is difficult to concentrate on egg sandwiches, cocktail sausages, orange jellies, crisps, Hula-Hoops, balloons and the birthday cake. She has switched off her BlackBerry but her mind remains on standby.

Tracey and Alena are on hand but they do not know the ropes. Tactfully, skilfully, Tilly takes command. She is an experienced children's party-giver: she has arranged many over the years. She never enjoyed it. She did it in the old days because it was expected – by her children, their friends, their friends' mothers. In particular the other mothers. Tilly wanted to earn the approval of the other mothers. The only constraint on her behaviour was peer-group pressure; the only sins the things Hermione and Alice and Caroline and Mary would think are sins. An affair? Everyone does it. Divorce? With a husband like Jomier, understandable. Pinching Max off Jane? These things happen.

And now? Jomier sits in an armchair in the corner of the room, talking politely to Tessa, mother of Tatty, and other friends of Sandra and Henry. Every now and then he looks at Tilly. He avoids meeting her eyes. She avoids meeting his. She does not talk to the other adults but busies herself with the children. She is the one to pour out the orange juice. She is the one to organise the musical bumps. Why so assiduous? Why does she put herself out for Henry in a way she did for Jomier only in the first years of their married life? Jomier remarked on this phenomenon when they were still married – the gradual shift of loyalty from husband to son. Was it a symptom of her general disenchantment with marriage? He then remarked upon the same phenomenon in other marriages and understood. Women are all over their husbands and boyfriends until they have had children.

Once the inseminator has served his purpose, they look to the future. The husband may still provide for the mother and her brood; his substance is eaten like the flesh of the male mate of the praying mantis. But it is the son, not the husband, who will be around when she is old and frail.

All this was a long time ago. When Tilly's eyes do meet Jomier's, as they must on occasion, this is what they express: 'It was all a long time ago.' The acceptance of this formula is meant to lead to civility, even friendliness, between Jomier, Tilly, Max and Jane. But Jomier does not accept the concept behind the formula – that time heals all. The man who is crippled because his wife pushed him down the stairs remains crippled even if he accepts that she was provoked by his slap of her face. Jomier remains crippled. He still suffers. He cannot look at Tilly's elegant legs without thinking of them parting for the loins of her hirsute lover.

Jomier looks around at Henry and Sandra's friends – men beginning to grow paunchy and bald; women starting to look used and tired. Do any of them have lovers? Probably not. They are from a different generation. They married later in life – wild oats scattered, curiosity satisfied, youthful passion spent. They expect fidelity once the commitment is made but feel no jealousy of former boyfriends. Their lovelife is linear. The exes are among their friends. No tormenting visions of fellatio and cunnilingus for Tony as he chats to Ted; no thought that the same tongue that now licks the cream smudged from an oozing eclair onto Ted's knuckle once slithered between the *labia minora* and *labia majora* of Jessica, his wife.

Latin – the language of anatomy and Catholicism. Why, after all these years, is Jomier unable to expunge the anatomical, the gynaecological, the venereal from his mind? He looks across the room at Tilly. She is stooping over Ned to persuade him to pass the parcel now that the music has resumed. Her figure remains slim; she makes the best of herself; she is well preserved – not mutton dressed as lamb but chic mutton in expensive smart-casual clothes. The skin is taut over her cheekbones but loose at her neck. There are wrinkles – no Botox – but the natural silver of her hair is streaked with gold. She is an elegant, handsome woman *d'un certain age* – dressed no longer to attract the male of the species but to appear as much in place in Kensington and Knightsbridge as she would be out of place on the Goldhawk Road.

Jomier thinks back thirty years to the time when they were giving children's parties for Henry and Louisa. Tilly had been softer, more easily amused, but always distracted by the toddlers' harassment and tired after broken nights. Less confident. Easton, the expensive analyst, and Maureen, the cheaper marriage counsellor, had both tentatively suggested that Tilly's initial attraction to Jomier had been because he was a confident, masterful, slightly older man. Her father's failings – drunk, depressed – had led her to seek an ersatz father as a mate. But the qualities that had appealed to her psyche as they set sail had grown less appealing as the voyage progressed. Confident became know-all. Masterful became bossy. Jomier's fastidious compulsion to keep everything shipshape had come up against the laziness of his crew. There had been misunderstandings from the very start. Jomier had assumed that his wife would make his breakfast and straighten the duvet on the marital bed. Tilly had grown up with servants: such things were done by others. She did not see herself as a member of the crew but as a passenger travelling first class. If they had lived together before they had married, these misunderstandings might have been resolved. But would it have meant that they would have chosen not to marry? No. They were in love.

Tilly picks up the paper torn from the parcel by the little fingers of covetous children. Tessa's Tatty has won the prize – a bejewelled plastic Princess made in China. Tilly takes the paper to the recycling bin. Tilly is no longer lazy. She now has servants in both her homes, and Henry and Sandra have Alena and Tracey; but Tilly has learned that even the grandest women now muck in. There are limits, of course: dusting, vacuum cleaning, cleaning lavatories with bristly brushes – she was not born for that!

Tilly is now confident. Gone is the bashfulness, the easy embarrassment, the timid feminine thing of sheltering behind the masterful man. When they had first married, Tilly had been a reluctant interface with the outside world. She pleaded with Jomier to make the calls – to the utility companies, to their friends. He issued the invitations. He booked the tickets. He made the plans. After the divorce he came to realise that this dominance had been illusory. He had been the front man, the factotum, not the boss. 'The Tylers love their Volkswagen Golf.' 'There's this villa in Umbria which Susie and John rented last year . . .' 'Let's have the Simpsons to dinner, with the Chalmers . . . and Max and Jane.'

Tilly is going around with a teapot to refill the mugs of Henry and Sandra's friends. Every now and then she glances at Sandra: her daughter-in-law is her only constraint. In some ways the two women are like-minded: Sandra too does not believe that she was born to dust, hoover or clean lavatories with bristly brushes. But nor was Sandra born to shop and gossip with her friends. Sandra's destiny is to study spreadsheets, take calls, send emails, hold meetings and fit in, where she can, her husband, her children, her friends. Tilly keeps an eye on her daughter-in-law because it has been known for Sandra to complain to Henry that his mother is 'taking over'. Their family. Their home. Mournfully, Henry has turned down invitations to Sunday lunch in Phillimore Gardens – roast leg of lamb, fresh mint sauce, glazed carrots, Jersey Royal potatoes – and trudged off to Tesco to buy a chicken to take home and cook himself.

So far Sandra is happy enough to let Tilly busy herself at the party. It leaves Sandra free to talk to the toddlers' daddies – the high-flying bankers, politicians and journalists who are their friends. Tracey lights the four candles on the birthday cake. It is placed before Ned. Henry takes out his Nikon Coolpix digital camera to catch an image of Ned as he blows out the candles. There is cheering and clapping. Ned becomes overexcited. He wriggles in his chair, catches the paper tablecloth with his foot which overturns a plastic cup filled with orange squash. Alena swoops to clear it up. Tilly steps forward to help Ned cut the cake. It is a step too far. Sandra puts down her mug of tea and comes forward with a large black knife. Tilly backs off. Sandra guides Ned's hand as he cuts the cake.

Jomier has been talking to Tessa, his friend from the playground, but now, on the pretext that she must see to her daughter Tatty, Tessa gets up and crosses the room. They have run out of conversation. Jomier is happy to be left alone. He is in existential mode. If the human body renews itself every seven years, is the Tilly who is talking to Henry's friend Tony a different person to the Tilly he married thirty-eight years ago? Has she in fact gone through five metamorphoses so that he should not be labelling her, in his memory, Tilly 1 and Tilly 2 but Tilly 1, 2, 3, 4, 5? Is that what is behind the concept of 'the seven-year itch'? It is not that a husband and wife have grown restless but they have changed into different people. The synapses that made up the brain of the Tilly who fell in love with Jomier have been replaced by synapses of a brain that falls in love with Max. No, that would have been Tilly 3. Tilly 2 was merely disenchanted because her husband had turned into someone who was not her type – Jomier 2. He had changed from a teasing lover into a routine husband; from a romantic revolutionary into a pedantic barrister who brought his work home – not just briefs in his briefcase but an adversarial manner when talking to his wife. The burned-out motor of the Miele vacuum cleaner was caused by a blocked nozzle: for weeks Rosa, their Galician cleaner, had been hoovering without any air, let alone dust, passing into the Miele's paper sack. Who was responsible? Rosa. But Rosa was acting as an agent for Tilly, therefore the buck stops with Tilly. Tilly: Machines are a matter for men. Jomier: Keeping house is a matter for women. Tilly: Who says? Jomier: Convention. Tilly: Fuck convention. Jomier: Including the convention that a husband provides for his wife? Tilly: You resent it, don't you? You fucking miser. You'd like to keep all your money for yourself.

Tears. Jomier remembers the tears. He had never hit Tilly but his sarcastic courtroom manner had on occasions made her cry. 'You're just better at arguing.' Sniff. Tilly would never admit that she was in the wrong. Her tears were not an admission of defeat. They were a symptom of frustration – that after a day dealing with dirty nappies, squabbling children, baby food, something for supper, overflowing washing machines, reproving nursery-school teachers (Henry had bitten Tamsin), and perennial anxieties about meningitis, measles, chickenpox, grommets, inoculations, she is now indicted and prosecuted by the man who promised to cherish her for the Galician cleaner's failure to notice that the nozzle of the Miele was blocked.

The tears. Jomier remembers them now with shame but then . . . A certain triumph? Easton the analyst had suggested that in incidents such as these Jomier had been driven by unconscious resentment to punish Tilly for the failings of his mother. Perhaps. Jomier does not want to think about his mother. He is still preoccupied with Tilly. He watches her as she talks to Humphrey. He wonders why, if this Tilly 5 is a wholly different person to the Tilly 3 who went off with Max, she still provokes feelings of resentment. Can he in all justice hold Tilly 3 to blame for shifting her affections from a man who bullied her about the blocked nozzle of the Miele to a man to whom Miele was, if anything, Miele Gesellschaft mbH, a company in which he might like to own shares? And Tilly 5 is not even Tilly 3. The svelte woman of a certain age who has now moved away from Tony to readjust the glittering plastic tiara that has gone askew on Samantha's head bears a certain resemblance to the harassed, downtrodden but still sexy young wife he knew in the 1980s, but she is not the same woman. Her responsibility for cheating on Jomier is less direct, even, than her responsibility in her former incarnation as Tilly 3 for the blocked nozzle of the Miele.

Jomier sums up. The woman who loved him turned into the woman who did not love him either because new configurations were made in replacement synapses or because he himself had changed. For neither of these developments could she be held to blame. She was not the same person she had been seven years before – neither in herself nor in Jomier's psyche. In his psyche, once she had children, she had become his mother and he reacted with the fury of a three-year-old to her perceived failings in that role. Just as there is justifiable homicide, so there is justifiable adultery and it is unreasonable for Jomier to continue to resent her understandable response to his punishment of her for the crimes of his mother.

Tilly turns and catches his eye. Something in his expression leads her to smile. Should she cross the room to talk to him? As she takes her first step, Jomier notices her pretty long legs. Do they still part to please Max? Do they still have sex? After all those years? The thought is enough. The defence case collapses. Jomier rises from his armchair and, avoiding Tilly, crosses the room to find Henry and Sandra and say goodbye.

## II

TEN DAYS HAVE passed since Jomier and Judith went to the cinema in Chelsea. If Jomier wishes to court Judith he cannot postpone proposing another date for much longer. Jomier has her email; he has her landline number; he has her mobile number; he has her postal address. Of the four, email is his preferred means of communication. Writing letters or even postcards has become cumbersome; texts are too fiddly; a telephone call is too immediate. It might be a bad moment. A brusque tone of voice may mean only that the person called is late for an appointment, or is longing to pee, but it can be mistaken for a brush-off. Email is good because the recipient can choose when he or she wishes to hear from the outside world. It can be short and to the point. There can still be brush-offs – a delayed reply, a non-committal reply, or no reply at all – but they will not be caused by bad timing or an importunate call of nature.

The only disadvantage to email, for Jomier, is the sight of the long list of names in his email address book. As with his digitalised postal address book, there are many 'contacts' Jomier has not contacted for many years and who have not contacted him. They lie in a neat column like gravestones in a war cemetery, not the names of the dead but of those who are dead to Jomier. Never again in this world will

Jomier communicate with Dr Harvey MacAdam, a private doctor he first consulted before the era of email when he thought he might have contracted a venereal disease from Max via Tilly. There was no rash; no discharge. It was merely the thought that perhaps Max on one of his business trips had had sex with a prostitute in Dubai or Bangkok. Dr MacAdam had gently told Jomier that there could be no diagnosis without symptoms; and, after Jomier had filled him in on some of the background to his anxieties, had given him the name of the psychoanalyst Easton whose fees were on a par with his own.

MacAdam, Marlowe, Miller, Moore – the names of men and women who had one time come into Jomier's life and now had left again. Some meant nothing to Jomier. Milson – who was he? A life-insurance salesman? An estate agent? A pupil in chambers? The solicitor acting for a client in a long-forgotten case? Jomier now wonders whether his inability to remember anything at all about Milson – jamesmilson@toddleoff.com – is a symptom of frontal lobe dementia or Alzheimer's disease. Or is the fault Milson's – a man inherently so uninteresting that his name triggers no memory in Jomier's mind?

Jomier prepares to email Judith. How did he open his last message? Was it with 'Dear Judith' or 'Hi!' He goes to his 'sent' file, recovers his last email and discovers that he had written 'Dear Judith'. He does so again. 'How about another movie?' He uses the word 'movie' instead of 'film' to counteract the fogeyish opening but ends 'With best wishes'. Almost immediately, he receives an answer. 'I'd love to how about next friday is there anything worth seeing judith xxx'. Jomier appreciates the immediacy of her reply: she must be sitting at her desk. The 'xxx' he knows denote three kisses — friendly smacks on the cheek, he supposes, not lingering smoochy saliva-lubricated intertwining of tongues. He emails back: next Friday is fine.

Suddenly — ping! Another email pops into his in-box. It is from tdclenaghan, alias Tom Clenaghan, a voice from the past. Tom is coming to London from New York at the weekend. He would like to meet up. Jomier is thrown. There is suddenly a danger of overloading the circuit of his social life. Jomier likes at least two empty days on either side of an engagement: less than that makes him feel that he is on a helter-skelter, and leads to a backlog of experience to enter in his journal. But he will make an exception for Tom. Tom is no Milson — no long-forgotten lost soul. He replies to tdclenaghan@clenaghan.org. 'Any time except Friday night.' 'A drink on Saturday? 6 at the Groucho?' 'Fine. Look forward to it.'

Jomier does not look forward to it. The pleasure he might take in catching up with Tom is less than the pain he must endure in going up west on a Saturday night — streets filled with loudmouthed yobs on their way to get pissed in Leicester Square; and, in Soho, humanity in pursuit of distraction spilling out on to the streets from the pubs and bars — smells of kebabs, onions, aftershave, sweat, cannabis, coffee, urine. And the Groucho Club — the other end of the spectrum to the Athenaeum on Pall Mall where Jomier lunches with his friend Theo — no fogeys here but cool copywriters, architects and corporate lawyers with the odd author to give the place its bohemian cachet.

And for a drink! Clearly Tom would not want to waste a whole evening on Jomier: he will have arranged to have dinner with someone pretty, someone powerful or someone rich. Or, if Tom runs true to form, someone pretty, powerful *and* rich. Since Jomier had first known him in London in the

1970s, Tom had worked on converting his roguish charm into cash. He coaxed commissions out of the editors and advances out of the publishers whom he met in the *salons* of fashionable *salonnières* where he played the role of court jester. His dishevelled, half-starved look made him attractive to women. So too his wit. Tom had kissed the Blarney stone: he had the gift of the gab. He made girls laugh. He put them at their ease. In this he was like Marco. Tom and Marco: Jomier's two womanising friends. They met only once – brought together by Jomier – and took against one another at once. Marco: elegant, suave, aristocratic, cosmopolitan. Tom: scruffy, furtive, Celtic – an upstart who had sneaked in by the servants' entrance and passed unobserved through the green baize door. Marco made love with an air of *noblesse oblige*. Tom was a sexual chancer. Like Maupassant's *Bel Ami*, his life plan was to nail an heiress – a girl whose daddy was both rich and influential.

Advantageous marriages are out of fashion: we are meant to marry only for love. Jomier, true to the zeitgeist, had disapproved of the opportunistic discipline his friend imposed on his heart. He had also thought him unlikely to succeed. Escorting the daughters of the rich is a costly business: they expect to travel in taxis, eat in expensive restaurants, sit in good seats at the theatre; they invite you to join them in villas in Tuscany or to stay at their parents' country houses – quite unaware that the cost of the cab, the restaurant, the tickets to Covent Garden, the flight to Pisa or the tips for their parents' servants are major items in the budget of a freelance hack. Tom's scruffiness was not an affectation: after the tips and tickets there was no money left for a wardrobe. Tom's clothes were threadbare; there were holes in the soles of his loafers. The girls found this enchanting: and finally the enchantment paid off. Arabella Marton became pregnant by Tom: as her father fumed and her mother urged her to go and see Mr Deventer in Harley Street, hot tears were shed at Marton Towers. Arabella refused to see Mr Deventer. She would have the 'Irish bastard', as her father termed his grandchild *in utero*, whether they liked it or not. The parents relented. There was a grand wedding in the parish church at Marton with the bride in a loose-fitting dress.

Jomier opens his journal on his computer and searches for 'Tom' to see how long that first marriage had lasted. Three, four years? The legitimate baby, a girl they called Rose, had been their only child. As soon as he had secured Arabella Tom started sleeping with other women. He thought it only reasonable while his wife was pregnant: 'Who wants to fuck a balloon?' He also thought it reasonable when she was no longer pregnant: 'Who wants to fuck a woman with oozing tits?' He thought it reasonable when the baby was off the breast and Arabella had recovered her figure: 'If you've been shagging all afternoon, you don't feel like it at night.' The shagging all afternoon was essential if Tom's novel was to be a success. Middle-aged women who edited the books' pages had to be motivated to provide promi-nent, favourable reviews. And it was absurd not to fuck the publicist who took him on tour since they were staying in the same hotel. So too the girl who sold foreign rights at the Frankfurt Book Fair. He denied these infidelities to Arabella but she knew and he knew that she knew. He got drunk and slept on the sofa; she cried herself to sleep in their double bed.

The entries in Jomier's journal tell the story. 'Tom off to New York.' 'Tom back from New York.' 'Tom going to live in New York to write for *Soho Soundbites*. A won't go with him.' 'Tom said to be dating Hannah Schultz of Schultz &

97

Beyerman.' 'Tom and A are now divorced.' 'Saw Tom in NY with his new girlfriend, Barbara Holmes of Holmes Oil.' 'Tom's getting married to Susie Aschenbach, daughter of his publisher.' Another marriage. Another child. Another divorce. More rich women – some now divorced like Tom – but no record of any more marriages to date.

Before his drink with Tom there is the movie with Judith. Jomier studies *Time Out* and the *Evening Standard* but can find no film that he wants to see. Jomier is fussy about films. He likes going to the cinema, particularly on a misty autumn evening – sitting in the dark, watching the ads and the trailers, the certificate from the censors, then the opening credits of the main feature – but rarely does he enjoy the film. Has Jomier changed? Or has the standard of movie-making declined? There was a time when the Americans made films with straightforward stories and tight, witty scripts: they can still be seen on afternoon TV or can be ordered from Lovefilm. No longer. Big names, big budgets and lavish promotion draw the crowds to watch crap. Jomier resists. He will only go to see a film if he has reason to believe it will be good. This was a point of contention with Tilly. Tilly liked to go with the flow of hype. The subliminal effect of write-ups in newspapers would make her want to see a film despite the damning reviews. Jomier had stood firm. He was damned if he would be suckered by the studios. Why pay to see a mediocre film in a cinema when you could watch a mediocre film on television for free? Or a good film on television – a classic – *The Third Man*, *Battleship Potemkin*, *La règle du jeu*? To which Tilly would reply that going to the movies, however mediocre the movie, was a night out.

In the event, Jomier and Judith agree that there is no film that they want to see. They go instead to an Indian restaurant and, over tandoori this and balti that, they dig deeper into one another's lives. Judith has problematic children. There is her daughter, the thirty-eight-year-old briefly married now on-the-shelf Ophelia who has not spoken to her mother for four years. Judith does not know why though she has theories. She thinks that Ophelia blames the collapse of her own marriage on her parents' divorce for which she blames her mother. 'Perhaps, looking back . . .' Judith now wonders whether, for the sake of the children, she should not have stuck it out with Beresford. 'But that's water under the bridge . . .' Her son Tim has had mental troubles, 'though one can hardly blame those on the divorce. He smoked so much dope when he was a teenager which was partly the fault of Alfredo.'

'Alfredo?'

'He was a Chilean painter I was seeing at the time.'

They discuss the possible link between smoking dope and schizophrenia, though Tim's condition is more like ME – lethargy, apathy, chronic fatigue.

'Depression?'

'That too.'

Tim is thirty-four. He lives in Devon with a girlfriend. She is a potter. Tim helps her with the clay. Tim's father, Beresford, pays him an allowance but 'of course he is terribly disappointed, having spent all that money on sending him to Eton'.

It is now Jomier's turn to talk about his children. He orders another half-pint of Cobra beer. What can he say? On the surface at least his children seem to have been unaffected by the divorce. He tells her about Henry and Sandra and Samantha and Ned. He tells her about Louisa and Jimmy and the five grandchildren he rarely sees – Fernando,

Roberto, Laura ('Lala'), Maria-Annunziata ('Nunci') and little Ysabel.

'Five children!' exclaims Judith.

'There's more space in Argentina,' says Jomier.

Judith: 'All the same!'

A whiff of political correctness? But also a whiff of musky scent as Judith leans forward to offer Jomier the last spoonful of *brinjal bhaji* from the oval metal dish. He declines. She takes it herself. A healthy appetite.

'I don't see them very much. And their grandmother is Catholic,' says Jomier as if this explains his failure to put a brake on this overpopulation of the world.

The moment of irritation has passed. The wrinkled skin on Judith's forehead is now smooth again. The cloud of disapproval that had appeared in her expression at hearing of Jomier's five Argentinian grandchildren is burned off by a warm smile. 'When all is said and done,' she says, 'one does one's best for one's children within the limits of the possible.'

Jomier agrees.

'Of course divorce is a trauma for children but if I had stayed with Beresford I would have become clinically depressed and now Ophelia would be blaming *that* for the collapse of her marriage.'

'Almost certainly.'

'There comes a time when children have to take responsibility for their own lives, don't you think?'

'I do.'

'And move on, psychologically.'

'Of course.'

'She's nearly forty, after all.'

'That's hard to believe.'

'I married young.'

'People must take you for sisters?'

'It has happened. And it didn't help.'

'And what about you?' Judith has told Jomier what went wrong with her husband but Jomier has not yet told Judith what went wrong with his wife. He hesitates to do so: Judith is a woman and women stick up for women when it comes to conflicts with men. Did not Judith herself say that she had been unfaithful to Beresford because she wanted to see what it was like to sleep with another man? Was this not Tilly's justification? *Did you really expect me to go through life having only slept with one man?* Yes. Jomier had expected that or, more foolishly, assumed it. The dual morality. What is sauce for the gander is not sauce for the goose. It was justified by David Hume. How could a man be expected to provide for his children if he had reason to believe that they might not be his? Why should he tend his property into his old age for the progeny of some other man? The fidelity of a wife to her husband and a husband to his wife was part of a personal compact; but the fidelity of the wife had social ramifications. It was the mindset of a different age which Jomier had thought eternal. He had not stopped to think how rapidly contraception and financial independence would lead to the unleashing of the feminine libido.

'My wife was called Tilly,' says Jomier.

'Was?'

'No. Of course. She's still called Tilly but she is no longer my wife. She fell in love with another man who was also married so we split up . . .' Jomier shrugs as if to say: 'That's the way of the world.'

'Ruth says she is very beautiful.' Judith looks sharply at

Jomier as if his reaction to what she says will reveal residual feelings.

'So people say.'

'And you?'

'Clearly I thought so when I married her.'

'You were in love?'

'Yes. Yes, I was in love.'

'And what went wrong?'

'Much the same scenario as yours, I suppose. Routine, drudgery, lack of sleep, lack of glamour, a stingy husband who takes you for granted . . .'

'Beresford wasn't stingy.'

'I didn't think that I was stingy – just careful with money.'

'Which you have to be, if you haven't got a lot.'

'That's what I thought but perhaps, looking back, I should have been more pound wise and penny foolish.'

'Meaning?'

'I was always ticking her off for leaving the lights on.'

'No fancy restaurants?'

'Or weekends in Paris. No.'

'No holidays?'

'Yes, there were holidays. Mostly with friends, particularly Max and Jane. And then it emerged . . .' Jomier sighs. 'It emerged that Tilly and Max were having an affair.'

'They fell in love?'

'I suppose they did, yes. Though I think at the time . . .'

'What?'

'It was more a sexual adventure. A jolly escapade.'

'What happened?'

'I found out.'

'How?'

'She lost her chequebook. We had a joint account at Hoare's in Fleet Street . . .'

'Why Hoare's?'

'My father banked there, and it is near to my chambers. I went in to get some cash. They gave me the lost chequebook. It had been found in the Strand Palace Hotel and sent back to the bank.'

'Had she paid for the room?' Judith seems more shocked by this possibility than by the adultery itself.

'No. It must have fallen out of her bag – perhaps knocked off the bed in the throes of passion.'

'So you confronted her?'

'Yes.'

'And she confessed?'

'Yes.'

'Was it a shock?'

'Yes.'

'How long had it been going on?'

'She said a year. I suspect it was longer.'

'You hadn't had suspicions?'

'No.'

'And his wife?'

'She said she didn't know but I now think that perhaps she did.'

'She didn't tell you?'

'No. She thought I'd make a fuss.'

'You'd been faithful?'

Jomier hesitates. 'There'd been a fling with a girl from my chambers.'

'Did Tilly know about that?'

'No.'

'No one else?'

'No.'

'Perhaps she knew and thought: tit for tat.'

'She didn't know.'

'She may have sensed it.'

'Feminine intuition? Perhaps. But it was really . . .'

'What?'

'She fancied Max.'

The waiter hovers. Neither wants coffee. They ask for the bill.

'You should forgive her,' says Judith.

'Oh, I have,' says Jomier.

She looks at him sceptically.

'Forgiven but not forgotten,' Jomier says.

'Scars?'

'The wound still festers . . .'

'And there's never been anyone since?'

The bill is placed before Jomier. 'Nothing significant.' He reaches for his wallet.

Judith picks up her bag from the floor. 'This time I insist.'

'I really would rather . . .' He hands a debit card to the waiter.

'Here.' She hands him £20.

'That's too much.' He hands back the £20 note.

She takes it and hands him a £10 note. 'Now it's too little so you needn't feel emasculated.'

They go out on to the Shepherd's Bush Road. 'What are you doing tomorrow?'

Jomier hesitates. He finds it difficult to remember what he is doing without consulting his digital diary. 'What day is it tomorrow?'

'Saturday.'

'Saturday. I'm having a drink with a friend who's over from New York.'

'And afterwards?'

'Nothing.'

'Then why not come to supper with me? I'm having one or two friends. Nothing grand.'

# 12

SATURDAY MORNING. THE first Saturday of the month. This is the day when Jomier sees to his finances. The custom dates from the days when he still worked and could not see to his finances on weekdays. Jomier was a barrister and barristers are self-employed. The clerk in his chambers had done some preliminary accounting, deducting the rent of the chambers and his own commission from Jomier's fees as they came in. But it had been up to Jomier himself to make returns for income tax and VAT. It was a process made easier thanks to the invention of the personal computer and accounting software. Jomier enjoyed it. He liked coming up with formulas on Microsoft Excel which would work out the VAT due on a gross sum; or, at the touch of a button, tell him what tax he should pay on a year's income; but even before he had owned a computer, Jomier had preferred to spend his Saturday mornings sitting at his desk doing his accounts to going with Tilly to the Portobello Road or taking his children to Holland Park.

Recent developments on the Internet now make it possible for Jomier to study his bank balances and investments online. His investments are in his pension fund. It is not large. If Jomier had been a civil servant like his father, he would have a generous pension paid for by the taxpayer, based on his final salary and linked to inflation. Since Jomier is not a civil servant, his pension depends upon what he has paid into his fund over the years. Early in his career as a lawyer it was difficult to pay in any money at all. His fees were modest and his costs were great. Jomier's parents and Tilly's parents had given them some money towards their first home but for that home to be in Notting Hill the sum had had to be augmented by a mortgage. Jomier did the sums and would come down from his study at midday on Saturday in despair. He would hand a printout of a spreadsheet to Tilly to make her cognisant of their financial plight. It would remain on the kitchen table unread.

Each family is like a small state. There is the Chancellor of the Exchequer (Jomier) and the spending ministries (Tilly, Henry, Louisa), and every year there is a quarrel about the allocation of resources – utilities, rates, income tax, food, versus clothes, dinner parties, holidays, school fees. Jomier favoured expenditure on 'plant' and 'infrastructure' – car, gas boiler, television, washing machine – whereas Tilly went for consumables – restaurants, parties, school fees, trips abroad. The most intractable dispute had been over contributions to a pension fund. Jomier turned thirty-five: he was now halfway through the biblical time span of three-score years and ten. It was time – high time – to start contributing towards a pension. Jomier took advice. The calculations were daunting. Huge sums were required to ensure a modest income in old age. His mind became befuddled with projections, estimations, tax benefits, annual increments, terminal bonuses: but it was clear that if he wanted to maintain a reasonable standard of living after retirement, he must make significant contributions towards a pension for the rest of his working life.

Tilly disagreed. Tilly was suspicious of financial advisers. She thought they had a vested interest in scaring her husband with visions of penury in a future that may never come. Her counterproposal: 'Something will turn up.' Jomier had pressed her. What would turn up? He, Jomier, might rise to becoming one of those barristers who earn a million pounds a year. Or he might become a judge who can go on working until he is senile and then retire on an index-linked pension. Might. Might. These were possibilities against the certainty of old age. OK. The certainties. His parents would die. Her parents would die. Their houses would be sold. Unless, countered Jomier, they had already been sold to pay for carers.

The conflict between Tilly's optimism and Jomier's financial-adviser-abetted pessimism had reached a critical point one summer when Jomier had told Max that they could not afford to share the rent of a villa in the Dordogne. Tilly was angry. More than angry – she fell into a tearful rage. For the first time in their married life, she had seized Jomier's Saturday midday spreadsheet printout and seen through her tears that a sum that might have been spent on their family holiday had gone on a nebulous 'pension contribution'. There were arguments. More tears. Sulks. Misery. Jomier had stood firm. It was the duty of a *pater-familias* to resist the jam today of a holiday in the Dordogne for the jam tomorrow of The Laurels Old Peoples' Home. In the event, that year, and in the years that followed, Max and Jane rented the villas and invited the Jomiers as their guests.

Was that Saturday the beginning of the end? Was it then that private thoughts about the alpha male who has no thought for the morrow because the morrow was secure in offshore trust funds first triggered a tingling in

Tilly's private parts? Jomier ponders the complex inter-action between the mind and the genitalia. Men are indelicate; there is no hiding the erections brought on by erotic images or sexual fantasies. Women are deli-cate and censor from polite discourse any mention of what takes place under their skirts – turgescence, tumes-cence, engorgement, secretions. 'We may perhaps say that the erotic personality rests on a triangular association between the cerebrum, the endocrine system and the auto-nomic nervous apparatus.' Havelock Ellis. The thought of munificent Max in the brain sends messages to Tilly's reproductive apparatus hidden slyly within her body – not an open, honest appendage like the male phallus but a sly octopus lurking behind the pubic lichen-fringed rock of her *mons Veneris* that emerges from the shadows not just to entangle Max but *en passant* to reach out with a spare tentacle and take hold of Jomier's pension. When they divorced, Tilly's claim to half of his pension fund was upheld by the Family Court.

Jomier reconciles his bank statements. Income and expend-iture are in balance. Jomier makes ends meet. The death of Jomier's parents came after his divorce. The care they had required in their old age had been covered by the Civil Service pension. After his mother's death, the flat in Holland Park had been sold and the proceeds, less inheritance tax and lawyers' fees, distributed to her heir, Jomier. All turned out as Tilly had predicted. Now the balance depleted by standing orders is replenished by dividends from Jomier's investments; and the annuities, bought from financial institutions with names that once anchored them in the British Isles – Scottish Widows, Norwich Union, Yorkshire Insurance – are paid into his account by anonymous globalised entities with names like those of newly discovered planets – Aegon, Axa, Aviva. What would happen, Jomier wonders, if like burned-out stars they became invisible through the telescope of his computer? Did not the twinkling Enron suddenly turn into a black hole?

Saturday 1 p.m. Jomier, having finished his accounts, makes himself a tuna-fish sandwich and eats it while listening to *Any Questions* on the radio. He then returns to his study, sits in his armchair with the *New York Review of Books* open on his lap and falls asleep. He wakes half an hour later and goes to the bathroom to splash his face with cold water. As he raises his head from the basin, he sees his reflection in the mirror of the medicine cupboard. Jomier still does not like what he sees – *un cocu, un pauvre con* – but he remembers his programme for the evening, with a possible denouement in Judith's bedroom, and he remembers too that behind the mirror in the medicine cupboard is Pfizer's magical potion that restores potency to the impotent – Viagra. Should he take a capsule with him to Judith's dinner party? Should he unobtrusively swallow it after the other guests have left – leaving the twenty-minute time lag before the drug takes effect for loading the dishwasher, a *digestif*, foreplay?

Jomier opens the cupboard door. The face of the *cocu* slides away and is replaced by a neat row of packets, tubs and bottles. Jomier takes the packet marked with the Pfizer logo, opens it, and looks at the capsules embedded in plastic and covered with thin tinfoil. There are three. There were four. The missing capsule tells a tale. Jomier would rather not tell the tale but memory is not always compliant. He smells heather. He is in Scotland. A house party. Old friends playing upper-class Edwardians with croquet, charades and corridor-creeping part of the game. Why is Jomier there? He is in his heyday as an available man. His divorce from Tilly is well in the past. Why not a second marriage in the future? It is a large house party with two unattached women of a certain age among the guests.

Jomier's host is Adrian Richards, a friend from his days at Oxford. His hostess is Adrian's wife Mary. No sooner has Jomier arrived at the crenellated shooting lodge than he wishes he was back at home. What is a house party but a protracted dinner party – the dredging of the mind for something to say not just in the evening but at breakfast, lunch and tea? Jomier does not fit in. He does not shoot grouse. He does not stalk deer. He does not fly-fish for trout on lochs and burns. He does not play bridge. Nor, in the past, did his friend Adrian. But Adrian has taken them up. He has used the money he has made managing the money of Saudi sheikhs and Russian oligarchs to build upon the foundations laid by his father who, on the day of his birth, had driven from Tunbridge Wells to Windsor to put his name down for Eton. Eton. Oxford. The Bullingdon. The Conservative Association. Eurosceptic speeches at the Union. Getting to know the right people. Chatting up their sisters. Marrying Mary Tattenham whose mother, Lady Clara, was the daughter of an earl.

Jomier sees nothing wrong with social climbing. It was the default preoccupation of ambitious young men in the nineteenth century and only temporarily replaced in the twentieth by unsustainable idealistic aberrations – Bolshevism, Existentialism, Hippyism. Now in London, at the turn of a new century, it is back in fashion and if Jomier has any criticism to make of his friend Adrian, it is only that he goes about it in too obvious a way. The ropes and hooks and karabiners of the mountaineer are too much in evidence beneath the pinstriped suit. His pink coat for hunting, his plus fours for shooting, his waders for fishing are all brand new. They expose him as a *parvenu*.

The smell of heather fades. The momentary hallucination gives way to the true-life odours of soggy shaving brush and toothpaste. Jomier is not in Scotland. He is in the bathroom of his house in Hammersmith. He puts the packet of Viagra back on the shelf of the medicine cupboard. The memories return. Viagra. Molly. Annie. Molly is Mary Richards' niece. She is there at the shooting lodge in Scotland with a friend and flatmate Annie. The two girls are in their early thirties: they are not 'of a certain age'. Annie is urban. She works in PR and lives in Barons Court. Like Jomier she does not shoot or stalk or fish. This leads to a fellow feeling. They chat on walks and when they find themselves next to one another at dinner. She is not a great beauty but she is fresh. White teeth. Clear eyes. Thick blonde hair. Unblemished skin. Also vulnerable. Unhappy. Her parents are divorced. Her father has cancer. Her brother is on drugs.

A boyfriend? She sighs. She has gone out with Molly's brother, then Toby Pierson, but that has just ended. He wouldn't commit. Not that she is in a hurry to get married. Half of all marriages end in divorce, like her parents' and Jomier's; and isn't it reasonable to assume that half of the couples who stay married do so out of lethargy or for the sake of the children or because they would rather put up with one another than downsize? 'In other words, there's only a one in four chance of being happy.'

'Wouldn't you like children?' asks Jomier.

'Yes, I suppose so. But what if I'd had a child by Toby that turned out as boring as he is?' So many of the men she knows are dull. School, gap year, university, a job in the City – blah, blah, blah. They never listen to women. They only want to show off how clever they are to their male friends. They don't know the difference between being clever and being wise.

'*Si jeunesse savait, si vieillesse pouvait,*' Jomier says with as wise a smile as he can muster.

'Oh, *vieillesse pouvait* all right. My stepmother is twenty years younger than my dad.'

'Don't you find that . . .'

'Unnatural? Not really.' Then, with a sidelong look into his eyes and the flutter of eyelashes: 'I don't think that age matters.'

Jomier catches a look from Mary at the head of the candle-lit table. The length and intimacy of his conversation with Annie has been noticed. 'We'd better *turn*,' he whispers to Annie and, with a funny little grimace to express reluctance, she does as she is told. Jomier turns too and talks to the older woman on his right – one of the two he has been invited to look over. She is intelligent, amusing and good-looking but, even as he listens to her describe the mystical beauty of sleeping under the stars in the desert in Oman, he compares her in his mind's eye with the younger girl behind him.

Oman. 'It was all arranged by Jamie Scott. He was at Sandhurst with the Sultan.' Sandhurst with the Sultan. Jomier feels like an extra in a 1930s film with raddled ladies talking in clipped upper-class voices about their friends who were friends with sultans and maharajas and the Prince of Wales. Where had Adrian found her? Central casting? Or was she a friend of Mary's – a lame duck who comes with the trousseau when you marry the granddaughter of an earl? She talks on. He listens, talks when prompted, and listens again. Finally it is time for the ladies to withdraw while the gentlemen gather round their host to drink port and smoke cigars. Another old-fashioned upper-class custom revived by Adrian to go with the Purdeys and plus fours.

# 13

THEY ARE BACK in London. Jomier has twice met Annie for lunch. She has been warm, friendly, interested, amusing. And she has been needy. Her father is dying. He is in pain. He is angry. Like Tolstoy's Ivan Ilych, he cannot understand how life around him can go on as before. He curses the doctors. He is vile to his young wife, Annie's stepmother. He is vile to Annie. ' "Rage, rage against the dying of the light," I suppose,' says Annie to Jomier. She has studied English at the University of East Anglia and so knows this line of poetry written by Dylan Thomas. Also Larkin's: 'They fuck you up, your mum and dad'. She feels she has been fucked up by her parents. 'Mum thinks Dad is being punished for leaving her. She doesn't say so, but I can tell.'

Jomier listens patiently. He is a shoulder to cry on – the kindly, sympathetic dad that Annie never knew. And she stands in for the absent Louisa. Frustrated paternal instincts are reanimated in his psyche. He longs to hug and hold Annie as he once did little Louisa, to stroke her hair and brush away her tears. But Annie is not little. And she is not Louisa. Within his psyche, the altruistic superego is harassed by a predatory libido that brushes aside any ersatz incest taboo. It takes advantage of that drowsy state when he is slipping into sleep, or first wakes in the morning, to screen porno imaginings of Jomier peeling off Annie's knickers and uncovering her pretty, pointed breasts. *I don't think that age matters.* Jomier reruns the clip of her glance when she said this – the flutter of her eyelashes, the bashful effrontery. If it does not matter to her, why should it matter to him? How many women are happily married to older men; older men to younger women?

Following the break-up of his marriage, Jomier had thought much about the nature of love. He has read Freud and Jung and Havelock Ellis; Erikson, Bettelheim and Simone de Beauvoir. He is satisfied that a man's appearance means less to a woman than a woman's appearance to a man. Celebrity, riches, power, authority will trump a receding hairline or a pot belly. He accepts that conjugal love is often shaped by the template of earlier familial relationships – brother–sister, mother–son, father–daughter. It would be wrong for Jomier to take advantage of Annie's dysfunctional relationship with her father to seduce her; but not wrong to respond to a psychic need which, though it might derive from that dysfunctional relationship, was now an unalterable feature of her adult personality.

In a waking state, the porno screenings cease. Jomier is able to reassure himself that his feelings for Annie are noble, disinterested, sincere, but that the nobility, disinterest and sincerity do not preclude an erotic component. He feels he may be falling in love and has reason to believe that his love is returned. He moves cautiously: it is not impossible that he has misread the signals. An appreciation of an older man's solicitude is not necessarily an invitation for him to make a pass. As he pays the bill after a third lunch at the Trattoria Umberto on Dover Street, he suggests an evening date. A movie? A play? Or simply supper? 'What about next week? Say Friday?'

She wobbles her head as if it will open her Filofax in her mind. 'Yes, I'm sure. I've left my diary at work.'

'I'll ring you.'

'No, honestly, don't bother. Friday will be fine. If I've anything on, I'll cancel.'

They kiss on the cheek as they part but her kiss lingers. Jomier returns to Hammersmith on the Piccadilly Line in a daze. *I'll cancel*. The misery of the depressed *cocu* has been transformed into a lover's exaltation. He is loved. He is in love. He almost skips as he walks across Ravenscourt Park and wants to embrace all the bored young mothers and sullen au pairs. How long will it be before it is Annie pushing a buggy containing their child? And it will be one in the eye for Tilly when she hears that he has pulled a girl around the same age as Louisa.

Back in his house, doubts set in – not doubts about his feelings for Annie or Annie's feelings for him, but whether he is up for an affair with a girl half his age. Will she want to go clubbing or to raves? Will he get on with her friends? Will he become a figure of fun like Professor Rath in *The Blue Angel*? Will he come up to the mark as a lover? His happiest imaginings are of hugging and caressing Annie, while the porno screenings make him uncomfortable. The question is not *si vieillesse pouvait* but *si cocu pouvait*. Since the trauma of his divorce, his loins have been largely quiescent. 'Farewell, sweet prince,' Jomier has said to his penis floating lifelessly in the bath: but the drowsy images of *Annie desnudas*, which started a flow of blood through the helicine arteries to the corpus cavernosa of his penis show that, unlike Hamlet, it is not dead. But enfeebled. The flow of blood is not what it once was. Is this a by-product of psychological emasculation or merely a symptom of age? How will he compare with Toby Pierson or Molly's brother whose name Jomier cannot now remember? For years he had made love to a woman (Tilly) who had had no yardstick against which to measure his skills as a lover. And when she had finally found her yardstick, she had clearly found him wanting. Was Max 'better in bed'? Or was he more exciting simply because he was different? Like all young women of her generation, Annie will have a stack of yardsticks. Can Jomier's skill and experience compensate for a lack of brute virility? Or can brute virility be restored?

Jomier makes an appointment with his doctor. He explains his anxieties. The younger man listens sympathetically. He knows something of Jomier's troubles: he is the one whom Jomier pesters with his cancer scares. He now takes Jomier's blood pressure. It is normal. He recommends Viagra. He can prescribe it but warns Jomier that the cost cannot be met by the National Health unless it could be shown that a relationship was imperilled by his erectile dysfunction. In other words: would his partner leave him because he failed to provide her with sexual satisfaction? Would it break up a family? No. The family is already broken; his partner has gone. It is precisely this that has led to the erectile dysfunction. Before that the erectile functioning was fine.

Jomier takes the prescription to a branch of Boots in Oxford Street. He pays £19.34 for four capsules of Viagra and £2 for a packet containing three condoms. Jomier does not resent the expenditure because he is in love. The thought of Annie provokes feelings of tenderness: he longs to see her again not so much for her body as for her solicitude and her smile. He is in no doubt that Annie reciprocates his love. Neither has yet used the word but both make no bones about the pleasure taken in the company of the other. The moment has come when they must either move forward or step back. Jomier feels the rectangular shapes of his purchases in the pocket of his jacket. There is no turning back. The die is cast.

Jomier emails Annie to say that he has booked a table at Garnier's restaurant in Bayswater. He had chosen Garnier's after a morning's dithering. It is no longer fashionable; the food is mediocre; the waiters elderly and complacent. But it has a plush, belle-époque decor, a carpeted floor and it is in a street where he will be able to park his car. The belle époque decor seems a suitable backdrop for an intimate dinner of an older man with a younger woman; the carpet means that he will be able to hear what Annie says rather than lose her words in the cackle and clatter bouncing off more fashionable tiled or wooden floors; and it will be convenient for wherever they may choose to go afterwards to have the car close at hand.

Annie arrives late. She apologises. She has been having a drink with some friends. She sits down opposite Jomier and smiles. She appears uninterested in her surroundings; accepts his suggestion of a champagne cocktail; and makes a perfunctory choice from the menu. She is in a mood he has not encountered before: soft and woozy, perhaps a little drunk. Her eyes look into his and, every now and then, she raises her hand to fiddle with her thick blonde hair. She wears a skirt and a top. A simple string of polished onyx hangs around her neck. The scene is set. Champagne cocktails. White tablecloth. Silver cutlery. Polished wine glasses. Mâcon-Villages. Brouilly. Annie drinks what is poured into her glass but eats little. Most of the *artichauts à la barigoule* and the skate with brown shrimp and capers are left on her plate. Jomier, on the other hand, empties his bowl of *soupe de poisson, rouille, Gruyère et croutons*, and eats all of his Elwy Valley rump of lamb, ratatouille and oregano. His head begins to ache: he regrets the champagne cocktail. She chats. He listens. Her father – as bad as ever. Her step-mother – demented. Her mother – trying to do the right thing. Her brother – out of rehab and a regular at AA. She talks about her friends. One of the boys she met earlier in the evening had said he knew Jomier. Jeremy Darton? Jomier remembers. He is the son of a cousin of Tilly's. 'And what did he think about your date with a friend of his parents?'

She shrugs, smiles, plumps up her hair. 'I didn't ask him.'

'What *would* he have thought?'

She shrugs again. 'Who cares?'

Annie tells Jomier about her former boyfriends and sundry male admirers – *la ronde de l'amour*. She had an affair with A at 'college' and only later, when she'd had other boyfriends, did she realise that he had a crooked penis. 'It bent sideways. No wonder it wasn't much fun.' She had an affair with B who was married and made out that he would leave his wife but it became quite clear after a while that he was really quite happily married so she dumped him. She slept with C to cheer him up after his girlfriend had dumped *him*. Everyone at work thought she'd had an affair with D, her boss, because they often went out to lunch together but she didn't fancy him and anyway he was married. E, F, G – but Annie does not use letters of the alphabet to disguise the identity of her former lovers. She gives their names – Molly's brother Dan, Johnny Gray, Simon Tapley, Toby Pierson. There hasn't been anyone since Toby. 'I haven't had sex for ages.'

Jomier listens – half flattered by her confidences, half appalled at her indiscretion. She goes on, filling in the gaps.

H, I, J. J for Jomier? What will she tell K, L, M and N about Jomier? Will his pot belly become a talking point like A's crooked willy?

Dessert. Dyspepsia now joins the headache caused by the champagne cocktail but Jomier eats on. Vanilla ice cream and hot chocolate sauce join the wine, brandy, Angostura bitters, fish soup, garlic mayonnaise, melted cheese, masticated lamb, ratatouille and oregano in his stomach. Annie cuts into her crème caramel with her spoon but does not eat it. The food is bad but not that bad. It is also expensive. The frugal Jomier chides the would-be debonair lover with the money wasted on uneaten artichokes, skate and crème caramel. The debonair lover ignores the frugal Jomier: he has other things on his mind. How to hold down the swill in his stomach; when to pop the capsule of Viagra.

Neither wants coffee. Jomier calls for the bill. Annie goes to the lavatory. Perhaps he should too. The bill arrives. Jomier tries to reason himself out of outrage. He tells himself that the management of Garnier's has to factor in rent, wages, pension contributions, business rates, depreciation of assets into the £35 bottles of wine and the £8 ice cream. He is paying for the ambience as much as the food. It is an investment in happiness for two. But Jomier does not feel happy. He feels nauseous. He loathes Garnier's. He is losing control of his mood.

Jomier braves the silent snarl of the taciturn waiters by leaving no tip beyond the 12.5 per cent service charge. He stands and walks the length of the restaurant to the cloakroom. There is a small panelled room with two washbasins and dim lights on the walls. Two doors lead from this antechamber: one marked 'Gentlemen', the other 'Ladies'. As Jomier makes for the former Annie comes out of the latter.

They cannot pass one another without touching. They touch. She puts her arms on his shoulders, her mouth close to his right ear and whispers: 'Hurry up.'

Jomier goes into the Gents. He does not stand at the *pissoir* but goes into the cubicle and shuts the door. Annie's two whispered words have excited his senses. His penis wavers in a state of uncertainty as to what function it is called upon to perform. Jomier waits. He cannot evacuate the urine from his bladder until the blood drains from the corpus cavernosa. Jomier ponders on this design flaw in the male genitalia. Women may not have the convenience of a penis but their urinary and reproductive functions do not have to timeshare a single tract.

What will Annie think he is up to? A slow detumescence. Then, like the points change on a railway line, the track suddenly opens to the bladder. Jomier pees. He empties his bladder, or as much of it as his enlarged prostate gland will allow. He zips up his flies, leaves the cubicle, washes his hands and returns to fetch Annie who sits facing away from him at their table. He lays his hand on her shoulder. 'Shall we go?' She turns and smiles. They go out into the street.

The cooler air does nothing to cure Jomier of his headache or dyspepsia. He now longs for only one thing: to go home and catch the tail end of *Newsnight*. They reach his Golf. Jomier presses the button on his key fob. The doors are unlocked. Annie turns towards him. The orange light from the street lamps makes her face look like a child's made up for Halloween. 'Shall we go clubbing?'

'I don't think I feel up to it.'

Annie laughs. 'I wasn't serious. Can you take me back to Barons Court?'

'Of course.'

They get into the car. Jomier starts the engine.

Annie: 'Molly's gone to stay with her parents.'

They drive west along the Bayswater Road. Jomier tries to plan a route to Barons Court in his befuddled mind. Like a tired nag, he longs to head home but, under Annie's direction, turns south on Kensington Church Street. The usual aroma of upholstery and windscreen wash has been replaced by the fragrance of Annie – scent, soap, a kind of musk. In Jomier's brain there is confusion. Contradictory messages are coming in from both body and mind. One voice tells him that he has got lucky: in a quarter of an hour he will be making love with a beautiful girl. Another asks if he knows what he is doing. Is he really going to have sex with a girl half his age? Is he going to add his name to the list of her lovers? Follow where so many have been before? Be drawn helpless by the gravity of desire into the black hole between her pretty legs? Dodge the asteroids of herpes, pubic lice and genital warts to plunge into a moist potpourri of E. coli, chlamydia, thrush, gonorrhoea and whatever else has been left behind after previous landings by Dan, Johnny, Simon, Toby et al.?

His body too sends signals that all is not well. The dyspepsia has turned to a mild nausea and his bowels have chimed in with a demand to void the fish soup. Jomier argues with his bowels: the fish soup is not due in the lower colon for two or three days. His bowels counter that something in the fish soup has arrived through his bloodstream and now wants out. As they drive down the North End Road Jomier mediates on the three-way squabble going on in his brain between the semen that wants out through his penis, the gas and excreta determined to leave through his anus, and the bile that threatens to exit through his mouth.

Jomier laughs.

'Why are you laughing?'

'Because life is a farce.'

'Why is life a farce?'

'Because I want to make love to you but I can't.'

Annie sits up, turns towards him, frowns. 'Why not?'

'I feel sick.' Jomier's eyes are on the road. He cannot see the expression on her face as she reconfigures her emotions.

'Do you *really* feel sick?'

'Yes, I really feel sick. It's the fish soup.'

Jomier stops the Golf at a red light.

'Turn left,' says Annie.

Jomier turns left.

'There, up on the right, by the pillar box.'

Jomier docks the Golf by the kerb.

'Do you want to come in?' she asks.

'To vomit?'

'Why not?'

Jomier shakes his head. 'I'd better go home.'

Annie leans forward and embraces him. 'You poor dear.' She opens the door. 'Will you call me?'

'Of course.'

'It was a lovely evening.'

'It was a mistake.'

'What?' She looks anxious.

'The fish soup.'

'You learn,' she says.

'Learn what?'

'Not to eat too much before . . . well, you know.' She opens the door.

'You're right,' says Jomier. 'I'll know next time.' *Si vieillesse savait*. He leans forward. They embrace again but don't kiss. She gets out. The door closes. He waits until she disappears through the door to her flat.

Jomier drives back to Hammersmith. The nausea is lifting but his gut remains taut. He opens his front door, disarms the burglar alarm and goes to his downstairs lavatory. He lets down his trousers. The cool wood of the lavatory seat caresses his buttocks. He relaxes the clenched muscles around his sphincter. Ecstasy – not perhaps the kind he had envisaged at the start of the evening but ecstasy all the same. Jomier has learned his lesson. Avoid fish soup on a date and, when it comes to the competing demands of the body, excrement takes precedence over semen. Shit trumps spunk.

Remorse. 'The higher part of one's body bends down to observe and judge the lower, and finds it monstrous. The sense of horror it experiences is what we call remorse.' Italo Svevo. The morning after his date with Annie, Jomier feels remorse. He is fed up with the lower part of his body – the stomach, the bowels, the balls. He blames his balls for leading him to Garnier's restaurant, his stomach for his greedy gobbling, and his bowels for their importunate and untimely demands. His stomach ignores his reproaches. It is a Saturday. He makes himself bacon and egg.

Later in the morning, Jomier begins to wonder whether the lower part of his body had not done him a favour. Does he really wish, now, that he had woken in a strange bed with a woman he hardly knows? Does he really want to shave with the razor she uses on her armpits in a bathroom strewn with drying knickers? Does he want to be preoccupied with post-coital post-mortems or encumbered with the demands that a 'relationship' inevitably entails? Would he not now be setting off with Annie to some art show in Dulwich or on a bike ride along the towpath of the Thames? How much better to spend the day alone – a trip to Waitrose, lunch listening to *Any Questions*, tinkering in his garden, preparing a supper of calves' liver and sautéed potatoes, reading the *New Yorker* while he eats it and then retiring with a cup of filter decaf to watch a familiar film on TV?

Jomier calls Annie. He apologises for the fiasco of the night before. He suggests they meet at the Anglesea Arms for Sunday lunch. She can't make it. Jomier is relieved. She may be hung-over and suffering, like Jomier, a measure of confused remorse. Or has she sensed the lack of enthusiasm in his tone of voice? Jomier says he will call her the following week. He does call her. They meet in her lunch hour at the Trattoria Umberto. Jomier tells that he is not really up to an affair. 'I'm afraid age *does* matter,' he says.

'Sex isn't everything,' she says. Without much conviction. Both reassure one another that they will remain the best of friends.

# 14

TOM CLENAGHAN AT the Groucho Club. They sit down on plush armchairs. Jomier drinks white wine; Tom whisky sour. They catch up. Tom's daughter by Arabella lives with a recovering drug addict in California. His son by Susie Aschenbach is a Wall Street whizz-kid. Tom asks after Henry and Louisa whom he knew when they were small but this eyes glaze over when Jomier tells him what they are up to. Tom is more interested in their old friends. Have they done well or have they done badly? Some have done well and others have done badly. Some have retired. Some are dead. Most are divorced. They go over bust marriages – Jomier's one; Tom's three. Jomier had not known about the third – a Puerto Rican art dealer.

'She represented Palavi, Boocher, Zatler, Blakeney.'

Jomier has heard of none of these artists but does not let on. And what had gone wrong?

'Oh, you know . . .' A roguish grin.

'She caught you with the receptionist?'

'That kind of thing.'

The effect of the Blarney stone has not worn off with time. Tom talks about himself. Jomier is happy with this: he would rather listen than talk. Jomier dislikes self-disclosure, particularly when there is little to disclose. He has told Tom about Annie on a previous visit. Tom was amused. Jomier does not want to tell him about Judith. He would not understand about the rekindling of a thwarted love from the past.

Tom tells Jomier about his blog. Jomier recalls receiving an email telling him about Tom's blog and feels embarrassed that he has not read it. The embarrassment is misplaced. Tom does not see Jomier as his target audience. He regards everything British as old-fashioned and provincial and says so. Jomier thinks that there are aspects of American life which are equally old-fashioned and provincial. Gas-guzzling cars. Slow trains. Groceries packaged in brown paper bags. He does not say so. He acknowledges the contribution to his life made by Microsoft, Apple, Google and Hollywood but believes nonetheless that Americans are inward-looking. They can recite the Gettysburg Address but know next to nothing about Julius Caesar or Napoleon. They converse only with themselves – the liberals with the conservatives, the blacks with the whites, the Jews with the Gentiles, the East Coast with the West Coast, the coasts with the hinterland. They have strong feelings about things that mean little to Europeans. Abortion. Israel. Imposing democracy on nations rich in natural resources.

Tom orders a second whisky sour and, after eating the maraschino cherry, lays into Jomier about the pusillanimity of the Europeans in the face of the threat posed by Islamofascism. Jomier has been subject to these attacks before. In the US Tom only mixes with the like-minded. Jomier is a welcome punchbag that he can pummel with neocon invective.

In their youth in London Tom had been a Marxist. He moved to the right around the time he started going out with Susie Aschenbach. The Aschenbachs were Jewish. So, it turned out, was Tom Clenaghan. One-eighth Jewish on his mother's side. Had Tom always known about this branch of his family tree? He said not. It had been a 'shameful secret' hidden from him by his parents. Tom's sister Susan, whom Jomier had once met at a wedding, denied this. None of the family had shown much interest in the provenance of their maternal grandmother. Their assimilation had been complete. An eighth Jewish? So what.

Susan said Tom had only made something of his Jewish origins after he had moved to the United States. Jomier too suspects a measure of opportunism in Tom's move to Zion. There were advantages in switching tribes beyond the hand of Susie Aschenbach. Leftism was out of fashion and Irish Catholics in America were a busted flush. Corrupt politicians. Paedophile priests. There were the Catholic Poles, Slovaks, Hispanics but they cut no ice with the literati of the *New York Review of Books*. Tom had married Susie in a synagogue. Had he also been circumcised beforehand like St Timothy? Or was he circumcised at birth?

There had been a time when Jomier put such questions to Tom. That time has passed. Here in the Groucho the one-time leftist chancer wears the mantle of a rightist pundit bestowed by chat-show hosts in the US – the scourge of Islamic fundamentalists and European appeasers. Tom recognises that Jomier is not an Islamic fundamentalist but is he a European appeaser? Is he aware that another holocaust is in the offing? That the Iranian president, Ahmadinejad, wants to wipe Israel off the map? Jomier listens, wondering what Judith will give him for dinner. When pressed by Tom, he mutters something about the plight of the Palestinians. The pundit's response is an Operation Barbarossa of invective. Jomier's attitude is all too typical of European anti-Semitism. He quotes Rabbi

Sidney Brichto: 'Deep down in the European consciousness, there lingers a conviction that the world would be better without the Jews.'

Can this be true? Better off without Groucho Marx – the iconic inspiration of the Groucho Club where Tom is now ordering his fourth whisky sour? Better off without Jesus, Josephus, Ben-Hur, Heine, Mendelssohn, Marx, Trotsky, the Freuds – Sigmund *und* Lucian – Charlie Chaplin, Isaiah Berlin, Woody Allen? 'That's nonsense,' he says to Tom, declining Tom's offer of a second glass of white wine.

'*Deep down*,' Tom repeats. 'You may not be aware of it. But it is revealed in your attitude towards Israel. To be anti-Zionist is to be anti-Semitic.'

Jomier counters with the names of anti-Zionist Jews. 'Yakov Rabkin? Israel Shamir?'

'Self-hating Jews.'

'Have you read their books?'

'I don't need to . . .' He waves his hand in the air dismissively. Like most pundits, Tom has no time to read books. He now lists other self-hating Jews and Jew-hating Gentiles who edit journals and run think tanks and foundations with names that mean nothing to Jomier, and then their right-minded neocon adversaries, all endowed by billionaire zealots. This is the essence of democracy: the war of ideas. Jomier recognises that when it comes to blogs and fees and stipends and invitations to appear on chat shows, one has to take one side or the other. He himself prefers to be *hors de combat*. He does not want to be asked to express an opinion because he does not have one. He too has no time to read books – not because he is appearing on television but because he is watching it – *Newsnight*, Wolfgang Petersen movies. Tom is now telling him that the time has come for a pre-emptive strike against Iran. Jomier glances at his watch. How much time remains before he must set off for Wandsworth? How much time before the world ends on the plains of Armageddon? Or there is no petrol for Jomier's Golf because Ahmadinejad has closed the straits of Hormuz?

Tom has moved on from Ahmadinejad to Putin. He hates Putin. Putin is destroying democracy in Russia and plans to reimpose Russian hegemony on the former Soviet republics. Jomier asks why the US is so anxious about democracy in Russia when it is so insouciant about the lack of democracy among its Arab allies – Saudi Arabia, Morocco, Egypt, Dubai, Abu Dhabi? Tom waves his stubby hand in the air. They are moving towards democracy. Russia is moving away from democracy. And they do not threaten American interests. Peace, democracy, access to the oil and natural gas of Central Asia. Jomier asks if it is wise to confront both Putin and Ahmadinejad at the same time?

'Where else are they going to sell their oil?'

'China? India?'

Again, a wave of the stubby hand. 'No pipelines.'

'Not yet.'

Tom leans forward, bringing his face closer to Jomier's. His cheeks glisten with boozy sweat. His eyes are bloodshot. *'Exactly whose side are you on?'*

A good question. Jomier is uncertain. He scribbles down an equation in his mind. Western adversarial democracy + chumminess with pro-Western Arab theocracies + support of Israel + proactive wars against anti-Western regimes (Iraq, Grenada, Serbia, Sierra Leone) versus chumminess with any regime that will keep the gas flowing to his Potterton boiler and Rangemaster stove, and oil flowing to the Jet petrol station on the Goldhawk Road + minding one's own business and leaving Iraqis,

Israelis, Palestinians, Grenadians, Bosnians, Kosovans, Afghans to stew in their own juice. Jomier tentatively favours the second option but recognises that he has not factored in the imponderables – truth, justice, jobs for peacekeepers and the makers of Toyota Landcruisers, salaries and benefits for those who work for the Foreign Office, the EU or the UN. There are also the unknowables. And the things we don't know we don't know. Is reason relevant to tribal conflicts? What is churning around in our collective subconscious as we consider the state of the world? Jomier thinks back to Sidney Brichto: 'Deep down in the European consciousness, there lingers a conviction that the world would be better without the Jews.' Perhaps deep down in the Jewish consciousness there lingers a conviction that the world would be better off without Russians? Perhaps Tom's loathing of Putin comes from a gene inherited from his pogrommed forefathers in the shtetls of the Russian Pale? Perhaps Jomier's failure to choose one side or the other comes from a Hugeonot gene which tells him that God has chosen some to be saved and others to be damned, and that there is nothing you can do about it because *the grass withers, the flower falls, but the word of the Lord remains for ever*.

Jomier knows that this *deus ex machina* will cut no ice with Tom because Tom does not believe in God. Tom's Judaism is tribal, not religious, which apparently is fine in the US where you can mix and match your beliefs – hence Zionist Christians, pro-choice Catholics and atheist Jews. But if there is no God, who chose the chosen race? Who promised the promised land? Jomier would like to ask Tom but knows that this would be construed as further evidence of his subliminal anti-Semitism. He says instead: 'I must go.'

'You haven't answered my question,' says Tom. '*Whose side are you on?*'

'I'm not sure,' says Jomier.

Tom snorts – a snort of contempt for all the shilly-shallying wishy-washy bystanders who kept themselves to themselves and minded their own business as Jews were rounded up and sent off to Auschwitz.

Jomier stands. 'It's been good to see you.'

Tom, too, heaves himself up on to his feet. 'Dear boy . . .' He embraces Jomier. 'It's been like old times.' The curtain has come down. The ham actor leaves the stage. He is back in his dressing room wiping off the greasepaint. Jomier would like to congratulate him on his performance but fears that might be a step too far. They part. Jomier goes out into Dean Street. Tom sinks back into his chair.

## 15

JUDITH OPENS THE door to her house in Wandsworth.
'Oh good.' The expression in her eyes suggests that she
means what she says. Jomier apologises for being late. 'It
doesn't matter.' Each implants a kiss on the other's two
cheeks. Judith leads Jomier down her narrow hall and into
her living room. There are four other guests – two women,
two men. Judith introduces Jomier to her friends. She
tells them: 'We knew each other as children.' Then, turning to smile at Jomier: 'Well, rather more than children.'
Jomier takes it that this remark is necessary to explain the
presence of a stranger among old friends. Jomier sits down
on a sofa next to one of the women. She tells Jomier that
she is called Annabel. Judith brings him a glass of white
wine.

So far so good. While he talks about this and that,
Jomier looks around him at the furniture and the pictures
on the walls. All are fine but faded: the unravelled strands
of seagrass on the floor covering and saggy loose covers on
the sofa suggest that both were fitted some years ago. The
sponge-painted pink walls must date from the 1990s. The
white paint has yellowed on the bookshelves built in the
embrasures on either side of the marble mantel. There is an
elegant davenport and some drawings and watercolours in

fine gilt frames. Standard lamps cast pools of dim light on to the floor.

One of the male guests is tall and balding; the other is stocky and small. Jomier is glad of their contrasting appearance because he has already forgotten their names. Both are slightly younger than Jomier: one, he learns, is an art dealer; the other a publisher of books on flora and fauna – a niche market, he tells Jomier, which makes him an adequate living.

They go down to eat. The stairs lead into a large kitchen. There is an old double-doored American fridge; an Aga; a yellow Marmoleum floor; bright prints on the pale blue walls; burgundy blinds; a long oak table. The lights have been dimmed: candles are lit on the table. Judith asks Jomier to sit at the far end between Annabel and the second woman, Marion, who is small and scrawny and cannot conceal her curiosity about Judith's new *beau*. She is the partner of Gus, the stocky publisher: they met on the Internet five years before. She has two grown-up children by a husband, Simon, who is now married to Ursula, an art historian writing a book on the Russian cubist painter Natalia Goncharova. Ursula is twenty years younger than Simon. She wants a baby. He does not. Marion's curiosity about Jomier competes with the pleasure she takes in talking about herself. This suits Jomier. He gives non-committal answers to her questions and then asks: 'And you?'

She laughs – hilariously. '*Me?*' She tells him her life story. Parents academics – north Oxford – went to the same school as Judith – lost touch with her after they both married – Simon and Beresford chalk and cheese – met up again later in life. 'It's a bit the same as with *you* and Judith, isn't it? You knew her when you were young?'

'Yes,' says Jomier. 'Though not well.'

'She married too soon. So did I, for that matter. I was twenty-four which in fact didn't seem young in those days. In fact it seemed quite old and I was pregnant and in those days it was bloody difficult to get an abortion and in fact my parents were quite religious so it would really have upset them if I had though I'm not religious and I probably would have done if it was as easy as it is now. Stupidly I once said this to Joe –'

'Joe?'

Marion grabs the bottle of red wine in front of her in the table, tops up Jomier's glass and fills her own. 'My eldest son. He took it badly. Stupid of me, really. But stupid of him too because of course as soon as he was born I loved him to bits and still love him to bits despite what we've been through but at that time he was just a cluster of cells in my womb and I can hardly be blamed for being in two minds as to whether I wanted that to go on growing if it meant marrying Simon whom I did love, or thought I loved, but who I knew was a little dodgy because he'd had oodles of gay experiences at school – starting with the cricket coach at his prep school and then on to public school where he was cox of the eight which so far as I can make out means that you are buggered by all and sundry . . .'

'Do you know what this is?' asks Jomier, glancing down at the sprig of vegetal substance held on the prongs of his fork.

'Seaweed. Judy's into healthy eating. She's not a vegan – don't worry –' hilarious laughter – 'or even vegetarian . . . I mean, she will eat meat and fish but when it comes to a *salade composée* she goes for seaweed. I'm a fish and chips and steak-and-kidney pudding person myself. And the roast beef of old England! So is Gus, thank God. It's one of the things we have in common. That and sex!' Hilarious laughter.

The plates are cleared away. Jomier notices that Gus has not eaten his seaweed. Did he and Marion establish their shared preference for traditional English cooking over the Internet before they met? And their love of sex? He thinks of their slobbery kisses – drool mixed with gravy after a gluttonous *Tom Jones* (the movie)-style feast. Interests: travel, folk music, food and sex. Is sex the presumed endgame of all Internet dating? Or can you click on to a section where 'chaste woman seeks celibate man for company, conversation, going to art exhibitions, the theatre, walks on canal towpaths on a Sunday afternoon'?

Jomier turns to Annabel who is sitting on his left. They already know something about one another from their conversation on the sofa. Now they build on these foundations. Annabel is harder work than Marion. She lacks Marion's exuberance and interest in herself. Jomier understands this lack of interest: she is not interesting. Her husband Rupert, the tall balding man sitting next to Judith, is an art dealer. Annabel met him when studying at the Courtauld Institute: he was an MA student writing a thesis on Boucher and Watteau. They have been married for thirty years. Jomier gains the impression that Rupert has done well dealing in French eighteenth-century painting. They live in Chelsea. Their two sons went to Eton: one now works for Christie's, another for Morgan Stanley. They have a house in Wiltshire.

Annabel is better-looking than Marion. Jomier can see that she must have been pretty when she was young. Pretty as a picture. A Boucher. A Watteau. Had Rupert seen her with plump thighs and pink nipples flying through the air on a garlanded swing? Or had he considered her a safe investment? A wife who would look good and never stray? Unlike the pretty women painted by Boucher and Watteau,

Annabel is not a coquette. There is not a trace of flirtation in her manner. Her demeanour is of the Dutch School – more a Rembrandt or a Vermeer. Has she ever been unfaithful to her husband? Has she ever been tempted? Have the Valmonts who made a play for her been thwarted by her implacable dullness? She is telling Jomier about her grandchildren. Rosie has been offered a place at Bute House but inexplicably they – her son and daughter-in-law – are determined to send her to Norland Place. Certainly, Norland Place is closer to their house in W10 but Cynthia doesn't work and so could easily take her to Bute House in the Prius or share a school run with other Bute House parents.

Jomier is prepared to summon up views on the rival claims for excellence of Norland Place or Bute House – or, for that matter, Wetherby's, Notting Hill Prep, Bassett House, the Hall – but his mind grows numb. It is not the subject matter that deadens his brain but Annabel's monotonous tone of voice. There is no cadence. No inflexion. No puff comes from the lungs to give an emphasis to this syllable or that. The sound is hypnotically dreary. Jomier feels himself falling into a trance.

'You may not like this.' Jomier is saved from stupor by Judith's voice. She has walked the full length of the table carrying two plates – one for Annabel, one for him. She places them before them.

Jomier looks down at what is on his plate. He recognises the mound of wild rice, the sprigs of broccoli, even the cubes of glazed marrow; but what are the browned rectangles lying on top of the rice? He turns to Marion. 'Are these fish fingers?'

Hilarious laughter. 'God forbid! It's grilled tofu.'

'Tofu?'

'You must have had tofu before. Stir-fried in a Thai restaurant? It's normally tasteless but this –' Marion pokes the rectangle of tofu with her knife – 'has been soaked overnight in an achiote marinade. Achiote powder, cayenne pepper, crushed garlic, salt, pepper, brown sugar . . .'

'What is achiote?' asks Jomier.

'God knows. Some spice from the rainforests. You'll have to ask Jude. It's actually quite yummy. It's certainly better than her Peruvian lasagne.'

'Does she never cook meat?'

'Oh, yes. Steamed capon with salsa verde – that's pretty yummy, too. Boiled beef. Slow-cooked leg of lamb. It comes out pink, rather like pastrami. Gus misses the grease. But the achiote tofu is her mainstay: it's horribly healthy and amazingly cheap. I mean, look at her. Doesn't she just *glow* with good health?'

Is this just the sales talk of a best friend? Jomier looks down the table towards his hostess. She is talking to Rupert the art dealer. From where he sits she seems flawless. The candlelight might be from a bank of votive tapers at an altar of the Virgin. She does glow with health. She glows with beauty. She glows with an ancient Asiatic wisdom which teaches that love flourishes on a light diet of grilled tofu, seaweed and wild rice just as it drowns in a swill of fish soup, garlic mayonnaise, melted cheese, masticated lamb, ratatouille and oregano.

An impious demon, an anti-Cupid, whispers in Jomier's ear: she has put you at the far end of the table because she looks better at a distance. She has put you between a raddled lush and a blank blancmange to make herself look better than she is. Candlelight flatters. *You have never seen her in daylight!* These poisoned arrows of the anti-Cupid miss their mark. They are deflected by the magnetic field that love creates around the lover. Already *crystallisation* is taking place. The shabbiness of Judith's drawing room; the *haut* bohemian decor of her kitchen; even the achiote-marinated tofu are all as perfect as her smooth shoulders and tumbling hair.

Annabel talks to the man on her left. Marion talks to the man on her right. Jomier is free to rest his eyes on Judith. Then, before he has time to look elsewhere, she turns away from Rupert the art dealer and meets Jomier's eye. She smiles, raises her eyebrows, tilts her head. How is it going? Annabel? Marion? The tofu? Jomier gives a amused shrug. She laughs with her eyes. The intimate wordless communication of lovers.

The evening continues. Goat's milk panna cotta with a blackcurrant coulis. A choice of Fairtrade coffee or dandelion tea. Jomier is happy and his happiness invests a charm that he lavishes upon Annabel and Marion, and applies in a more masculine form when they go back up to the drawing room in conversation with Gus and Rupert. He is not impatient for them to leave. He has surrendered to his karma. He basks in his dulcet emotions. He has lost interest in the capsule of Viagra in the inside pocket of his corduroy jacket. Jomier is holistic. Fatalistic. What will happen will happen. What will be will be.

What will happen does happen. What will be comes about. Rupert and Annabel, Gus and Marion leave together. Rupert and Annabel shake Jomier's hand as they take their leave, saying how nice it has been to meet him and how they hope to meet him again. Gus too shakes his hand. 'Cheers.' Marion lurches across the room to say goodbye to Jomier: she hugs him, kisses him and whispers: 'You lucky man!' Judith sees her guests to the door. Jomier waits in the drawing room, his back to the gas log fire. Judith comes back into the room. 'I'm sorry about Marion. But she's an old friend.' She glances anxiously at Jomier. His expression reassures her. She goes to him and places her hands on his shoulders. 'I'm so glad you came.'

'Shall we clear up?'

'Oh no. That can wait.'

Jomier reaches round with his right hand to draw her gently towards him. He lowers his head. She raises hers. They kiss. The kiss continues. The bodies entwine. Jomier moves her back towards the sofa. She falls back gracefully, her weight on his arm. Jomier moves his lips to her shoulders, her throat, her neck. She takes a deep breath, clutches his back but starts to slip off the sofa. They break apart and sit up. 'This is rather teenagerish, isn't it?' says Judith. 'Let's go upstairs.'

# PART TWO

## 16

CHRISTMAS. A BAD time for the divorced. Who spends it with whom and where? It is Jomier's turn to celebrate the birth of Christ with Henry and Sandra or, more properly, Henry and Sandra's turn to spend it with him. Jomier's house in Hammersmith is smaller than Henry's house in Queen's Park – cramped even for a neat nuclear family + grandfather. It makes more sense for Jomier to go to them but there is nothing special for Henry and Sandra and Samantha and Ned in celebrating Christmas in their own home. It is also a waste of the precious Christmas–New Year holiday to spend it in London. They want their children to breathe fresh wintry air. Knowing this, Jomier once rented country houses from the Landmark Trust. This made Christmas costly but he considered it a price worth paying for a happy Christmas. But the Christmas was not particularly happy. A happy Christmas requires thought and preparation. Jomier did what he could. A turkey from Lidgate's. A Stilton from Paxton & Whitfield. A box of holly from the Shepherd's Bush market. It was not enough. A rented house is not a home. There was no woman's touch. Sandra was too busy, her touch on the keyboard of her BlackBerry until midday on Christmas Eve. Tilly had been good at Christmas. Jomier knows that Sam and Ned and

Henry and Sandra would rather spend Christmas in luxury in Wiltshire with Tilly and Max.

On the years when it is not Jomier's turn to spend Christmas with his son Henry, his daughter Louisa invites him to spend it with her in Argentina. His most recent visit was the year before. He had flown to Buenos Aires via Madrid, squeezed like a tinned sardine in the economy class of Iberia Airlines. Like a tinned sardine. Jomier usually eschews similes, particularly hackneyed similes, but as he sat suffering at 35,000 feet he could think of no better comparison for his condition. Peas in a pod? They are fresh and fragrant. Matches in a matchbox? They have space to rattle. Only sardines are squashed and oily and malodorous like Jomier's fellow passengers in economy class.

Jomier in Argentina. He spends one night with Louisa and Jimmy in their flat in Buenos Aires, then drives with them in their jeep to their estancia in Corrientes. He remains there for two weeks. Also staying are Jimmy's two brothers, their wives, their children. The brothers are tall and healthy and dull like Jimmy: their wives streaked-blonde, long-legged, chic – lazing like sleek whippets on the leather sofas, gossiping in Spanish, calling to their children as they rush past.

And there is Jimmy's mother, the terrible Doña Adelina. She is small and dark and old and devout and autocratic. She speaks no English. Jomier no Spanish. She dislikes walking. Her eyesight is failing. Only her peripheral vision is acute. She sits on a wooden rocking chair pointing out crumbs with her stick. Dark-skinned women with Indian physiognomies scuttle to sweep up the crumbs. Jomier is a crumb but not one that could be disposed of by a dustpan and brush. Doña Adelina occasionally addresses him in Spanish: one of her sons translates. 'You are a Protestant?'

'My ancestors were Protestants.'

'Humph.' Then: 'Thanks to the Inquisition, there were no wars of religion in Spain.'

'But a particularly unpleasant civil war with a religious dimension, I seem to recall.'

'Humph.'

It is midsummer in the southern hemisphere – the weather is hot. Jomier sits on the veranda of the estancia while his three little granddaughters – Lala, Nunci and Ysabel – study him from a distance. Can this grey-skinned old man really be their *yayo*? The two older boys, Fernando and Roberto, practise their English. They are tall, healthy, tanned, good-looking. Their English is good: less of their father's Chiquita-banana lilt; a touch of a US drawl. Their English teachers are Irish Christian Brothers. They watch undubbed American films on DVD.

Louisa is enchanting. Louisa is superb. She speaks gently in good Spanish to the servants and teases her mother-in-law, the terrible Doña Adelina. '*I* was once a Protestant, *yaya*. Can you really trust a *converso*?'

'Humph.'

Jomier to Louisa, out of earshot of Doña Adelina: 'Have you become a Catholic?'

Louisa: 'It makes things easier . . .' She does not want to talk about it. She is busy running the household but whenever she passes her father she smiles. She is pleased he is there. Or so it would seem. On Christmas Eve they eat sparingly – rice and vegetables. It begins to grow dark. The family go to their bedrooms, not to prepare for bed but to get ready for midnight Mass. The boys wear suits. The girls, pretty party frocks. Louisa comes into the living room, her head covered by a mantilla. 'Would you like to come?' Jomier shakes his head. Folklore. Superstition. He understands that it makes things easier, but cannot believe that she believes it – an all-powerful deity arriving from outside the space–time continuum covered in mucous and blood. 'Twixt pissing and shitting are we born.' Tertullian. Human beings have no choice. But God?

They leave. Jomier reads. Should he wait up for their return? Or go to bed? If he goes to bed they will wake him or, worse, whisper and tiptoe around the house. He returns to his book but cannot concentrate. Jet lag. Fatigue. Old age. He gets up from his chair, goes out on to the veranda and stands listening to the noises that come from the dark – dogs, cats, insects, frogs. He goes back into the living room, takes a cigarette from a pack of Achalay *con filtro* left by Jimmy, lights it and returns to the veranda. He has not smoked a cigarette for several years but the setting demands it. Warmth. Darkness. Strange sounds and scented air – eucalyptus, horse dung, smoke from wood fires. He draws on his cigarette and feels dizzy. He sits down on a slatted chair. He feels half happy to be alone, half unhappy at being left out.

They return – all cheerful, the eyes of the little girls gleaming with excitement at staying up so late. The servants appear, aprons over their Sunday best, with dishes of tapas. Jimmy and one of his brothers open bottles of Mendozan sparkling wine. A glass is given to Doña Adelina, enthroned on her chair; another to Jomier. He hesitates, then takes it. The adults, the children, the servants mill around, joking, laughing, teasing. Louisa urges her father to eat the tapas – squares of bread with cheese, chorizo, mashed-up egg. Jomier listens to his eleven-year-old grandson Fernando talk about rugby in a croaking, breaking voice. Over the boy's shoulder he watches Louisa as she stage-manages this opening of the Christmas celebrations. She does it well. She is like her mother. She was always like her mother. She is like Tilly before the Fall. Or perhaps Tilly at the time of the Fall. She must be older than she looks. Sunshine. Servants. None of the debilitating drudgery under dark skies that ages the middle-class housewife in England.

Louisa catches his eye and gives an amused look as if to say: 'I know Fernando's a bore but so are all the boys of his age in Buenos Aires and he's so proud of you and pleased you are here. It gives them great prestige at school to have *un abogado inglés* as their grandfather.'

Doña Adelina gets to her feet. It is time for bed. Embraces. 'Happy Christmas.' Louisa hugs her father. 'Is everything all right?'

'Everything is perfect. Happy Christmas.'

Christmas morning. Jimmy takes Jomier on a tour of the estancia. Jomier feels that the shaking of his liver and kidneys as the hard-sprung old Land Rover bumps over the pampas is doing him good. Jimmy talks about the political situation in Argentina. Cristina Kirchner is a big disappointment as president; her husband Néstor still calls the shots. Her attempt to increase the tax on soybean exports was iniquitous: Jimmy's uncle led the opposition to the measure in the Senate. Jimmy's family are big in soybeans. Do they cut down rainforests to plant more soy beans? So far as he knows, Jomier has never eaten a soybean so cannot understand the world's insatiable appetite for soybeans. He would ask Jimmy but prefers to avoid giving him a pretext to go on talking. But Jimmy is a mind-reader. He tells Jomier that soybeans are the world's most versatile vegetal source of protein. Soya milk. Caramel. Tofu. It is also the staple of most animal foodstuffs. There would be no hamburgers served in McDonald's in Jakarta were it not for soybeans grown in Argentina. By using soybeans as a supplement to their diet of grass Jimmy can double the number of cattle on the estancia. He has diversified into Kobe-style beef by crossing the Wagyu bull that he imported from Japan with locally bred Aberdeen Angus. He exports it to the US where Kobe-style steaks are all the rage.

An Anglo-Christmas dinner. Turkey. Sausages. Stuffing. Bread sauce. All the trimmings. Mendozan white, Mendozan red. Mumm Cordon Rouge with the Christmas pudding. Treacly black coffee. Cohiba cigars. Crackers. Excitement. Shrieks from the little girls. They withdraw to the living room. Mounds of gifts rise from the floor. Before they are opened, the family sings carols around the tree. Louisa plays the piano. Jomier recalls her music lessons with Miss Pearson in Princedale Road; the steady progress from Grade 1 to Grade 8. A wave of nostalgia for the dark damp streets of Holland Park breaks over him: celebrating Christmas in the heat of high summer feels wrong. And the sausages served with the turkey were gristly and spicy, not crisp and bland and bready as they are in England.

Jomier's grandchildren are well disciplined: only little Ysabel, as she sings carols, lets her eyes wander towards her pile of presents. They come to the last verse of the last carol – *Adeste Fideles*, 'Oh Come all Ye Faithful'. Louisa then looks towards Doña Adelina, enthroned on an armchair. *Muy bien*. That is the signal. The children, 'joyful and triumphant', make for the piles and open their presents. The grown-ups linger. Jomier readies himself for the polite thanks of his grandchildren for his disappointing gifts. Jomier is not good at choosing presents for others. He finds it impossible to imagine what they might like. It was always Tilly who did the Christmas shopping. Jomier had only to buy a present for her. Tilly always changed it. In the end, she had bought his gifts to her herself: he had only to wrap them up.

Nor do others find it easy to choose presents for him. A silver-framed photograph of the five grandchildren from Louisa. A leather humidor from Jimmy. A maté gourd and silver straw from one of Jimmy's brothers. A gaucho shirt from the other. A tie from Doña Adelina. Jomier will bin them all when he gets back to England. All except the photograph. He will put that on the baby grand piano that he keeps tuned for Louisa's occasional visits to London.

In the cool of the evening, the boys go riding with their uncles. Jomier and Louisa go for a walk. 'I am so glad you came,' she says. 'It gives you a chance to get to know the children.'

'They are enchanting,' says Jomier.

'Not too like the von Trapps?'

'The von Trapps?'

'*The Sound of Music*.'

Jomier laughs. 'They're no worse for that.'

'You won't have had time to see it, but they're all quite different. Fernando is like his father which is good but Roberto is more curious, intellectually, and so is Lala; they bicker terribly but that's because they're so alike. Nunci is just like her granny Adelina – another despot in the making – and Ysabel . . . I don't know. She's not really like anyone much.'

'They are enchanting,' says Jomier again.

'It's a wonderful country to bring up children if you're not poor. There's the sun and so much space. I watch out for some of the less attractive qualities that you find out here so that I can nip them in the bud.'

'What sort of thing?'

'You must have noticed it in Jimmy and Doña Adelina – in all of them, in fact. The way they treat the servants. An arrogance. A contempt for the poor – "losers", they would call them though not in my presence.'

'The spirit of the conquistadors,' said Jomier. 'Everyone starts with nothing so the poor are only getting what they deserve.'

'They didn't start with nothing,' says Louisa, 'and they're meant to be Catholics which should mean a love of the poor.'

'Is that what you tell them?'

'Of course.'

'And what do they say?'

'That you can't expect *una inglesa* to understand.'

They walk on for a while in silence. In his mind Jomier compares the wide views and open spaces of the *estancia* with the cramped confines of Queen's Park. 'But you don't regret it?'

'Living out here?'

'Yes.'

She thinks. 'I do miss England. I miss you and Mummy and Henry and Sandra and am sad not to see their children growing up. I wouldn't have stayed here if it wasn't for Jimmy.'

'And you don't regret *that*?'

'Marrying Jimmy? No.' She smiles. 'He has his limitations, but all husbands do, don't they, after a while? And sometimes limited people are easier to deal with. I mean, men out here – men like Jimmy – have very simple and straightforward expectations of their wives. They want them to bear their children and run their homes and put up with their intolerable old mothers whereas in England . . . I don't know . . . everything seems to depend upon a *relationship* between two rival bisexuals both working and both cooking and both parenting so that neither needs the other except for some kind of psychological ego boost which is hard to sustain over the years.'

'Your mother didn't work,' says Jomier.

'No. She fell between two stools. Girls of her generation and her background didn't expect to have to earn their living so they didn't train for a career and so felt demeaned when the feminist zeitgeist downgraded motherhood to the status of office cleaning.'

'You can't blame me for that.'

Louisa hesitates. 'No. No one blames you for the change in the zeitgeist.'

'But for other things?'

'No, not *blame* exactly . . .' Then: 'Let's not talk about it. What's done is done.'

They move on to books. Louisa reads a lot. With servants to shop, cook, clean, wash, iron, garden, she has the time. She buys the *New York Review of Books* in Buenos Aires and has the *Week* and the *Literary Review* sent out from England. She makes a double-click purchase on Amazon of any book she thinks looks enjoyable or interesting. She has read all the novels on the Booker Prize shortlist and thinks that the judges made the wrong choice of the winner. Jomier has read none of the novels on the Booker Prize shortlist and so cannot discuss their merits or demerits with his daughter. She is puzzled by his lack of curiosity about contemporary fiction. 'Surely now that you've retired you have the time?'

Jomier: 'I like rereading classical authors. Chekhov. Stendhal. Dostoevsky.'

She nods. 'I like those too.'

They walk for a while in silence. Jomier does not say

what he is thinking. 'You read so much because you are bored by your life in BA.' Or: 'All the arts have been taken over by charlatans.' Or: 'Without the vested interests of teachers of Eng. lit. in our universities, and the missionaries the faculties send out into the media, modern fiction would shrivel to the true proportions of its mediocrity and be blown away by the public's indifference.' He has these thoughts but does not express them. He does not want to spoil Louisa's pleasure as a new book arrives from Amazon. He does not want to remind her of his negative outlook on life which was perhaps at the back of her mind when she said 'not *blame* exactly . . .' meaning 'yes, you were to blame because you were cold and unromantic and stingy and sneered at Mum for reading modern novels and going to exhibitions at the Whitechapel Gallery with her friend Susie'.

Jimmy's brothers and their wives and their children leave on Boxing Day for Punta del Este. Jimmy and Louisa and their children will join them there for the New Year. Louisa half-heartedly suggests to Jomier that he might go with them to the Uruguayan resort. Jomier fakes regret that he cannot accept because his return ticket to Europe on 29 December cannot be changed. He looks forward to getting back to Hammersmith: Jomier has in fact been looking forward to getting back to Hammersmith from the moment he checked in at Heathrow. He is suffering from the heat. Louisa tells him that it would be cooler on the beaches of the South Atlantic Ocean, then smiles sadly and says: 'You never really liked the seaside.' The seaside. She does not mean Worthing or Felixstowe but the pebbly beaches of Patmos or Corfu – family holidays, mostly with the Stutzels – Max, Jane, Hayden and Chuck. The sadness in her smile suggests to Jomier that this too – this dislike of heat and glare and heat rash and sand in his socks – his grey pink-spotted body in boxer-short trunks next to Max's bronzed hirsute torso on the puttering caique – was part of the 'not *blame* exactly . . .' – the qualities that were not his *fault* but surely contributed to her mother's disenchantment. 'If it wasn't for the ticket . . .' She knows this is not true. He knows she knows.

The last days are difficult. He has lost his novelty interest for the children who get on with their pursuits. He goes for walks with Louisa. They sit on chairs on the veranda in the evening drinking pisco sours. Both father and daughter hear the clock ticking and want to make the most of what remains of their time together but they have said all that there is to say. She is a grown woman. The bonds between them are historic. He has his life. She has hers. The love he feels for her is so acute that it is painful but how can he express it? He had hugged her and cuddled her and helped her with her homework until she developed breasts and it seemed inappropriate to feel them pressing on his chest. And her curriculum was beyond him. What were the unspoken, unconscious, explicit influences on her formation? Neither wants to ask, to analyse, to dissect. The silences between them grow longer. Jomier has heard all he wants to hear about Louisa's life in Argentina. There is not much to say about Jomier's life in London. He cannot tell her about his unhappiness – the wretchedness he still feels all these years later because her mother left him for Max.

On the last night of his stay, Jomier cannot sleep. He has eaten and drunk too much. The pisco sours, the Mendozan red, the T-bone steaks, the *dulce de leche* dessert, a last Cohiba, the Johnnie Walker Black Label as a nightcap, the heat, the mosquitoes or imagined mosquitoes. And his thoughts. About Louisa. Like and yet unlike her mother. Wiser. More measured. Her feelings under control. Does she really love Jimmy? Or has she learned from the breakdown of her parents' marriage to mistrust romantic love? To play safe. Is there, at the back of her mind, a sense that if things had been otherwise in her childhood she might have taken a greater risk in her choice of a husband? 'Not *blame* exactly . . .' She is affectionate towards Jomier. She is scrupulously kind. But perhaps she *does* blame him for giving up too easily – for capitulating before the zeitgeist which says that, after a daughter has reached the age of puberty, a father no longer has a role to play. A source of authority? Patriarchal claptrap. A personification of the superego? Cod psychology. The guardian of her chastity? A cover for incestuous desire. So Jomier had backed off. He had given up. He had given up his role as guide and mentor and left Tilly and the zeitgeist to urge her on. Have fun while you can. Play the field. Don't marry too young. But Louisa had known better. She had crossed an ocean to find a husband who, unlike her father, would kill a wife who made love with another man.

Jimmy and Louisa drive him back to Buenos Aires: the children remain with Doña Adelina at the estancia. Jomier had said he would take the train. They would not hear of it. They park the jeep at the airport and hover while he checks in. At the departure gate, Jomier turns to Jimmy. 'Many thanks. It's been a wonderful Christmas.'

'*Adiós.*' A crushing bear hug. A last thump on the back.

'Oh Dad,' says Louisa. She hugs him gently. There are tears in her eyes.

Jomier: 'Come to London.'

'We will soon, I promise.'

He gathers together his hand baggage, his ticket, his passport and, just before passing out of sight behind the screen, turns for a final wave but they have gone.

# 17

NOW IT IS Jomier's turn to spend Christmas with Henry but a new factor has entered into the equation. Judith. Jomier and Judith are now an item. They have been going out since the early autumn. They do not live together but meet up twice a week – midweek and at the weekend. Jomier returns home after meeting up with Judith on a Wednesday evening for a movie or an Indian, but the Saturday-night date lasts until the Sunday evening. They sleep over in one another's houses, mostly in Judith's. Both have met one of the other's two children: Judith has been to Sunday lunch with Jomier together with Henry, Sandra, Samantha and Ned.

Both have used the word 'love'. Judith: 'Oh, oh, oh I love you so much . . .' This during sex. Jomier: 'I do believe I'm in love' – this neither a mature nor premature ejaculation but the excited, surprised observation of a scientist conducting an experiment on himself. Over a biryani in a Keralite restaurant on King Street in Hammersmith. What had prompted his declaration? The touching eagerness with which she was eating? Or the disappointment he felt when she told him that she would be away at the weekend visiting her son in Devon? His dates with Judith had become the high points of his week. On a Monday morning he looks forward to Wednesday; on a Thursday he looks forward to Saturday. He is saddened, even angry, when she goes away – to teach at a week-long residential yoga retreat in Andalusia or to spend a weekend in Devon.

Jomier has not met Judith's son Tim. He forms an image of a muddled idle loser whose depression is a pretext for living on handouts from his father; and his girlfriend, Tamara, the potter, a toughie who sees a secure future in caring for the son of a rich banker. Jomier acknowledges that this image may be distorted: it is seen through the prism of a mother who feels at once guilty and jealous, exasperated and detached. Jomier wonders what Judith was like as a mother when the children were small. As a sixty-something-year-old lover she is all a sixty-something-year-old man could want: but as the parent of a toddler, an adolescent? Jomier is not so sure.

Jomier has met Judith's daughter Ophelia. After the four years of silence, she is back on speaking terms with her mother. Jomier first met Ophelia when she turned up unexpectedly at her mother's house in Wandsworth to find Jomier at breakfast in dressing gown and pyjamas. Judith was upstairs taking a bath. Ophelia had sat at the kitchen table with Jomier waiting for her mother to come down. 'I heard that Mum had a new bloke,' she says, taking a cup of coffee from Jomier. No word of thanks. She is wearing a low-cut black dress: there are mascara smudges around her eyes. She has lost the keys to her flat. She had gone out with a girlfriend and had met this man and they'd gone back to his flat and she hadn't realised until the morning that her bag had been nicked. Jomier wonders why this divorced woman in her late thirties is picking up men in bars and getting so drunk that she does not realise that her bag has been stolen. Is this going back to square one in the dating game? Is life now a game of snakes and ladders? Or did she never grow up? She does not seem happy. Nor is she embarrassed. By the admission of a one-night stand. Or finding her mother's lover in his pyjamas. She is only surprised by the pyjamas. 'I've never seen a bloke wearing pyjamas,' she says. 'Not even my dad. All the ones I've known sleep in boxer shorts or nothing at all.'

'It's a generational thing,' says Jomier.

'Yeah, I suppose.'

Judith comes down. If she is annoyed or embarrassed by her daughter's appearance, she does not show it. Her voice is as supple and controlled as her movements. 'Poor darling. What a bore.' She takes a spare set of keys to Ophelia's flat from a bowl on the mantel and hands them to Ophelia. 'Would you like to stay and have some breakfast?'

Ophelia shakes her head. 'I'll go back. I need a shower.'

Jomier agrees. A post-coital aroma — scent, sweat and glandular secretions — mingles with that of coffee and singed toast. Jomier too would like to take a shower: no doubt he too exudes a post-coital aroma.

Ophelia stands. She is basically pretty but there are signs of wear-and-tear. No sun. No space. No servants.

'She does it on purpose,' says Judith as she returns from seeing her daughter to the door.

'A cry for help?'

'I've done all I can. And anyway, she thinks I'm the problem, not the solution.'

Jomier goes up to take a shower. Judith has put out a large fluffy bath towel on an armchair in the bathroom. The bathroom is large — the size of a bedroom — with framed pictures on pale yellow distressed walls. On a dressing table there are tubs of oils and unguents; on the shelves jars of bath salts and bottles of bath oil. Placed around the bath are coloured candleholders: Judith has treated Jomier to a soak – lying for an hour in candlelit gloom with hot scented water up to his chin. Aromatherapy. A physical and mental cleansing. A spiritual detoxification. Jomier had emerged from this bath and passed through to Judith's bedroom wrapped in the large fluffy towel. He had lain back against the cushions at the top of the bed while Judith unwound the fluffy towel and caressed his scented skin. Her body, lean from yoga and a diet of tofu and wild rice, had hovered over his like a morning mist on a Chinese scroll. Controlled. Artful. The Kama Sutra.

There is a time for taking a bath and a time for taking a shower and now, following Ophelia's visit, and in unfiltered daylight, it is time for taking a shower. The shower head is attached to the mixer taps at the head of the bath. There is a slightly grubby shower curtain. The fixtures in the bathroom date from the eighties or nineties when Judith first moved in. The paint is peeling on the side of the bath and at one end, where water has penetrated into the wood, the panel has warped. The pressure is weak. Water dribbles over Jomier's body, alternately scalding and cold. Should Jomier offer to pay for the installation of a thermostatically controlled Dornbracht power shower of the kind he has in his house in Hammersmith? He considers the idea, then relegates it to the pending file in his mind. Judith might be offended by the implicit criticism of the present shower. She might see in the offer a premature presumption that she would like him to move in. It would be expensive and, if their relationship was not to last long, money wasted. Judith never takes showers.

Jomier has met Ophelia on two further occasions – once when she had gatecrashed a Sunday lunch (poached capon, salsa verde) that Judith had given to introduce Jomier to another group of her friends; once on a Sunday evening when she returned Judith's Peugeot which she had borrowed for the weekend. 'I'm so sorry, Mum, I got a ticket parking on the Mall outside the ICA.'

It was after this third meeting that Judith had said to Jomier: 'She's going to spend Christmas with her father, thank God.'

'And Tim?'

'Tim too.'

'So what will you do?'

'I don't know. Go off somewhere. Or celebrate it here on my own.'

'Why not come to me?'

'Would your children mind?'

'Of course not. Or, better still, they could go to their mother and perhaps we could spend Christmas abroad.'

Jomier brings up the subject of Christmas with his son Henry and daughter-in-law Sandra during Sunday lunch at their house in Queen's Park – roast beef, roast potatoes, Yorkshire pudding cooked by Henry. He floats the idea of a change in the established routine. 'Judith's on her own. We thought we might go to Venice. Could you manage Christmas without me?'

Incredulity. Henry and Sandra struggle to grasp the meaning of what Jomier has just said. Then, after two or three seconds of incomprehension, the penny drops. Sandra turns towards Henry with a boardroom look which says: 'Handle this carefully. For fuck's sake don't blow it' – while Henry's expression, like a fast-forwarded recording of a TV weather forecast predicting showers with sunny intervals, shows first an astonished delight, then a feigned regret. 'Of course, if that would suit you.' He turns to his wife. 'What do you think?'

'I'm sure we could manage,' says Sandra.

'We could go to Granny Tilly's,' says Samantha.

'I dare say,' says Henry.

'Hooray, hooray, hooray,' says Sam.

'Hooray, hooray, hooray,' echoes Ned.

'Venice can be lovely in winter,' says Henry.

# 18

STANSTED. THEY ARE flying Ryanair to Treviso: tickets out of Heathrow were too expensive. Jomier would have been prepared to pay the extra but Judith has insisted that she will pay for herself and he senses that she has not got much money. Their original intention was to take the Underground to Liverpool Street and then the Stansted Express but Judith has a large suitcase: it is difficult to travel light in winter because of the bulkiness of warm clothes. They take a minicab: Jomier pays and enters the £70 into the mini-spreadsheet on his Palm Treo. The airport is crowded: the Christmas rush. They wheel their suitcases towards the check-in desk for Treviso. They join a long queue. Judith holds Jomier by the arm. She is excited. Jomier does his best to persuade himself that he too is excited but sneaks an envious look towards 'Arrivals': in a week he will be back.

They reach the front of the queue. They present their printouts and passports. There is extra to pay for consigning two suitcases to the hold. Judith offers to pay. Jomier: 'Isn't it simpler if I pay for now and we settle up later?' Judith agrees. They join new queues to pass through security and passport control. At security a uniformed Sikh searches Judith's hand baggage. He passes her tub of cold cream and small bottle of Body Shop eau de toilette but singles out a can of Klorane spray-on deodorant. Aerosols may not be taken on to the plane. Judith is angry but impotent against the Sikh stickler for anti-terrorist regulations. How is he to know that Judith is not a jihadist or a reanimated sleeper from the Baader–Meinhoff gang? The Klorane spray-on deodorant is consigned to a plastic bin.

'You can buy some more in Venice,' says Jomier.

'No, I can't,' she snaps. 'It's almost impossible to find.'

'Deodorant?'

'Klorane. You can only get it in France.'

'What's so special about Klorane?'

'There's no aluminium.'

'Aluminium?'

'Other deodorants use aluminium. It gives you breast cancer.'

Jomier waits while Judith goes into the WH Smith bookshop. She comes out with two paperbacks in a plastic bag and a copy of the *Independent*. They now start the long walk to a far-distant gate reserved for the skinflint passengers of Ryanair. Judith takes his arm again. 'I'm sorry I got cross.'

'Don't apologise. It's maddening.'

They reach the gate and sit waiting for their flight to be called. Judith reads the *Independent*. Jomier enters the sum he paid for the checked-in baggage on to his Palm Treo.

They are summoned to board the Boeing 737. Cold-eyed *Mädchen in Uniform* herd them down a ramp onto the tarmac. They walk in the drizzle towards the plane, climb the steps and shuffle like sheep in a sheep dip looking for empty seats. Jomier and Judith have elected to travel from Stansted to Treviso but they have not paid for 'priority boarding'. They must sit where they can. Judith finds an aisle seat: Jomier squeezes in between an Italian matron and a bronzed hunk en route to the skiing slopes of the

Dolomites. Travel, 'mankind's diabolical invention which, for complication, fatigue, danger, time wasted, and nervous expenditure has no rival except war: with the difference that travel costs the shirt off your back, whereas in war at least one is paid for'. Costas in Montherlant's *Pity for Women*. In the 1930s, when the novel was written, the shirt off your back bought you a ticket to Venice on the Orient Express: now, for one dirty sock + the 50p wheelchair charge, you are packed into a Boeing. Like sardines.

At Treviso, Jomier and Judith drag their suitcases out of the barn-like terminal building to the coach waiting to take Ryanair passengers to Venice. They lift their suitcases into the belly of the coach and join the queue to get in. Jomier climbs the steps, taking out his wallet to buy a ticket. No, no. The driver waves him off. He must buy his ticket in the terminal. Jomier and Judith squeeze past the passengers standing behind them. Should they leave their bags on the bus? Jomier is afraid it might depart without them. Their suitcases are now hidden behind a wall of other suitcases, holdalls, rucksacks . . . Jomier breaks down the wall to retrieve them. They walk back into the terminal, find the ticket counter, wait in a queue to buy tickets, buy the tickets (€9 × 2 = €18), and once again make their way out of the terminal. The coach has gone. Will there be another? They return to the terminal to try and find out. '*Si, si. Un altro . . .*' They return to the coach stop and wait.

Pale winter sunlight. From the vaporetto taking Jomier and Judith along the Grand Canal, *La Serenissima* looks superb. But she is incontinent. They disembark at the Ponte dell'Accademia and find, when they reach the Sestiere Dorsoduro, that they must walk on duckboards to reach their hotel. The ground floor of the Albergo Manzoni is under water but the hotel itself remains open for business. The concierge behind the desk neither apologises nor explains. He shows Jomier and Judith to their room. It is small but light with a fine view of the Giudecca and the church of San Giorgio Maggiore. There is a shower and lavatory in a windowless annexe. The concierge explains that the *sala da pranzo e chuiso* but breakfast can be brought to their room. The room is chilly. With a certain reluctance he stoops to switch on an electric radiator on the wall.

It is now late afternoon. The light is fading. Jomier and Judith agree that it is too late to start sightseeing. The smell of singed dust rises from the radiator. Jomier and Judith remove their damp shoes and lie under the bedclothes to rest. 'This is no good,' says Jomier. 'We'll upgrade tomorrow.'

At seven, they walk out on to the duckboards and rise above sea-level as they pass the Accademia and find a small restaurant near the Fenice. It has been recommended by an online website but Jomier pretends that he knows it of old. It is not wholly a pretence. Jomier certainly ate at a restaurant like this restaurant somewhere around the Fenice when he was in Venice with Tilly thirty years before. Over supper he confesses to Judith that this might not be the same restaurant or, if the same restaurant, it may be under new management. Judith smiles. She does not complain. They are both hungry. The food is not bad. Mozzarella and tomato salad, *risotto ai funghi, scaloppine al limone* for Judith: *bresaola, linguine napolitana* and a veal chop for Jomier. A bottle of Chianti. No pudding. No coffee. No *grappa*. No sex once they are back at the hotel. An early night. *Reculer pour mieux sauter* . . .

The next morning the waters have subsided: a mournful African is mopping up the muddy residue in the lobby of the hotel. They check out and move to the five-star Hotel Palazzo Solaia. Jomier has told Judith that he will pay. She has said 'nonsense' but with less conviction than before. 'Well, I'll pay for the upgrade,' said Jomier. They are offered a 'Christmas package' by the hotel: two nights in a deluxe double room, complimentary buffet breakfasts, a bottle of prosecco, home-made sweets and biscuits on arrival, a Christmas surprise, and Christmas lunch in the hotel restaurant to include wine. Judith hesitates. Jomier can see a 'Isn't this rather vulgar and horribly expensive?' look on her face. Jomier jumps at it. €670 per person plus the extra nights at a special rate.

Judith is happy. Jomier is happy. Judith is happy because there is a bath tub, not just a shower; Jomier is happy because there is a multi-channelled 18-inch TV. Judith does not take a bath. Jomier does not switch on the TV. It is only eleven in the morning. Culture comes first. They start at the Piazzetta San Marco, water still glistening on the flagstones from yesterday's flood. Jomier points to the four bronze horses on the portico in front of the cathedral and tells Judith how they were taken from the Forum in Rome to Constantinople, then stolen from the Byzantines and brought to Venice, then taken by Napoleon to Paris and only returned to Venice after his fall. *Sic transit gloria mundi*. Not mass transit but transit of the spoils of war. The bronze horses. The relics of St Mark, plundered from Alexandria.

It is cold. They go into Florian's and find an empty table. They order cappuccinos. The cappuccinos arrive, large cups with generous, creamy froth sprinkled with chocolate powder. They sip them. Jomier laughs at the moustache left on Judith's upper lip. She laughs too, wiping her mouth with a paper napkin. Most of the others in the cafe are, like Jomier and Judith, North Europeans or Americans of a certain age. They do not mind. They are happy, away from their judgemental children. They finish their cappuccinos. It is time to move on. Jomier calls for the bill. He hands the waiter a €50 note. There is scant change. Jomier puts the receipt into his wallet.

Jomier now leads Judith across the square to the Museo Correr. Judith asks whether, given the artistic treasures that are available in the churches and galleries of Venice, they really want to look at a display of pottery and local costumes. 'Wait,' says Jomier. He leads her past the display cabinets to one of the paintings hanging on the wall, Carpaccio's *Two Venetian Women*. 'Ruskin,' he tells Judith, 'thought this the best picture in the world.' They stand looking at the Venetian painter's depiction of pigeons, a peacock and two old whores.

'And you?' asks Judith.

'What?'

'Do you think it is the best picture in the world?'

'No.' He laughs. They leave.

'Let's go to the Accademia,' says Judith, taking Jomier by the arm. She talks with a familiarity that suggests she knows Venice as well as, if not better than, Jomier. Both have been there before; both want to impress the other with their familiarity with *La Serenissima*, but both are reluctant to go into detail of their previous visits because they had been in the company of former lovers – or, in Jomier's case, a wife. Jomier is also reluctant to admit that his previous visit was thirty years before, or that his knowledge of Venice comes from guidebooks and the Internet, not a cosmopolitan persona. The little restaurant behind the Fenice; Ruskin's 'gem' in the Museo Correr . . . Why did he feel he had to pretend to Judith that he knew his way around Venice? Why do men feel that they have to impress women? Why do women make men feel that they have to impress them?

Veneziano – Paolo and Lorenzo; Bellini – Giovanni and Gentile; Giorgione, more Carpaccio, Titian, Tiepolo, Canaletto, Guardi, Veronese . . . Jomier and Judith study the paintings conscientiously and, every now and then, point out on some canvas a poignant depiction or masterly touch. Jomier drops his pose as connoisseur: it is quite evident that Judith knows more about art than he does – particularly Titian and Tiepolo. Jomier finds that he dislikes the work of both those painters but does not say so: he is not so sure of Judith that he dare risk appearing to be a cultural dunce. He does dare sigh at some point and say: 'Isn't it time for lunch?' 'Of course,' says Judith – brought down to earth by Jomier's carnal needs.

They go to Harry's Bar. It is now two o'clock. There is a table. The menu lists the dishes on offer in both English and Italian. Jomier is irked to see that a dish offered in Italian does not appear in English translation. He asks the waiter what it is. 'A Venetian speciality. Not for tourists. You no like.' The man speaks disdainfully. Jomier's hackles rise. He orders the dish. The waiter shrugs. Judith chooses a salad. Jomier's choice, when it arrives, is inedible – chunks of gristle in a viscous sauce. He eats what he can. Judith says nothing. When they have finished, the waiter clears his plate piled with chunks of masticated gristle. His glance and demeanour express what he does not say. *'Imbecille!'*

Both would like to return to their hotel for a siesta but the winter day is short. Daylight fades. Churches, *scuole*, museums close. They do the Scuola dei Calegheri and Santa Maria Gloriosa dei Frari before calling it a day. They are back at the Hotel Palazzo Solaia by five. They rest. They read. Jomier catches CNN news at seven. He sees that there are pay-to-view channels with recently released movies and an 'adult' option. Jomier is tempted by one of the movies but not by the porn. Why watch when you can do?

Jomier and Judith have not yet made love on their king-sized double bed. They are waiting for the most opportune moment when neither is tired nor bloated. Jomier must plan ahead: he has to take a tablet of Viagra half an hour or so before. Subsequent to that first coupling when the novelty and romance had done the work of the drug, Jomier has had to call upon Pfizer's elixir to boost the pumping power of his heart. He has made no secret of this from Judith; she too makes use of unguents that would be unnecessary for a younger woman. They are able to laugh at their physical shortcomings and agree that they do not detract from the end result. In Judith's case, as observed by Jomier, that is self-evident; in Jomier's case, as observed by Jomier, it was, like his familiarity with Venice, a few steps short of the truth. The actual sensation is not as pleasurable as he remembers it; indeed, at times it verges on pain; nor is ejaculation as ecstatic – not the gusher from a newly tapped oil well but a coughing splutter from a rusty pump.

But here they are, two lovers in a luxury hotel with a king-sized bed. Eschewing sex is not an option. Both rest. Jomier nods off. When he awakes, Judith is in the bath. She returns to the bedroom wrapped in a huge, fluffy white towel. Jomier goes to the bathroom. He washes down a capsule of Viagra with water from the disposable plastic tumbler. He stands in the shower, streams of hot water cleansing his body. He returns to the bedroom, also wrapped in a huge, fluffy white towel. He lies down beside her. She is reading one of the novels she bought at Stansted. He closes his eyes and waits for the Viagra to take effect. At the first stirrings, he tilts his body so that he can look into Judith's eyes. She removes her glasses, puts them on the bedside table and turns towards him. Her look is loving, sensuous, inviting. He kisses her – a pleasant, lingering kiss with touching tongues. Her lips are not as plump and cushioning as those of a younger woman; he can feel her teeth beneath her skin. No doubt she can feel his. Jomier thinks of the skull on one of the tombs in one of the smaller churches they looked into that afternoon. The thought does not stymie his desire: there is still flesh on the bones of them both. He pulls the towel away from her body; it is still pink and warm and moist and fragrant from her bath. He kicks away his own towel. They make love.

## 19

It is Christmas Eve. Jomier and Judith, well wrapped in overcoats and scarves, walk out into the street. Elegant decorations hang from the palazzos; bright shop windows display their wares festooned with glitter and tinsel. They dawdle at a Christmas fair – little stalls vividly lit selling biscuits, panettone, sugared fruit, glazed chestnuts, orange segments coated in dark chocolate. They walk on. They choose a restaurant at random. It is warm. The waiters are friendly. They eat well. They come out of the restaurant into the crowded street. They follow the flow of people and find themselves in St Mark's Square. People are making for the basilica.

'Midnight Mass,' says Judith. 'Shall we take a look?'

'Why not,' says Jomier. A folkloric experience. Fine music, perhaps. A free concert.

The basilica is dark and filled with people. Banks of candles and the dim bulbs of huge chandeliers cast a faint trembling light on the arches and domes. The smell of candlewax and incense thickens the air. The Mass has started. A booming chant comes from the darkness. The vestments of the patriarch and his acolytes sparkle at the high altar. Judith peers over shoulders. She is entranced by the spectacle. Jomier too is impressed: here is something that transcends tourism.

Marco Polo, Christopher Columbus, Vivaldi, Casanova – all would have seen what he is seeing if they had stood where he stands now. Little has changed in a thousand years. He looks at the faces of the Venetians around him. Have they been drawn by the spectacle? By tradition? Or do some of them, like his friend Theodor, believe?

More singing. More scuttling around the altar. Chanting in Latin. Readings in Italian. Jomier starts to feel claustrophobic – suffocated by the smoky air. He leans down and whispers into Judith's ear: 'Shall we go?' She hesitates, her eyes still fixed on the glittering figures at the altar. Then, as if with an effort of will, she turns away and says: 'OK.'

They push through the crowd to reach the door of the basilica. Out on St Mark's Square, Judith takes Jomier's arm. 'Wasn't it beautiful?'

'Yes, but . . .'

'I know. The incense. It makes one dizzy. I had the feeling that the whole thing was genuine.'

'Yes, though . . .'

'What?'

'I wonder how many in that crowd actually *believe*?'

Judith squeezes his arm. 'You're so *literal*. I mean, one can believe in the sense of accepting that an ancient and touching myth about a child born in a manger is true because it is beautiful like a painting or a poem or a sonata.'

'Born of a virgin?'

'Yes, well, that's perhaps not so beautiful if it is taken to demean sex. But Christmas celebrates the *birth* of Jesus, not his conception – immaculate or otherwise.'

'The Immaculate Conception . . .' Jomier begins, meaning to tell Judith that the Catholic dogma refers to the conception of Mary, not of Jesus, but he has resolved not to be a know-all and so leaves the sentence unfinished.

Judith does not seem to notice. She squeezes his arm again and gives a little shiver. 'God, it's cold.'

Christmas Day. Breakfast is brought to their room. They open the presents that each has brought for the other: a racing-green cashmere jersey for Judith from Jomier; a blue check shirt and speckled red tie for Jomier from Judith. And smaller parcels: Floris bath essence for Judith from Jomier; a pair of fleece-lined leather gloves for Jomier from Judith. Each unwrapping is followed by an expression of delight and a kiss. However, they are adults and understand that the expressions of delight may be pro forma. Judith has retained the receipts for the shirt from Kilgour and the tie from Paul Smith. Jomier has retained the receipt for the cashmere jersey from Harrods.

They laze around. Judith is reading Margaret Atwood's *The Blind Assassin*, Jomier Italo Svevo's *Senilità* – or, in this English translation, *As a Man Grows Older*. Jomier chose the novel because it was written just across the lagoon in Trieste. Jomier likes to read books that pertain to the place he is visiting: *The Leopard* in Sicily, *Dubliners* in Dublin, *Portrait of a Lady* in Florence; *I Promessi Sposi* in Milan; *The Bridge on the Drina* in Mostar; *Anna Karenina* in Moscow; *A Sentimental Education* in Paris. By entering into the lives of characters created by an author who knew the city, you get behind the flat two-dimensional surfaces of palazzos and paintings. What were they like, those Doges with the funny bumps on their hats? What went on in the minds of Carpaccio's two old whores? What were those Venetians thinking in St Mark's Cathedral during midnight Mass? As Jomier grows older he feels increasingly frustrated by the limits of tourism – looking at churches, castles, palaces, paintings, statues, the constructs of the dead; and only interacting with living humanity when presenting his credit card or taking euros out of his wallet.

There is *Death in Venice* but Jomier has read it and anyway the novella is about Germans and Poles, not Venetians; he thinks he is more likely to get under the skin of Italians living on the Gulf of Venice by reading Svevo rather than Thomas Mann. Jomier had also been attracted to *Senilità* by its title but is disconcerted to discover that the hero Emilio is only forty. Is forty the old sixty just as sixty is the new forty? Jomier reads on to find out but is only on page 32 when Judith finishes *The Blind Assassin* and suggests walking out into the city. Jomier is now used to the speed with which Judith reads novels. He is both impressed and dismayed by the way she finishes one and starts another without pause for breath. Jomier sees this as a kind of promiscuity: surely a reader who has been moved or stimulated by a work of literature should reflect for a while on what she has just read? However, he agrees about a walk. It is foolish to be in Venice and spend the few hours of daylight reading novels in a hotel. They dress. They step out. There is a pale wintry sun. They stroll towards the Rialto Bridge.

'How was the novel?' Jomier asks Judith.

'Not one of her best.' Judith takes his arm. She likes taking his arm and squeezing it. Jomier likes his arm to be taken and squeezed. Mostly. Sometimes he feels the gesture is proprietorial rather than loving. More a clipping of a leash on to a collar than a caress.

'It's about relationships within a family . . .' Judith is talking about the novel by Margaret Atwood.

'Often problematic,' says Jomier.

'You've told me very little about *your* family,' says Judith.

'There's not much to say,' says Jomier.

'I don't believe that,' says Judith. 'There's always something to say.'

'Well,' says Jomier, 'I had a father who was a civil servant who never made the grade he felt he deserved so became embittered and deliberately dull.'

'What does that mean – deliberately dull?'

'He read a great deal and loved music but talked only about the trivia of domestic life.'

'Was he happy with your mother?'

Jomier shrugs. 'Hard to tell. They never quarrelled. It might have been better if they did. I sometimes think he felt . . .' Jomier hesitates.

Judith prompts him: 'Felt what?'

'That he had let her down . . . by not making the grade.'

'She would like to have been Lady Jomier?'

'Yes.'

'Was she nice to *you*?'

'In her fashion.'

'What was her fashion?'

'I was her project. She wanted me to succeed where my father had failed.'

'Was she affectionate?'

Again, Jomier hesitates. He feels uncomfortable talking about his parents. 'Not as such. She thought any overt expression of feeling was vulgar.'

'You didn't feel loved?'

'She regarded love as something given. You did not need to show it.'

'No hugs?'

'No. A wintry smile if she was pleased. A pained look if she was displeased.'

'How sad,' says Judith.

'She had been brought up in an old-fashioned upper-class household. Nannies. Governesses. She saw her parents only for half an hour before bedtime.'

'No loving role model,' says Judith.

'No one is taught parenting,' says Jomier. 'You can take courses in almost anything, and almost everything is subject to regulation and control, except the one thing that has a greater bearing on human happiness than anything else – how to bring up a child. As a result, we make mistakes which are handed down from generation to generation.'

'But your children sound fine,' says Judith.

Jomier reflects; then: 'Tilly was good with the children.'

They have reached the Rialto Bridge. Jomier is about to tell Judith how, thirty years before, he and Tilly had come to the Rialto Bridge from the same direction and after crossing it had got lost in the narrow streets looking for the Museum of Modern Art. He changes his mind. This recollection of a happy moment with another woman might not be something that Judith would want to hear. Jomier stops the words from leaving his mouth but the memory remains in his head. An impromptu winter holiday. He had finished a long trial and felt rich. They had left the children with Tilly's parents, flown to Turin, hired a car and driven across the Po valley, staying in Parma, Ferrara and Padua before arriving in Venice. There were no tourists. They were almost alone in the restaurants and hotels. Tilly had been so fresh and pretty and happy. There was no Max, only Jomier: love brimmed over from her eyes when she smiled.

The memory now makes Jomier feel sad. He fights this sadness: he struggles to prevent his mood spiralling down into a pit. The past is past. The Tilly who loved him is dead. The Jomier who loved Tilly is dead. He is in love with someone else – an attractive woman, albeit a yoga teacher and no spring chicken, but healthy, cultured, companionable and accomplished in bed. Judith does not notice the struggle going on in his mind: she has let go of his arm and is examining a bead necklace displayed on a stall on the Rialto Bridge. She asks its price, then shakes her head. She wants the necklace but feels she is being taken for a sucker. She haggles. She is an experienced haggler from the souks of Morocco, the casbahs of Damascus, the markets of Kerala and Rangoon. Tilly had never haggled. She was too much the grande dame. Jomier does not haggle either. He puts himself in the shoes of the Venetian. Tourists are there to be fleeced.

Judith strikes a deal. She buys the necklace. 'Don't you think it's pretty?' Bright blue glass beads linked together by a delicate silver chain.

'Is it for Ophelia?'

'No, it's for me.' Jomier has said the wrong thing. Judith's tone turns sharp. 'I spent a fortune on her Christmas present.'

'What did you give her?'

'A pair of Camper boots.'

Jomier is prepared to believe that Camper boots are expensive and so says: 'That's very generous.'

'What did you give your children?'

'CDs. I gave Henry *Parsifal* and Louisa *Don Carlos*.' Jomier wishes he had not raised the question of Christmas presents. He is wearing his fleece-lined gloves but notes that Judith is not wearing the racing-green cashmere jersey. It remains, carefully folded and half rewrapped, in their hotel bedroom.

A clock strikes midday. It is time to return to the hotel for the inclusive Christmas lunch. They have wandered further than they realised and are the last to enter the hotel restaurant. They are shown to their table – far from the window looking out on to the canal, close to the swinging doors into the kitchen. Tinsel and glitter decorate the table; crackers lie parallel to the knives and forks. There are other couples of a certain age sitting at tables for two but there are also tables for six or eight – families with grannies and in-laws and children and friends. Next to Jomier and Judith sits a party who are talking German: they are either Germans or Austrians or Swiss. Bottles of wine uncorked on the table are already half empty: they have got off to a flying start. A thickset freckled fifty-year-old with cropped orange hair sits facing Jomier. '*Prost.*' He raises his glass. Jomier nods and smiles. His wine glass has not yet been filled: he raises it all the same. '*Prost.*' A woman and a man with their backs to Judith and Jomier now turn and raise their glasses. '*Prost.*' Again, Jomier and now also Judith raise their yet-to-be-filled glasses. The man who has turned – heavy, genial, bald – notices that their glasses are empty. '*Ja, das geht nicht.*' He grabs hold of a half-full bottle of sparkling wine and stretches over to fill their glasses. He cannot reach their table. He stands. 'No, no . . .' Jomier tries to fend off this impulsive generosity. Impossible. Fizzy wine splashes into their glasses. Now the whole table of friendly Teutons turns towards them. '*Fröhliche Weihnachten! Prosit Weihnachten!*' Jomier and Judith raise their half-filled glasses. 'Thank you. Happy Christmas!' They drink.

'Did you know Brian?'

Jomier searches his memory in an effort to remember who Brian might be.

'Ruth's husband, Brian. Did you know him?'

'Yes. Not well. He seemed nice enough. I don't know what went wrong.'

'He was under-sexed. They hardly ever made love.'

Jomier thinks of Ruth's large behind. 'Perhaps he didn't fancy her?'

'Then why did he marry her?'

Jomier thinks of his social-climbing friend Adrian Richards. 'Was she smart? Or rich?'

'Both. But she's got through most of her money. And Ralph doesn't bring in much.'

'Ralph?'

'You know. Her present man. The one who worked for the BBC.'

Jomier does not want to talk about Ruth's love life. He is also uncomfortable discussing what constitutes being over- or under-sexed. What are a wife's reasonable expectations? What are a husband's? What are the reasonable expectations of an older woman with an older lover? Does she have memories of non-stop sex on her last visit to Venice? With Beresford? With Alfredo? Jomier assumes that Judith had been there with Beresford. Judith must realise that he had been there with Tilly. That is only to be expected. It is Alfredo, the Chilean painter, who is beginning to irk Jomier. Was it from him that Judith learned about Titian and Tiepolo?

Judith is telling Jomier how Ralph had come with Ruth on one of her yoga retreats in Andalusia. It had been like having a disruptive pupil in class. He had said that he preferred the exercise regime of the Royal Canadian Mountain Police; and as to the spiritual aspects of yoga, both the Yama and the Niyama were found in all religions, and there was not much to choose between a yogi and a Christian monk. He had skipped the morning sessions to go into Seville to buy the *New York Herald Tribune*.

Judith's account of Ralph's resistance to yogic detachment is amusingly told. She makes it quite clear to Jomier that she takes the mystical dimension of yoga with a pinch of salt. Yet proselytism is not wholly absent. 'You should try it one day,' she says to Jomier.

'To improve my posture?'

'To achieve detachment.'

'Some might say that I was already quite detached enough.'

'It's a different sort of detachment.'

'In what way?'

Judith hesitates. 'Avoiding issues isn't the same as being detached.'

'Don't we all avoid issues?'

'They fester.'

'We've both avoided talking about our previous visits to Venice.'

'I don't mind talking about them.'

'Were you here with Alfredo?'

'Alfredo? Good heavens, no. I came here with Beresford, twice, and once with Giles.'

'Who is Giles?'

'Someone I went out with.' Judith is speaking gently, like a nurse with a patient.

'Before or after Alfredo?'

'After. Two or three years ago.'

'And what happened to Giles?'

'We weren't really suited. It didn't last long.' She leans across and touches Jomier's hand. 'At our age one can't really mind, can one? After all, you must have been here with Tilly.'

At long last two waiters appear at their table, one with the antipasti – first of the seven courses – the other to fill their glasses with the half-bottle of Asti Spumate that is included in the price. Jomier is grateful for the distraction. He has thrown down the gauntlet – 'we are avoiding talking about our previous visits to Venice' – and now Judith has picked it up; but is he ready for a duel of competitive reminiscences? He does not want to tell her about the holiday with Tilly. He is not detached. He feels wretched. He grieves for his lovely young bride. He mourns over the death of his marriage. He longs for his children and grandchildren. What is he doing celebrating Christmas with vulgar Germans or Austrians or Swiss and the discarded fuck-bag of Beresford and Alfredo and Giles and God knows who else? He should be in Hammersmith watching Sam and Ned unwrap their presents; or at the estancia with Louisa and little Nunci and Ysabel listening to Fernando's talk about rugby and feeling Jimmy's clap on his back.

Jomier enjoys life in retrospect more than he does at the time. In this, he is the opposite of a Guarani Indian, who lives in the present. Jomier knows this. One day he will savour happy memories of this Christmas lunch at the Hotel Palazzo Solaia with a woman who loves him. She sits opposite him talking gaily about this and that, certainly aware of the psychic turbulence in the head of the man she is with but quite confident, as a frequent flyer, that resistance to the stress and strain of such turbulence is factored into the design and tolerances of the aluminium struts and rivets of the wings of their affair.

She is also confident that if she were to be permitted to take over the controls of the Jomier 737 she could fly it above the turbulence to a calmer karma at 38,000 feet. She can show Jomier how to detach himself from his feelings of anger, frustration, regret. None of this is put into words but her very serenity is a sales pitch for one of her retreats in Andalusia. This in itself is an annoyance. More than an annoyance, Jomier feels that it is a threat to his identity. What is he if not a nexus of anger, frustration, regret? What would he write in his journal if he had no anxieties, no complaints? Jomier feels wary of this soothing femininity matched to the contemplative mysticism of the East. He sees Judith as a huge, soft, smiling yin waiting to envelop and absorb a puny, muddled yang.

The antipasti is good – Parma ham, Milano salami, mozzarella cheese, artichoke hearts, stuffed eggs, small slabs of foie gras. The pasta is superb – soft, plump raviolis stuffed with lobster with a lobster bisque sauce. The half-bottle of Asti Spumante – too sweet but tolerable because cold – had been replaced by a 75-centilitre bottle of 2005 Canaletto Montepulciano d'Abruzzo which Jomier finds as good as any Italian wine he had ever tasted – indeed, better than most wines from anywhere else. Judith agrees. The food and the wine improve Jomier's mood. He regains his confidence that the inclusive Christmas offer by the Hotel Palazzo Solaia is good value after all. He even manages to talk about Tilly and their trip to Venice without feeling tearful; indeed, it dovetails into a discussion about love and marriage and maturity or the lack of it or what one means by maturity. How can a man and a woman at the age at which Judith and Beresford and Jomier and Tilly first married expect to remain compatible with an immature choice? Was it not inevitable that the choice would be made for the wrong reasons – to satisfy the unconsciously absorbed ambitions of parents perhaps, or to escape from an unhappy home? Is it not likely that those couples who *do* remain married for forty or fifty years, do so at the cost of an arrested or perhaps distorted development? It was one thing for the Victorians and Edwardians, where wives were not expected to develop in any meaningful way, but even these marriages, as we now know, were not what they seemed, with men like Dickens having second families and women, at least among the Edwardian upper classes, having children by their lovers.

The turkey, which the chef at the Palazzo Solaia must have felt he should prepare for the English and American guests at the hotel, is less bland and more delicious than the traditional English Christmas turkey – with fresh herbs in the stuffing, a spice-impregnated bread sauce, brittle fried potatoes, fresh spinach and a sauce too noble to be designated gravy. The *dolci*, too, are up to the same standard: Jomier eats both a rum baba and, in place of Judith who declines a dessert, a slice of semifreddo ice-cream cake. *Espressi*. More San Pellegrino for Judith. A glass of Marsala for Jomier. Then they are drawn into a chain of cracker-pulling by the Germans, who are, it turns out, Bavarians, not Austrians or Swiss.

## 20

JOMIER LIES ON the king-sized bed in the Palazzo Solaia watching Judith's legs rise in front of her torso and meet behind her neck as she practises her yoga on the carpeted floor. She is wearing a leotard. The black fabric clings to her body. Jomier finds Judith attractive in her leotard; he feels a faint tingling in his groin; but the Viagra is all used up.

This is their last day in Venice. They have been there a week. Both are looking forward to getting back to normal but both feel that the holiday has been a success. After the psychic turbulence Jomier had encountered while waiting for the antipasti and Asti Spumante at the Christmas lunch, all has been plain sailing. Plain flying. Beyond the turbulence, not above it. They had seen things of great beauty during the day and, during the long evenings, they have been to a concert at the Palazzo Barbarigo-Minotto, Verdi's *Nabucco* in the Teatro Malibran, the temporary home of the Fenice Opera Company and, on the Tuesday, seen an English-language movie in the Giorgione Movie d'Essai. In the early evening, before going out, they have rested in their hotel: Judith has done her yoga while Jomier has read his novel or watched BBC World News or entered the day's expenses on his Palm Treo. They have taken baths and showers and made love and tried different restaurants: both agree that Italian food is the best in the world.

There have been no awkward silences at table: they now find that they can talk about their childhoods, their marriages, their families with ease. The only time they have spent apart was when shopping; Judith said she preferred to shop alone. Jomier went out hunting for a pair of Italian shoes but all he saw were too spivy and expensive. He bought a wallet for Henry, necklaces for Sandra and Sam, and a model Maserati for Ned. Judith has been more successful: she has bought shoes, a skirt and three tops. 'Italians are so stylish,' she said.

Judith finishes her yoga. Jomier looks up from his book. Judith comes to lie beside him on the bed. She is not out of breath and the odour of her perspiration has been made fragrant by whatever deodorant she found to replace the confiscated Klorane. 'Our last day,' she says.

For a few moments they discuss what they might do with this last day; then Jomier says, without premeditation: 'You don't think we should move in together when we get home?'

Judith looks down at her bosom, flattened by the tight leotard, and picks off a piece of white fluff that has come off one of the fluffy white towels. 'You wouldn't want to live in Wandsworth.' Then, as if realising that her considered reaction to his dramatic proposal showed that she had been considering the idea herself, she turns and smiles at him and says: 'Could you bear it?'

'We've managed well enough in a single room for a week,' says Jomier.

'I mean Wandsworth.'

Jomier thinks of the dribbling shower. 'Does it have to be Wandsworth? Couldn't we both sell our houses and buy one together?'

Judith pulls herself up: her thinking has not yet gone this far. 'Pool our resources?'

'Why not? We should be able to buy something in Notting Hill.'

'Or Chelsea?'

'Or Chelsea.'

'I'm *longing* to move,' says Judith; then, as if this confession might be construed as an ulterior motive that detracts from the romance of Jomier's suggestion, she adds: 'to start afresh.'

'With me?'

'Of course with you.' She snuggles up, her head on his chest. Jomier likes this. Or he thinks he likes it. Tilly had never snuggled up like this. Not with him. Perhaps with Max. Jomier strokes Judith's hair. It is thinning but she is far from bald.

'Could you put up with Ophelia?' asks Judith.

'I'm getting quite used to Ophelia,' says Jomier.

'And what about Henry and Sandra?'

'What about them?'

'Won't they disapprove?'

'I don't think so. Why should they?' He asks the question and at once comes up with one or two answers. Will this cohabitation lead to marriage? Will Jomier's equity in the new house pass on his death to Judith? Will that transfer be for her lifetime or outright? Will Henry and Louisa see their inheritance spent on rehab for Judith's children?

Judith shrugs. 'I don't know. They might not like it.'

'I should think they'll both be relieved,' says Jomier, 'to think there'll be someone else to push me around Holland Park in a wheelchair.'

'Or the Chelsea Physic Garden,' says Judith.

'Or the Chelsea Physic Garden,' repeats Jomier.

'Not quite yet, I hope,' says Judith.

Jomier squeezes her lycra-clad knee. 'Not quite yet.'

Jomier returns from Venice a happy man. Even the ghast-liness of the return journey on Ryanair – vaporetto to the Piazzale Roma, bus to Treviso Airport, more sheep dip, more sardines – does not pollute the happy feeling that he loves and is loved. As if to prove that their plans are well founded, providence finds them two adjacent seats on the plane. Judith is reading an Ian Rankin thriller that she bought at Treviso Airport: Jomier estimates that she has read six novels since they left London while he is only on page 137 of *Senilità*. This no longer irritates him. Why should it irritate him? How much better a woman buried in a novel than a woman holding forth. He thinks Judith is perfect or as perfect as he can reasonably expect. Certainly, she is second-hand but then the brand-new Tilly proved unreliable. So too his Golf. That was also new and proved problematic. Jomier sees himself as a man in a car lot suddenly finding a model he has always longed for. A gull-wing Mercedes. One of those big-bonneted old Volvos or a curvy two-stroke Saab.

They part at Liverpool Street Station. A kiss. A hug. Judith goes to wait in line for a taxi – the black money-eating scarabs edging forward to devour their prey. Jomier trundles his suitcase down the escalator to the westbound Central Line platform in the bowels of the earth. The train is crowded. Passengers knock their shins on Jomier's suit-case. An automated voice warns Jomier that Shepherd's Bush Station is closed. He alights at Holland Park and waits in the drizzle for the 94 bus. One comes and goes: it is full. Jomier cracks. He hails a taxi which takes him on the last leg of his journey home.

\* \* \*

Jomier is happy to be home. Jomier is always happy to be home. Tilly was never happy to be home. To her a holiday was a break from drudgery and routine: after returning from Tuscany or Provence or Crete, she sulked for a week. It exacerbated her disgruntlement to see Jomier's spirits rise as he sat down at his desk in his study, to open the mail that had arrived *in absentia*, calculate the cost of the holiday and write up his journal.

Since his divorce Jomier has adjusted his back-to-normal routine. He no longer rushes to open his post or look at his email because he knows it will mostly be computer-generated junk mail and spam. The spreadsheet, too, can wait until the morning – a pleasure held in reserve. Jomier goes to his bedroom to unpack his suitcase. He puts dirty clothes in a pile on the floor; a clean shirt back into his shirt drawer, jerseys into his jersey drawer; clean socks into his sock drawer; suits and trousers onto hangers in his wardrobe. Every item has its allotted place. Jomier takes the pile of dirty clothes to the bathroom and puts them in the laundry basket from which his Brazilian cleaner Maria will remove them when she comes in after the New Year. He takes a thermostatically controlled power shower. Then, cleansed from head to foot, he changes into fresh but familiar old clothes, cooks himself a simple supper, reads *The Economist* while he eats it at his kitchen table, then moves through to his living room and settles down in front of his Panasonic Viera flat-screen TV.

At ten the next morning, Jomier calls Judith. As a rule, Jomier only makes calls when he has something to say but he knows that lovers are expected to ring to whisper sweet nothings into one another's ears. He says, 'I miss you' and 'It felt odd going to bed alone', both of which were sincere expressions of his feelings. Jomier does miss Judith in the sense that, after a week in her company, he is conscious of being alone. It has also felt odd lying in a bed by himself after a week of sleeping alongside Judith. But were the awareness of his solitude or the oddity of going to bed alone altogether unpleasant? There is a certain ease in being alone, and while Judith's warmth had been agreeable, so too in another way is it agreeable to lie in a bed by oneself. At times when she had faced him on the mattress of the king-sized bed in the Hotel Palazzo Solaia, and he had breathed in the air she had just exhaled, he had felt stifled: moreover, there was borne on that air a faint aroma of stale wine and rotting food. Jomier had turned his face away. He was then out of range of Judith's exhalations but not out of earshot of the guttural rattle that emanated from her half-open mouth as she fell into an inebriated slumber.

Jomier also snores and no doubt a malodorous miasma is borne by the air from his lungs as he exhales. There had been some mention of snoring, even a purchase of earplugs, but clearly no suggestion that the downside was in the same league as the upside of sharing a bed – the warmth, the hugs, the sex and post-coital oblivion. No suggestion *then*. And now? Judith says she misses Jomier. She agrees that it seemed odd going to bed alone. But she does not propose getting together that day. Neither does Jomier. They both need space. They both need time alone. *Reculer pour mieux sauter*. Judith is leaving the next day to spend the New Year with Tim in Devon and Jomier has much to catch up with on the hard disk of his Sky+ Box.

Jomier spends the morning working on the spreadsheet 'Venice'. It is a Saturday and, since Jomier has always spent Saturday mornings doing his accounts, he can easily discount the inner voice that accuses him of undue haste in calculating Judith's share of the cost. So too the suggestion that he should forget about her offer to pay for herself. Jomier knows that he has more money than Judith and could afford to pay for the whole thing; he senses that this would be the chivalrous and romantic thing to do. But Judith has said that she wants to pay her share. She is a woman of today. She would surely feel insulted if Jomier were to ignore her offer.

The inner voice persists. Perhaps Judith, on this matter, is not as principled as he supposes. He ignores it. He downloads the spreadsheet from his Palm Treo onto his computer. Most of the calculations are simple: he divides them by two. The costs of the hotels are more complicated. The bill from the Hotel Palazzo Solaia incorporates the €670 per person for the Christmas package which included two nights in a deluxe room, complimentary buffet breakfast, a bottle of prosecco, home-made sweets and biscuits on arrival, a Christmas surprise (what was it? Jomier cannot remember), and the Christmas lunch in the hotel restaurant with the excellent wine. There are also the four extra nights @ €250 (discounted from €285) making the basic cost of the stay at the Hotel Palazzo Solaia €2,340. In fact it had been €3203.18 because of breakfast (not included on the extra nights), some room service, laundry, drinks from the minibar and at the bar, the *Herald Tribune*, calls by Judith to her children on Christmas Day.

Jomier has promised to pay for the upgrade but what element of the Palazzo Solaia bill constitutes the upgrade? And what expenses would they have incurred if they had they remained at the Albergo Manzoni? If they had stayed at the Albergo for six more nights, Judith's share of the cost would have been a mere €240 (6 × €80 = €480 divided by two). This makes the four extra nights at the Palazzo Solaia easy to calculate: Jomier pays €760, Judith €240. But what element of the two-night inclusive Christmas package constituted the cost of the room, and what the inclusive breakfasts, Christmas lunch, home-made sweets, Prosecco and so on? Jomier proceeds on the basis that the cost of the room is the same as the 'special rate' they paid for the rest of their stay: thus he pays €420 and Judith €80 for the room. This leaves the balance of the special offer (€840) to be divided by two. In retrospect, €420 per person seems a great deal of money to have paid for the welcome pack of prosecco, home-made sweets, etc., buffet breakfasts and a seven-course Christmas dinner; but the wine was excellent and the food superb. Nothing is for nothing. They had a wonderful week in a comfortable hotel in the centre of the most beautiful city in the world.

But this reassurance that the money was well spent does not solve the vexing question of apportionment of expenses on the spreadsheet. Judith could argue, says Jomier's patient but all the same tiresome inner voice, that if they had remained at the Albergo Manzoni and eaten a simpler Christmas dinner in a local restaurant, it would have been cheaper than the seven-course lunch at the Palazzo Solaia. And they could have found breakfast for less than €40.

The provisional figures for the stay at the Hotel Palazzo Solaia now stand at €2,111.59 for Jomier and €1,091.59 for Judith. Working on the premise that Christmas dinner in a good restaurant would have cost €120 a head at the very least, Jomier knocks €300 off the €420, Judith's share of the bundled Christmas dinner, welcome pack, etc., but divides the €863.18 for miscellaneous extras by two. This he considers generous because, apart from the *Herald Tribune* and a couple of Camparis at the bar of the hotel, the extra costs had been incurred by Judith – a massage, telephone calls to her children (he had called Henry and Louisa on his mobile: she had not arranged 'global roaming' for hers), laundry (surely she could have taken her dirty knickers back to London) and bottle after bottle of San Pellegrino from the minibar. The final tally for the Albergo Manzoni and Hotel Palazzo Solaia is €2,451.59 for Jomier and a paltry €831.59 for Judith.

Jomier now turns to the other expenses of the trip which he has downloaded from his Palm Treo. The list is long, starting with the Ryanair tickets to Treviso, the taxi to Stansted, the baggage charge, the bus from Treviso, the Albergo Manzoni, supper that first night, coffee at Florian's, lunch at Harry's bar, tickets to museums, *scuole*, the opera; rides on vaporettos; one gondola; more coffees, more lunches, more suppers. All these Jomier divides by two. Finally, with one last click, he comes up with a grand total for the whole trip – €4,243.18 Of this, Jomier's share is €2,931.59 and Judith's €1,311.59 or, with the euro at 1.34 to the pound, £978.80 sterling. Surely that will be within her budget. She can hardly have expected to pay less.

# 21

IT IS THE second Friday of the new year. Jomier is sitting with Judith in the Taj Mahal Indian restaurant in Wandsworth. This is the first time the two have seen one another since they parted at Liverpool Street Station. They meet and kiss and cling to one another in a prolonged embrace. Only the intoxicating smell of curry and a sense of decorum leads them to put the demands of their stomachs before that of their loins. A predictable but perfect evening lies ahead. Poppadoms. Chicken jalfrezi. Bhindi bhaji. Fried rice. Naans. Raita. One pint and one half-pint of Tiger beer. A new pack of Viagra in Jomier's pocket. Judith's house and bed nearby.

They catch up. Judith laughingly describes the hippy discomfort of Tim's farmhouse in Devon, and the grungy neighbours who gave a party to celebrate the New Year. 'They smoked joints and drank cider. I promise you! Home-made cider to toast the New Year!' Jomier describes the equally ghastly party given by his friends the Hamilton-Russells. 'Everyone still hung-over from Christmas. And all that forced bonhomie.'

Their stomachs satisfied but not bloated, Jomier and Judith return to her house. They kiss in the kitchen and then, while Judith goes up to her bedroom, Jomier fills a glass with water to wash down the capsule of Viagra. He goes upstairs. They make love. They lie back contented.

'Are we going to start house-hunting?' asks Jomier.

She raises her head and looks into his eyes 'Do you *really* want to?'

'Of course. Why not?'

'Why not . . .' She repeats his words as if there are a number of reasons why not. Has she been here before? With Alfredo? With Giles? Jomier grows drowsy. Judith switches off the light. They fall asleep.

Breakfast. Jomier's breakfast during the week consists of muesli, toast, orange juice, and tea with a coffee chaser. Judith is puzzled why he needs to take caffeine in two different forms. She makes it clear that she would rather he took no caffeine at all. She thinks a lemon and ginger infusion would be enough. But she does not insist and on Thursday morning, after their midweek dates, Jomier has been able to eat his habitual breakfast in Judith's kitchen. Weekends have proved to be trickier because Jomier, on Saturday and Sunday mornings, likes a traditional English breakfast of grilled bacon, tomato and fried, poached or scrambled egg. This has posed a problem for Judith. The smell of burning pig-flesh first thing in the morning makes her feel nauseous. Until now she has put up with it: grubs on hooks are also unsavoury but they are effective as bait when catching fish. But once the fish is caught? Jettison the bait. Jomier comes down on this second Saturday of the new year to a breakfast of muesli, toast, tea, coffee, a poached egg, grilled tomato and two slices of Waitrose's best honey-roast ham.

Jomier is disappointed. There is something about a crisp rasher of smoked bacon which nothing can replace. Is it because it is forbidden to Muslims and Jews? A perk for Christians like keeping one's foreskin? Or is it just the fatty, salty taste? Jomier puts a brave face on it. Love demands compromises, particularly at their age. What do things like bacon or a dribbly shower or guttural snuffling or mildly *mauvaise haleine* matter when one is in love? Moreover, Jomier does not want to raise peripheral issues like bacon when there are more important matters to be dealt with: settling up after the holiday in Venice and finding a house in Notting Hill.

Jomier goes up to Judith's bathroom, shaves, takes a dribbly shower and gets dressed. He comes down wearing Hackett cords, a Boden check shirt and a heather-coloured jumper from Browns – clothes he bought before Christmas under Judith's direction. Judith has dressed before him: jeans, shirt and Jomier's Christmas-gift jumper which has miraculously changed colour from racing green to powder blue. It is a crisp, cold day. The sun is shining. Judith has cleared up the kitchen. The dishwasher gurgles. She smiles at Jomier. They are ready to set out.

'Before we go,' says Jomier, 'shall we just deal with this?' He has in his hand the folded sheet of white A4 paper upon which is printed the Excel spreadsheet 'Venice'.

'What is it?' asks Judith.

'The costs of our trip.'

Jomier places his actuarial masterpiece on the table.

'It's been quite complicated to work out because of the upgrade to the Hotel Palazzo Solaia which of course I will pay as I said I would, and the cost of the extras. If you look here –' Jomier points to a column – 'you'll see that I have paid the extra cost of the upgrade less your share of the notional costs we would have incurred had we remained at the Albergo Manzoni.'

Judith does not look. She opens her handbag and takes out her chequebook. 'How much do you want?' Her voice is tight. Abrupt.

'Your share is . . .' Jomier begins, running his finger along the figures at the bottom of the spreadsheet; then, with a delayed awareness of Judith's changed tone of voice, asks: 'Are you sure you *want* to pay your share?'

'Of course. Just tell me how much.'

'Well, with an exchange of pounds to euros of around 1.34 . . .'

Judith sits down at the table and opens the chequebook. 'How much?'

'£978.80.'

Judith fumbles in the bottom of her bag for a pen. She finds one, uncaps it and holds it poised over the chequebook. 'Say that again,' she snaps.

'Call it nine hundred pounds.'

She ignores his munificent offer.

'Nine hundred and what?'

'Really, that's fine.'

'Seventy-nine pounds?'

'Seventy-eight.'

'Sixty pence?'

'Eighty pence.'

She fills in the cheque, tears it out, hands it to Jomier.

'You are sure?' says Jomier.

'Of course I'm sure.'

'You don't want to look at the spreadsheet?'

Her jaw clenches. 'Shall we go?'

They drive north over the River Thames, through the flat-lands of Fulham and up the Aussie corridor of Earls Court into Kensington; then north from Kensington to Notting

Hill. They are silent. Jomier senses that the settling up has put Judith into a bad mood. He cannot understand why. His own feelings have been hurt by her refusal to look at his spreadsheet. The ingenuity of the calculations and the generous presumption in her favour in the allocations will now never be appreciated: neither by Judith nor anyone else.

They find a meter on Ladbroke Square, park the Golf and walk to an estate agent on Kensington Park Road. They look through the window at the display of houses posted for sale – photographs of elegant terrace houses with 'details' beneath. The prices are stupendous. They are expressed in millions with a simple decimal point. £2.3 million. £3.75 million. Each decimal point is one hundred thousand pounds. No need to spell it out as 'three million, seven hundred and fifty thousand pounds sterling' or even show the zeros: £3,750,000.

'Ridiculous,' says Judith.

'Absurd,' says Jomier.

Both realise that, even if they were able to sell their present houses for £1 million apiece, they would then only be able to afford the meanest of dwellings in Notting Hill. Jomier thinks of his former home on Blenheim Crescent. £3 million? £4 million? And the house Tilly shares with Max on Phillimore Gardens? £8 million? £10 million?

Perhaps they should look in North Kensington? Jomier makes the suggestion. Judith accepts it. Jomier further suggests leaving the car where it is and taking a 52 bus from outside the Pentecostal church opposite the estate agent: but Judith has seen from the corner of her eye the human stream that has erupted like volcanic lava from the Notting Hill Gate Tube station and is pouring down Pembridge Road. 'Let's go by the Portobello Road,' she suggests. Jomier agrees – relieved that a note of gaiety has come back into her voice.

The lava moves slowly. It is composed largely of Continental Europeans – French, Germans, Italians – shopping for bric-a-brac in the Portobello Market, Britain's *marché aux puces*. Judith too, it seems, is on the lookout for a bric-a-brac bargain. She pushes through a loden-green wall formed by the backs of German tourists to look at . . . God knows what. Jomier remains behind the wall, waiting patiently while Judith looks, fingers, questions, considers, rejects. They move on. Progress is slow. Somewhere, on one of the many stalls, is something that Judith covets – or would covet if she knew it was there. A silver sugar bowl, perhaps, or an amethyst brooch. Jomier masters his exasperation. Are they looking for houses or trinkets? He recalls the ornamented surfaces in the drawing room of Judith's house in Wandsworth and compares them in his mind's eye with the clear clean shelves of his house in Hammersmith. Cosy clutter versus anal minimalism. In their shared dwelling in North Kensington, which will prevail?

Judith buys a bowl. It has an oriental look. She shows it to Jomier.

'What is it for?'

'Don't you like it?'

'Yes, it's lovely.'

'I might give it to Tim.'

'Wouldn't that be coals to Newcastle?'

'You're right. I'll keep it.'

'And use it for what?'

'Dried rose petals.'

'They gather dust.'

She takes his arm and squeezes it. 'You're *so* philistine.'

They leave the Portobello Road and join Ladbroke Grove just before it passes under the Westway – the motorway on stilts that carries BMWs from Beaconsfield into central London. In the dark area beneath the viaduct, tramps lean against the concrete struts clutching cans of Special Brew. An aroma of urine mingles with that of diesel on the crisp morning air. They are now in North Kensington, that part of London that has been up-and-coming for the past fifty years. They walk along Oxford Gardens, Bassett Road, Chesterton Road – streets that have defied gentrification. They pause by houses flagged with estate agents' boards. 'We'd be no better off here than in Hammersmith,' says Jomier.

'Or Wandsworth,' says Judith.

## 22

SUNDAY LUNCH IN Queen's Park with Henry and Sandra. Jomier goes alone. He is without Judith. Both have agreed that it is best for each to break the news to their children of their proposed cohabitation in the absence of the other. Judith also thinks she should cook lunch for the emotionally needy Ophelia – the quality time that Ophelia feels she was denied as a child when her mother was off with Alfredo, Giles, et al. Jomier has not seen his son, daughter-in-law and their children since before Christmas: in the new year they had gone skiing in Courchevel with their friends the Crockford-Tylers. Sam and Ned run to embrace their grandfather. Sandra kisses him on both cheeks. Henry too embraces his father. He has mulled some wine. The children beg to taste it. Henry gives them a sip. Samantha stumbles around pretending to be drunk. Ned follows her, rolling and laughing, round and round the mound of plastic toys they have been given for Christmas.

Henry has cooked a chicken with roast potatoes and Brussels sprouts. He is in a benign mood – relieved, Jomier suspects, that the holiday season is over and he has returned to the calm of his office. Sandra is preoccupied: Tracey, the Australian nanny, has chosen this moment to go skiing herself. She will not be back for another week. Sandra feels that Tracey should have fixed her skiing holiday to coincide with theirs rather than falling in with the plans of her Aussie friends. But she does not want to lose Tracey and so has had to swallow her irritation and try and work out if the taking and fetching of children to school can be undertaken by Alena the au pair alone.

Henry and Sandra go through the permutations of this nanny crisis as they eat lunch. Jomier has no suggestions other than offering his own services as auxiliary au pair should they be required. Henry too affects detachment: Sandra's staff is her affair. This annoys Sandra as much as Tracey's holiday plans but she tries not to show it. Clearly there has been some pre-nup agreement that nannies and au pairs were her responsibility while cooking chickens was his.

Only after they have moved on to a dessert of stale mince pies, and the children have retreated to watch CBeebies on the television, do they talk about Wiltshire and Venice and Courchevel. Henry is reticent about Wiltshire. 'All very comfortable.' Max's sister Lydia had been there with her husband and children. Max has converted one outbuilding into a giant playroom with a billiard table and another into a mini-cinema with a Bluetooth DVD player and 56-inch plasma TV. Henry had called Louisa on Christmas Day and again on New Year's Day from Courchevel. 'She said she hadn't been well.'

'It's all those pisco sours and the *dulce de leche*,' says Jomier.

'No doubt,' says Henry. 'Or perhaps it was just flu.'

Jomier wonders why Louisa had said nothing to him about being ill when he called her from the Hotel Palazzo Solaia. Perhaps she had sickened after Christmas. Should he have called her on New Year's Day?

'And Venice?' asks Henry. 'How was it?' He puts the question cautiously – almost reluctantly – and, as he asks it, Sandra turns away. Neither wants to hear about sexagen-arian sex.

'We had to walk on duckboards to reach our hotel,' says Jomier.

'It was flooded?'

'On the first day. We upgraded.'

'To the Danieli?'

'No, to a hotel called the Palazzo Solaia: but it was good.'

'Expensive?' asks Henry.

Jomier shrugs. 'You get what you pay for.'

'Not always.'

'In this case, I'd say we did. The Christmas dinner was good.'

Jomier does not want to talk about the costs of the Hotel Palazzo Solaia because it reminds him of his spreadsheet and Judith's *froideur*. He describes the wonderful art galleries and churches and *scuole*; the Christmas markets, the tucked-away restaurants, midnight Mass in St Mark's. 'And we got on so well,' he adds, 'that we decided to move in together when we got back.'

Silence. Sandra looks at Henry. Henry says: 'That's wonderful.' He says this but does he mean it? Jomier's son sounds like a politician caught off guard. Then: 'Will you get married?'

'I wouldn't have thought so. It hasn't come to that as yet.'

'Will you move in with her,' asks Sandra, 'or will she move in with you?'

'The idea,' says Jomier, 'is to pool our resources. Sell our houses and buy a new one together.'

Again Sandra looks at her husband. What are the ramifi-cations? What's the downside for us? Henry does not meet her glance. He is trying hard to think of what will make his father happy. 'I am really pleased,' he says. 'She really seems to suit you and it can't be easy . . .' His voice tails off.

'To commit at our age?' suggests Jomier.

'Yes, I suppose that's what I meant. Once bitten, twice shy.'

'One values companionship as one grows older,' says Jomier.

'Of course,' says Henry.

'And what about her children?' asks Sandra.

'They're grown up,' says Jomier.

Sandra nods. It takes little imagination for Jomier to imagine what she has left unsaid: 'I know they're grown up but from everything you've told us about the daughter and the layabout son in Devon they might turn out to be a nightmare and a drain on your resources and ergo eat into your grandchildren's inheritance.'

The fiscal implications have also struck Henry. The effort of thinking about what would make his father happy has been too great to sustain. He returns to default. 'Would you jointly own the new house?' he asks.

'That's the idea.'

'Are your present houses of equal value?'

'More or less, I think. We haven't got to that.'

'It's just that if one of you were to die . . .'

'We haven't got to that either.'

'I mean, I'm delighted for you,' says Henry, 'but there are various factors that will have to be taken into account.'

Jomier is not upset by his son's condescension. He feels it reflects well on his upbringing that Henry has grown so well into the role of paterfamilias that he now treats his father like a King Lear: compare and contrast with the dropout Tim living off his father with his potting mistress in Devon. Jomier also sympathises with Henry's anxieties:

he too is made uneasy by the thought that the equity tied up in his house in Hammersmith should find its way via a 50 per cent stake in a house in Notting Hill to Judith and from Judith to the demented Ophelia and the ne'er-do-well Tim. 'I'm sure something can be worked out,' he says. 'There would have to be safeguards.'

'And is now the time to make the move?' The question is put by Sandra whose fingers never leave the pulse of the property market.

'The market seems strong,' says Jomier.

'Overall, yes,' says Sandra, speaking in her crisp office voice. 'But while you would certainly get a good price for your houses, there has not been the same feeding frenzy in Hammersmith and Wandsworth as there has been in Notting Hill.'

'What about Chelsea?' asks Jomier.

'Just as bad,' says Sandra. 'I really would doubt that the joint proceeds of your two houses would get you anything nice.'

Jomier suspects this may be true. 'Then we'll get a bigger house in Wandsworth or Hammersmith,' he says.

'It might come to that,' says Sandra.

Henry goes to the stove to make coffee. Jomier asks Sandra about the Crockford-Tylers with whom they went skiing. He is not interested in the Crockford-Tylers. He asks the question to direct their conversation away from the property market and his plans to share a house with Judith. It has made him feel uncomfortable. The idea of life with Judith in Wandsworth or Hammersmith is subtly different from the idea of living with Judith in Notting Hill or Chelsea.

After lunch Ned says he wants to see boats so they drive in convoy down to the river. They go for a walk in Fulham

Palace Gardens. They pass the memorial to those who died fighting for the Republicans in the Spanish Civil War. Henry says that the Republicans, had they been victorious, would have set up a Stalinist tyranny; and that it is therefore wrong that those who fought for them should be commemorated as heroes. Jomier suggests that at the time people did not know of Stalin's atrocities. Henry counters that the facts were there, but were airbrushed out of public dialogue by Communist fellow-travellers in the media and academe. Jomier thinks back to his leftist youth – demonstrating in Grosvenor Square with his friend Marco. What had they thought about the gulags, or Mao's Cultural Revolution? He cannot remember. 'Communism,' he says to Henry, 'draws on humanity's belief in its own perfectibility.'

'A chimera,' says Henry.

'No doubt,' says Jomier.

'A dangerous chimera. Like the Muslims' belief in a universal caliphate.'

'Perhaps one day,' says Jomier, 'there will be a memorial to the young Pakistanis from Bradford who went to fight for al-Qaeda in Afghanistan.'

'Unlikely,' says Henry.

'A hundred years ago,' says Jomier, 'it would have been thought unlikely that there would be a large mosque in Regent's Park.'

Sandra walks ahead following Samantha and Ned on their scooters. She does not like men's talk – politics, history, cars – but accepts that it is something she must put up with when her father-in-law comes to lunch. Jomier would like to have more to say to her than he does about children, schools, the property market. He would like to talk to her about corporate law but does not understand what it is she does in her office in Holborn. He does not understand what

Henry does either, or what anyone does in the City that brings them such rich rewards.

They look at boats on the Thames. Then they part. Henry and Sandra throw scooters and children into the back of their four-year-old E-Class Mercedes Estate. Jomier drives back to Hammersmith in his Golf. He has much to think about. Should he ring Louisa? What time is it in Buenos Aires? He does not feel up to it. His mind goes on standby as his Panasonic Viera television springs to life.

## 23

THE FOLLOWING WEEKEND, it is Jomier's turn to host the tryst with Judith. On the Friday night they go to a movie with Ruth and Ralph. The Gate Cinema. Pizza Express. Then back to his house in Hammersmith where they make love. The next morning, Jomier brings Judith breakfast in bed. This saves her from the smell of singed pig's flesh and allows him to read the Saturday edition of *The Times* in peace.

They drive south to the river and look around Chelsea. Jomier is forced to make a number of concessions in its favour. There is a lively atmosphere on the King's Road on a Saturday morning; there is no equivalent of John Sandoe's bookshop in Notting Hill, nor anything approaching that paradigm of department stores, Peter Jones. Judith argues that there are fewer smug fund managers in Chelsea than there are in Notting Hill; Jomier counters that the haute bohemians you find in the Chelsea Arts Club or living on barges on the Thames are no better. In any event, after collecting lists of properties for sale, both are obliged to accept Sandra's judgement that the sums raised by the sale of their two houses would not be enough to buy a decent-sized house in either Chelsea or Notting Hill.

'It looks as if it's going to have to be Hammersmith,' says Judith.

'Or Wandsworth,' says Jomier.

Both are being considerate as lovers should be considerate. Neither means what he or she says.

They return to Judith's house in Wandsworth where she prepares a scratch lunch from the cling-filmed leftovers in her fridge. The long afternoon. Jomier reads Judith's weekend *Guardian* and snoozes in an armchair. Judith stretches out on the sofa and reads a novel. Jomier wakes feeling muzzy and suggests a walk on Wandsworth Common. Judith says that she is all walked-out after the morning traipsing around Chelsea. Jomier goes out on his own. He does not go far. It is growing dark. He is in alien territory. Anywhere south of the river is as threatening as Amazonia. He might get lost. Or mugged. He does not go on to the common but walks along residential streets. Lights have been switched on in ground-floor rooms but the curtains left open. Jomier glimpses tableaux of life in Wandsworth. Not so different to Hammersmith, surely?

He comes across a cluster of estate agents and peers yet again at properties posted in their brightly lit windows. The houses seem much like Judith's. There do not seem to be any that are larger. It would have to be a big house to provide Jomier with a study and accommodate all his books. Or would he have to throw some away to leave space for the bric-a-brac? Jomier is suddenly weary – not physically weary from walking but mentally weary from wrestling with the idea of moving house.

He returns to have tea with Judith in her cluttered kitchen. They should return to Hammersmith because this is Jomier's weekend. Two sirloin steaks from the fancy butcher on Turnham Green Terrace are waiting in his fridge. So too aubergines, tomatoes, courgettes, garlic. Neither can face the drive through Saturday-night traffic. Judith rustles up some supper – *pasta al pesto* – wholemeal pasta, organic pesto. Afterwards Jomier looks in the *Guardian Guide* to see what is on TV. *Under Siege 2* is showing on Five. Jomier hesitates to suggest it: he knows that Steven Seagal is not to Judith's taste. Nor is Judith's TV suited to major motion pictures: it is small and self-effacing, kept hidden under a table behind one of the sofas. She has no Sky+ Box or DVD recorder. She thinks TV is bad karma. But she knows that Jomier likes watching TV and is prepared to compromise. They settle down to a documentary about global warming on Channel 4.

The following Tuesday morning. Jomier is at his desk in his house in Hammersmith entering those passages in his journal that cover the middle years of his marriage to Tilly. They are dull. Trials, his attempts to become a QC, the children's schooling, dinner parties, holidays, weekends. Are they dull because he was dull? Had he always been dull? He scrolls back to the earlier years – his adventures with Marco and Tom. He misses Marco. Marco had been caustic and funny and, with Marco, Jomier had been caustic and funny too. Had Jomier's wit been a mere echo of Marco's? Or did they laugh about life only because they were young? If Marco had not succumbed to his family's exclusive disease, Frycht's anaemia, would he have changed like Tom? Like Jomier? Become dull? A snob? Married a Habsburg? Dropped Jomier? Or would he have come out of the closet? Set up house with a gay lover in a loft in New York? Jomier will never know. Marco's life is like an old paperback that has disintegrated – the glue dried out on the spine. The central sections are lost. Only the first chapters remain and the last page. Death ends not just what is but what might have been.

Tilly had laughed as much as Marco. She had made Jomier feel that he was funny. Jomier taps the 'Page Down' key on his keyboard and reads about their first encounters. Their first dates. How fresh we are when we are young. No template. No matrix. No mould. Each willing to be shaped by the other – as malleable as dough. No, he had not been dull when he had been young. Life had dulled him just as it had dulled his father. A seed of dreariness sowed in both at their conception like original sin. The Huguenot gene. And in Tilly? The seed of deceit? Had she always thought 'this is the first: there will be others' or 'he'll do for now'? Or had she thought 'this is for ever'? Or 'this is for ever . . . for now'? Is that all love can ever be? For ever for now? If one does not choose to fall in love then can one be blamed for falling out of love? Was it culpable of Tilly to fall for Max? Was it culpable of Jomier to become dull? All agree that it is wrong to be insincere. To lie. To pretend. Does that make it wrong for a lover to put his best foot forward? To hide little weaknesses from Judith such as a penchant for watching *Under Siege 2* for a third time? Jomier did not pretend to Tilly that he was someone other than he was: he could not know that with the passing of time he would become dull. But is he now pretending to Judith that he is someone other than he is? Is Judith modifying the opinions she expresses to suggest a greater compatibility than in fact exists?

There have been gentle arguments over breakfast and in Indian restaurants, but also silences. Judith clearly feels strongly about certain things. Global warming. Palestine. Religion. The Murdoch Press. Feminism. Gay marriage.

Reproductive rights. Her morning newspaper is the *Guardian*. Jomier's is *The Times*. She questions the morality of reading a Murdoch newspaper. Jomier says it costs less than the *Guardian*. She gives a little snort as if to say this is an inadequate excuse. Would she rather he read the *Telegraph*? Another snort. 'If you really want to start the day with a picture of some minor member of the royal family in wellington boots.' Jomier does not: this is why he does not take the *Telegraph*. He takes *The Times* because it is the most innocuous of the morning newspapers.

'It's hardly liberal,' says Judith.

'No, libertarian,' says Jomier.

They discuss the difference between liberal and libertarian. It becomes clear that liberalism is the nearest thing that Judith has to a religion. Liberalism is being non-judgmental about people's sex lives but hyper-judgmental about profits and pollution and fox hunting and Tesco and Margaret Thatcher. Jomier argues that libertarianism is more relaxed than liberalism. Liberalism nags. It fosters an industry of nagging do-gooders who get jobs advertised in *Society Guardian* that are funded by the state – time servers in education and the social services more interested in their incremental wage increases and pension rights than the development of children or well-being of the poor.

It is now that Judith goes quiet. She lowers her head to hide the furrows in her brow. She does not want to get into an argument with Jomier. She does not want to risk alienating this last available man. She does not yet know Jomier well enough to realise that Jomier argues for the sake of arguing. Arguing has been his profession. If he has opinions, they are contradictory and cancel one another out. As a follow-up question to Pontius Pilate's 'What is truth?' he asks, 'What is Justice?' As an idealistic young barrister he had set out to save the innocent from wrongful conviction but the innocent had proved elusive. The clients he defended were always guilty of the crime with which they were charged – drug smuggling, benefit fraud, credit card scams. They were guilty – but could they be blamed? A tramp is prosecuted for stealing a shirt from Marks & Spencer; George Soros degrades sterling and goes free. The wonder to Jomier is not that there is so much theft but that there is so little. Why is the underclass so docile? Why do those living in the tenements of White City put up with the conspicuous consumption of the rich in Kensington or Belgravia? Why is there not a constant, endemic, freelance expropriation of the expropriators? Why do not the wretches on unemployment benefit or the minimum wage, who will never prosper in the society in which they live, set fire to the bankers' mansions, storm the private gardens of Ladbroke Square, throw bricks through the windows of Lidgate's and Maison Blanc, and torch the Range Rovers and S-Class Mercedes? Where are the Bakunins or the Proudhons crying 'All property is theft!'?

These anarchic thoughts are all that is left of Jomier's youthful ideals. Little by little he became part of the system. Like his father and grandfather before him, he has both benefited from, and worked to perpetuate, the ascendancy of the middle class. The fees he has been paid by the state for defending thieves and swindlers were spent on a private education for Henry and Louisa so that, like him, they should be better educated and more articulate than their peers from comprehensives. He owns property – a freehold in Hammersmith – shares, corporate bonds, a Dell computer, a Volkswagen Golf. He is a 'have' who, through his council tax pays policemen to protect him from the 'have-nots' and, through his income tax, funds social benefits which ensure that the 'have-nots' become 'have-a-littles' and so are not driven to a dangerous desperation.

'You are a cynic,' says Judith.

Jomier does not deny it. He remembers from his youth a *pensée* of Pascal's: 'We cannot enforce justice so we justify force.' The state is a bourgeois mafia, a protection racket, that camouflages its self-interest and extortion with high-minded rhetoric. The rich grow richer. The poor remain poor. Politicians and civil servants feather their own nests. Today's statesmen would no more forgo their large inflation-proofed tax-funded pensions than George Washington or Thomas Jefferson would have liberated their slaves.

Will Judith be able live with Jomier's cynicism? Will Jomier be able to live with Judith's faith in the perfectibility of mankind? Is either convinced by the other's stance? Jomier suspects that Judith suspects that his cynicism is a cover for Thatcherite reaction. Jomier suspects that Judith's progressive views are a matter of fashion rather than reasoned conviction. There are little inconsistencies. Even hypocrisies. Judith's carbon footprint is greater than Jomier's. She travels a great deal – to Devon, to India, to Italy, to Spain, to France. Every year, she holds her yoga retreat in Andalusia: half a dozen disciples must fly to Malaga. 'But sometimes they take the train which is powered by electricity.'

'Generated by nuclear power!'

Judith is silent for a moment: she does not quite know where she stands on nuclear power. Then: 'The warmer weather saves on the central heating!'

A further inconsistency: Judith's mixed feelings about her ex-husband, Beresford Grant. They have talked much in Venice about what might have happened if Judith had not married so young; if Jomier had sent that letter; or if Jomier had re-entered her life after she had split up with Beresford ahead of Alfredo and Giles and whoever. 'We might even have had children.' However, Jomier notices, or thinks he notices, a difference in her speculation of *what might have been* with *what she wished had been* which went with *what would have been* if she had been more worldly-wise. Despite her yogic detachment, Judith is unable to prevent a look of annoyance coming on to her face when the talk turns to her successor, Beresford's present wife Bridget. It is clear that Judith regards her as in some sense a usurper. It is somehow wrong that Bridget has the run of the houses in London, Gloucestershire and the South of France. Judith tells Jomier rather more than he wants to hear about Beresford's triumphs in the City: how he had teamed up with Izzy Raub to form Raub Asset Management in the 1980s, then sold it to Deutsche Bank at the top of the market.

Judith is clearly impressed by Beresford's success as a financier. She kicks herself for not seeing more clearly which side her bread was buttered and somehow arranging to have extra-marital sex on the side. 'I was so stupidly idealistic.' But what about Beresford's carbon footprint? The three houses? The six gas-guzzling cars. Jomier has challenged her with this inconsistency. She has frowned and pondered. Jomier feels that he has committed a solecism. Inconsistency, like menstruation, is a female attribute that one knows about but does not mention. But Jomier has got it wrong. The frowning and pondering is not an admission of inconsistency: it is expression of annoyance that she must apply her mind to showing that Jomier is wrong and she is right.

In due course Judith presents her argument. Beresford's three houses have live-in staff. His cars have drivers. If the staff did not live in Beresford's houses they would live elsewhere. If the drivers did not drive Beresford's cars they would drive cars of their own. Their dwellings might be smaller than Beresford's mansions but they would be less ecological: Beresford has put solar panels on the roof of Le Nid de l'Eveque. Nor would their old bangers be as fuel-efficient as Beresford's Range Rover or S-Class Mercedes. Thus Beresford's overall carbon footprint is much the same as anyone else's.

Jomier is convinced. Or he pretends to be convinced. He does not give a toss about Beresford's carbon footprint. He does not particularly care about global warming. *Après moi le deluge*. Does the world deserve to continue? If there was a Hebrew deity, a 'He Who Is', looking down at humanity in the twenty-first century, would he not conclude that things were just as bad as they were prior to the Flood? The rich shopping in Bond Street or the rue de Rivoli for £2,000 handbags and £20,000 watches while children in Africa sift the dirt for grains of wheat? What would he make of the massacre of the innocents *in utero*; or the scientific experiments on a week-old embryo that might be an incipient Vermeer or Tolstoy or, following the Hebrew deity's way of thinking, the yet-to-come Messiah himself? Is it not time to wrap up the human project? To turn up the temperature of the solar winds and let humanity frazzle? 'No more water. The fire next time.'

Jomier has not expressed this view to Judith. First, it would expose *him* to the charge of inconsistency: he does not believe in a Hebrew deity or any other kind of deity – neither a He nor a She nor an It who is. Second, he fears that an admission of indifference about the fate of the universe would be a deal-breaker: no more movies or Indians with Judith; no more Kama Sutra sex. How could Jomier (she would ask, and Jomier puts the question to himself) deny his children and grandchildren the right to enjoy the life that he has enjoyed? Cut short little Samantha's progress from Norland Place to St Paul's to Oxford to a profession to a marriage to a fund manager and a daughter who goes to Norland Place and St Paul's and Oxford and a profession . . . ad infinitum? Just because Jomier's life has turned sour does not give him the right to deny others a chance to be happy. And surely Jomier's life is no longer sour. It has turned sweet again. He has Judith.

The telephone rings. It is Henry. 'Dad, I'm worried about Louisa.'

Jomier listens. He accepts that Henry is worried because he so rarely rings Jomier from his bank. 'Is she no better?'

'She seems to be worse and I really don't know if the doctors out there are any good.'

Out there. Argentina. A long way away. Jomier has spoken to Louisa; she has told him of her tiresome illness. 'It's not the Third World,' says Jomier.

'They seem to be thrashing around,' says Henry. 'At first they said it was glandular fever – the Epstein–Barr virus. Now they're talking about ME.'

'Have you spoken to Jimmy?'

'Yes. He sounds alarmed. Apparently she's getting weaker by the day.'

'I'll ring her,' says Jomier.

'Persuade her to come to London,' says Henry.

Jomier eats his lunch listening to *The World at One*. Terrorist atrocities abroad. Political bickering at home. He only half concentrates on what he hears. He is thinking about Louisa. He does this reluctantly. It is painful to think of her suffering: intolerable to envisage her seriously ill. Jomier is willing to suffer himself; he is sanguine about death and would be happy to donate his kidneys, liver, heart or bone marrow to any of his children or grandchildren. He is less willing to witness the suffering of his children or grandchildren. For this reason he has not dwelt on Louisa's recalcitrant virus. He has accepted Louisa's assurances that some days are better than others, that she is sure to get better in the end.

He calls Buenos Aires. He speaks to Louisa.

Her voice is weak but its tone cheerful. 'It's such a lovely morning. I wish you were here.'

'Are you in bed?'

'Yes. But I'll get up for lunch.'

'What are your symptoms?'

'Oh, you know . . . weakness, lassitude. I think they call it chronic fatigue syndrome.'

'Are you in pain?'

'A bit achy, like having flu.'

'What do the doctors say?'

'They tested me for brucellosis but that was negative. Also for sarcoidosis – all these illnesses one never knew existed!' She laughs. 'Ow, ow, it hurts my ribs when I laugh.' She goes on laughing. 'They injected me with something radioactive and did a scan. But that came up negative. They're still talking about the Epstein–Barr virus and then there's ME.'

'We think you ought to come to London,' says Jomier.

'I know. Henry told me. Mum thinks so too. So does Jimmy. But there are the children . . .'

# 24

JOMIER SITS IN the reading room of the London Library.
He has come here, as he does every week, to escape from Maria
as she cleans his house and washes his clothes. The reading
room is like the libraries of the nearby London clubs – the
Reform, the Travellers', the Athenaeum. It has deep leather
armchairs in which members may read or doze. The subscription is expensive; Jomier could buy the books he borrows at
less cost through Amazon or AbeBooks, but that would mean
knowing in advance what books he wanted to read. In the
London Library he can wander through the labyrinthine stacks
to look at books he does not know had been written. Novels by
forgotten novelists. The memoirs of unremembered diplomats
and statesmen. The reminiscences of obscure old princes and
divas who once had their day in the sun – the celebrities of
yesterday and the day before and the day before that. It is like
walking through a cemetery with little tombstones that one
can pull out of the ground to learn about the deceased.

> He would confide as unto trusted friends
> His secrets to his notebooks; turn there still
> Not elsewhere, whether faring well or ill.
> So that the old man's whole life lay revealed
> As on a votive tablet.

Horace. From Horace in the first century BC to Jomier in the twenty-first century AD, a fraternity of diarists leave their lives to posterity in words – tablets, papyrus, scrolls, parchment, books, memory sticks. Epitaphs on gravestones are mere markers: *De Profundis* says much more about Oscar Wilde than the lip-marks of venerating gays on his tombstone in the Père Lachaise. There is more to Marx than 'Workers of All Lands Unite' chiselled on to his tombstone in Highgate Cemetery. But for every *De Profundis* or *Kapital* there are ten thousand books by forgotten authors. Transient vanity? Perhaps. '*Vanity of vanities, all is vanity*' – Ecclesiastes. '*All that me, me, me . . .*' – Updike. His judgement on contemporary fiction. And his own? Will Updike's novels one day be stacked unread by future generations like those of Nobel Prize-winners such as Bjørnson, Eucken, Carducci, Benavente, Reymont, Deledda, Heidenstam? Who now reads Sully Prudhomme, Romain Rolland or Roger Martin du Gard? Is each generation doomed to T. S. Eliot's 'provincialism of the present' – the spin-off from a belief in Progress; the assumption that we are more humane and enlightened than our forefathers; that each generation builds on the knowledge of the one that has gone before; that art like science is progressing towards an endgame of total enlightenment when mankind will have created all that is worth creating and knows all that it needs to know?

It is ten to one. Jomier leaves the London Library and walks across St James's Square in the spring sunshine towards the Athenaeum on Pall Mall where he is to lunch with his friend Theo. The Athenaeum is almost empty. So too was the London Library. It is officially a workday but most workers are not working: they have already left London for the bank holiday weekend. Theo is not displeased. He clearly enjoys having the club's waiters and flunkeys at his beck and call. As they drink dry sherry, Jomier teases his friend. Should a devout Christian be quite so happy to be served rather than serve? Theo: the best form of charity is employment. It provides not only a livelihood but also self-respect. How much better that Andro the Croatian, Bekim the Albanian, Clarita the Filipina should serve Theo and Jomier in Pall Mall than loiter unemployed on the street corners of Zagreb, Tirana or Manila. (And better, thinks Jomier, that the Brazilian Maria should now be ironing his shirts than selling her body on the streets of Rio de Janeiro.)

Jomier admires Theo for the clarity with which he assesses the good and the evil of the smallest actions in everyday life. How much more enjoyable is lunch at the Athenaeum when one knows that each mouthful is, in some small sense, a good work. Theo has not only expressed these views to Jomier but to a wider audience through talks to the Oxford Newman Society and articles in the *Telegraph*, the *Spectator* and the *Salisbury Review*. They enrage his Catholic co-religionists who, since the Second Vatican Council, have put all their eggs in the basket of social reform. Their Jesus is a Nye Bevan of antiquity; his curing of lepers a pilot for the National Health Service; his feeding of the Five Thousand a dry run for the UN's World Food Programme. They do not like to hear Theo's message that it is better to buy a flat-screen TV made in China than sign a standing order for Christian Aid.

As they eat their lunch, Jomier tells Theo that when in Venice at Christmas he and Judith went to midnight Mass at St Mark's Basilica. Theo listens but does not put any follow-up questions. He does not ask about Judith. Though he was happy to be a shoulder to cry on at the time of Jomier's divorce, he prefers not to know about Jomier's extra-marital amours. What was the position of Thomas Aquinas on sex with a post-menopausal woman? Is it the ontological equivalent of buggery or ejaculating into a condom? Jomier does not ask. He listens to Theo hold forth on Venice – a maritime empire built on trade – a proto-type for the British Empire and, like the British Empire, brought down by its involvement in wars in its hinterland – for Britain Flanders, for Venice the Valley of the Po.

Jomier is used to Theo's lack of curiosity about his private life. Or any other aspect of his life. Theo has no interest in people as such. His interests are on the one hand financial – markets, probabilities, risks – and on the other theological – eschatology, ethics, exegesis. He takes particular pleasure when the two combine. From the decline of Venice he moves on to the fissure between Latin and Orthodox Christianity that runs through the Balkans with Islamic enclaves left by the retreating Ottoman Turks – hence the different religious affiliations of Andro the Croatian (Catholic) and Bekim the Albanian (Muslim) – and ends over coffee with the hypothesis that thanks to idiotic altruism one or other would soon be out of a job.

How so? Theo explains. Well-meaning *dirigistes* in the US have encouraged banks to provide mortgages for poor people who have now defaulted on their loans. The loans had been sold on in packages to other banks and no one knows which are good and which are bad. 'Imagine,' says Theo, 'a huge balloon held up by a thousand little helium-filled party balloons.' A delinquent toddler has pricked some of the little party balloons with a pin. They start to lose their buoyancy. The big balloon begins to sink. It is difficult to sift the pin-pricked party balloons from the undamaged party balloons. Can it be done before the big balloon hits the ground? Probably not. No one now wants to put their party balloons beneath the canopy of the big balloon. Can it be kept afloat by more party balloons provided by the taxpayer? Perhaps, but even so the big balloon must shed ballast. Factories will close. Businesses fail. Hedge funds will go under. Jobs will be lost. Belts will be tightened. Inessential expenditure curtailed – holidays, restaurants and subscriptions to London clubs.

Theo sits on the committee of the Athenaeum. He fears that there will be cancelled subscriptions and a consequential need to prune the staff. Andro, Bekim and possibly Clarita may be dismissed – all because the well-meaning Democrats could not leave well alone. Will Theo be affected? No, quite to the contrary. Theo is ahead of the game. He is 'shorting' a number of banks. He advises Jomier to put any assets he might have into cash.

Jomier returns home in a gloomy mood. He turns on his computer and checks his emails. There is one from Henry. 'Louisa and Jimmy are coming to London next week. Can you meet them at Heathrow and take them to the Hampton Clinic?' Jomier replies: 'Yes.' There is another from a building society announcing that interest rates are to go down on their online accounts. That expects no reply. Take it or leave it, sucker. We lured you into depositing your money with us with the promise of a high rate of interest and now we are lowering it little by little because we know you can't be bothered to shop around for a higher rate and open yet another account. Correct. But if Theo is right, it is not the interest that he is getting on his bank deposits that should worry Jomier but the fall in value of his funds. Jomier fights through a thicket of account numbers, passwords and customer IDs to access his bank accounts, pension funds and ISAs. The funds are all down – some more, some less.

Clearly the fund managers paid by Jomier to care for his money have lacked Theo's perspicacity. Jomier is enraged. Why pay fees to these supposed masters of the universe if they do no better than anyone else? He does not trust them. He suspects that they dump the worthless stocks of their prime clients like Max onto their sub-prime clients like Jomier. All Jomier's rancour against the bankers and oligarchs that went into abeyance when he fell in love is now reignited by the idea of a shrinking pension fund and diminishing income.

Jomier must retrench. He must economise. He must cut his coat according to his shrunken cloth. But where are the cuts to be made? Jomier rarely travels or buys smart clothes or goes to the theatre or eats in restaurants other than the weekly Indian with Judith. Judith! Judith clearly is an expense or, if no great expense as such, a potential for expenditure drift. He thinks back to the cost of Christmas in Venice. True, she had paid her share, albeit a discounted share; but the ill will with which she had paid it – the brisk grumpiness with which she had written out the cheque – made it clear to Jomier that she had not expected him to take up her offer to pay her way. And Jomier had learned his lesson. He now always pays for the movies and Indians. He says 'we'll settle up later' but that later never comes.

And there is the Viagra. Jomier punches the figures on the rubbery buttons of his electronic calculator. Two capsules a week means £250 a year! Add extras for holidays and he should budget for an annual expenditure on Viagra of around £300. Judith does not offer to make a contribution to that expense; he pops the pill discreetly; it is never mentioned; the fiction is maintained that he is aroused by the scent and sight and touch of this desirable woman. But as he looks at the number 300 on his calculator, Jomier asks himself whether Judith who, to judge from the sounds of pleasure that she emits as the rhythmic undulations of her well-tuned body gather pace, and the ecstatic cries as she arrives at her perfectly calibrated climax, does not in fact get more out of sex than he does? Indeed, does Jomier get anything much from sex any more beyond dubiously pleasurable sensations and the reassurance that he is still up to it – that he is still a man?

| A year of Viagra: | £300 |
|---|---|
| A year of Indians: | £1,500 |
| A year of movies: | £700 |
| Future holidays: | £3,500 |
| Gifts: | £300 |
| Miscellaneous: | £300 |

These estimates suggest that Judith will cost Jomier £6,600 over twelve months or, with tax at 20p in the pound on his investment income, a gross sum of more than £8,250 a year! And that is just 'above the line'. More worrying for Jomier, as he thinks about the effects of the global credit crunch on his personal finances, is the possibility that this expenditure on Judith is just the start. If he and Judith were to share a house, would she share the costs? Would she pay half the Council Tax? Half the utility bills? Or would she take the same 'How unromantic. How unchivalrous. How ungallant. How bourgeois. How penny-pinching' attitude that she had shown when he had presented her with the Venice spreadsheet? Was Jomier about to fall yet again for the age-old confidence trick perpetrated by women on men? Is he, for Judith, anything more than a cashpoint, handyman and perambulating vibrator?

Tilly: you know the cost of everything and the value of nothing. Had she been right? Was he repeating the same mistake with Judith? How can you measure the cost-effectiveness of love? Has it not always been incumbent upon the male of the species to cherish his chosen partner, and has not cherishing always involved some expense? And what if he had fallen for a woman whose self-esteem depended on eating at the Ivy, the Wolseley or the Café Anglais? Jomier should be grateful that no more is expected of him than stumping up for tofu and seaweed when they shop together at Whole Foods, paying for cinema tickets, and footing the bill for their weekly Indian.

Jomier dines with his friends the Richards – Adrian, the parvenu Eurosceptic, and Mary, the granddaughter of an earl. He does not take Judith just as Judith does not take him to dinner with some of her yogic friends. As a couple they remain semi-detached. It has been tacitly accepted that each should occasionally see old friends on their own. So far the convention has worked well: Judith has assured Jomier that he would be bored by Raphael and Madge Samuelson; Jomier that Judith would detest the Richards. He has described their reactionary views and explained their continuing friendship on the grounds that he and Adrian 'go back a long way'.

Would the Samuelsons be bored by Jomier? Would the Richards detest Judith? Is this implicit in the choice of friends whom they see as a couple and those they see alone? Put another way, would the Samuelsons invite Judith to their organic evenings in Islington if she had Jomier in tow? And would the carnivorous super-polluting Richards invite Jomier to dinner if they knew that the grungy Judith would come too? Jomier cannot answer for the Samuelsons but he knows the way the minds of the Richards work. He is also aware of his value to Mary as a single man. She does much entertaining: bankers, actresses, MPs, even government ministers. Almost everyone is someone but there is an occasional spinster cousin who has to be matched with a man in which case a no one like Jomier will do.

Jomier knows where he stands. He does not mind. Dining in a large elegant house in Kensington makes him feel that he still has a toehold on the right side of Shepherd's Bush. And after weeks of eating food that is either raw or steamed or poached, he looks forward to the thick mayonnaise on the lobster and the grease dripping from the joint. He enjoys the ice-cold vintage Krug, the mellow Chateau Très Cher 1986 and the plump Cohiba cigars. He likes the glittering candlelit table furniture, the crisp linen napkins, the silver knives and forks. If the price to be paid is making conversation with the spinster cousin, so be it. He is happy to pay it for the fare, and for the sharp conversation between movers and shakers which he sometimes joins in. He likes to think that in the corridors of power in the Palace of Westminster a junior minister might say to a senior minister: 'This interesting barrister I met at the Richards' had an excellent image for the sub-prime mortgage crisis – a lot of party balloons filled with helium holding up the bigger balloon of the American economy, some of which have been pricked with a pin by a delinquent toddler . . .'

Jomier also likes entering an account of dining with the Richards in his digital journal the next morning. He does not write with posterity in mind but this record of exchanges between significant people gives some weight to what might otherwise be judged another *Diary of a Nobody*. He may not be a Chips Channon or Woodrow Wyatt, but his thumbnail sketches of the different guests could possibly be of some historical interest in the future were Jomier's journal ever to see the light of day.

On the following Saturday night, over an Indian, Jomier tells Judith about the dinner with the Richards, every now and then making a mental note of something he has failed to enter in his journal. Judith listens. Jomier can sense that there is something in his narrative that seems to annoy her. She says nothing and, when he has finished, tells him about her week – an overnight visit by Tim from Devon to ask her to arrange an exhibition for Tamara's pottery in London ('Why does he think *I* have those kind of contacts: there's Karl's gallery but he won't want to show Tamara's folksy junk; Tim should ask his father for help, not me') and then ('inevitable . . . it had to happen sooner or later') fetching Ophelia from Islington police station after she had been arrested for driving Judith's Peugeot while drunk.

Jomier thinks Judith's difficulties with her two children are trivial compared to his anxiety about Louisa. He tells Judith that his daughter is apparently growing weaker and thinner and the specialists in Buenos Aires are at a loss. Judith listens. She sympathises. Her tone of voice becomes solicitous and feminine but Jomier can see that it requires an effort for her to show an interest in the suffering of someone she does not know. She feels for Jomier, her lover, not this piece of baggage from his past. She says: 'poor you', not 'poor Louisa'. She wonders if Louisa's illness may not be caused by eating too much meat. She tells Jomier that the per capita consumption of beef in Argentina is more than *three times* that of Britain – an absurdly extravagant use of potentially arable land but also, because of the need to cultivate soybeans to feed the cattle, the cause of deforestation which, together with the flatulence of so many animals, is a major contribution to global warming; and the eating of so much meat is a major cause of colon cancer and, no doubt, fatal diseases such as mad cow disease which they cover up to protect their exports. 'Has she been tested for Creutzfeldt–Jakob's disease?' Judith asks Jomier.

'I'm sure,' says Jomier. 'Anyway, the problem is with her blood, not her brain.'

A pause in the conversation as they await the bill. Then Judith says: 'I'd like to meet the Richards.'

'You'd hate them.'

'You seem to have enjoyed yourself at their dinner party.'

'Perhaps, but it's not your sort of thing.'

'You shouldn't presume that you will *always* know what is my sort of thing. And if Mary Richards is the daughter of Lord Atterton, then she must be some kind of cousin.'

'Granddaughter,' says Jomier.

'A cousin, then, two or three times removed.'

Jomier is aware that the egalitarianism that is bundled with Judith's liberal beliefs has not done away with a measure of self-identification with England's upper class. She concedes that her views are not those of the Richards' but feels that there will be a deeper affinity because of the Atterton connection. Jomier pays the bill; he waves away Judith's offer to split it, but it is clear that this gesture of mini-munificence is not sufficient to change her worsening mood. Judith is starting to think that Jomier does not want to introduce her to the Richards; that he will somehow be embarrassed by her despite her bona fide credentials as a cousin of Mary albeit two or three times removed. Is it her looks? Her age? Her views on capital punishment or global warming? Jomier knows that these thoughts are passing through her head but dare not nip them in the bud

by admitting the true reason behind his reluctance to introduce Judith to the Richards – viz. that, if he becomes half
of a couple rather than a single man, Mary Richards will
cross him off her list.

They return to Judith's house in Wandsworth. They make
love but their hearts are not in it. A mental estrangement
detaches them from the action of their bodies. Judith is
thinking that Jomier's reluctance to introduce her to his
grand friends the Richards means that at some level he is
ashamed of her. Jomier is thinking that Judith may not
only destabilise his finances but will also deny him any
independence. They nuzzle and kiss before turning out the
light but both are acting; they fall asleep thinking treason-
ous thoughts.

The thoughts persist at breakfast – for Judith muesli
and herbal tea, for Jomier coffee, a poached egg on wholemeal toast and Waitrose honey-roast ham. They unpack
the *Observer*. Jomier reads the news, Judith a feature on
binge-drinking by young women. 'What am I to do about
Ophelia?'

Jomier looks up. He does not want to think about
Ophelia: he wants to return to what he is reading about the
impending recession. 'There's probably not that much you
*can* do. What's done is done.'

'What do you mean – what's done is done?'

'You can't un-divorce. You can't reconstitute a happy
home.'

'You think it's that? My fault, in fact . . .'

Jomier shrugs. 'Not your fault as such but it seems likely
that the divorce is the cause; the attempt to anaesthetise her
unhappiness with alcohol the effect.'

'But *you* divorced and your children aren't alcoholics.'

'Or dropouts. No. Clearly behaviourism is not an exact science. And Tilly . . .' Jomier's voice tails off.

'Tilly what?'

'Well, once she married Max, she did provide them with a stable home.'

'And I did not?'

Jomier shrugs again. 'I don't know. Perhaps if you had stuck with Alfredo or Giles or whoever . . .' He waves his hand as if the list is too long to be remembered. 'It must be disturbing for a child not knowing who she is going to find in bed with her mother when she gets up in the morning.'

Judith stands. She goes to the window of her kitchen. 'I've just had bad luck, that's all.' Jomier suspects that she is crying.

'I'm sorry,' he says. 'I'm not saying that you're to blame, merely that causes have effects.'

'I'm sure they fucking do,' says Judith, 'and no doubt you were the cause of Louisa choosing to live as far from her fucking father as she could.'

'Quite possibly,' says Jomier, looking back at the paper.

'And now she's dying from mad cow disease from eating all that meat!'

Jomier does not answer.

'Which she wouldn't have eaten if she hadn't gone to live in Argentina, and she wouldn't have gone to Argentina if she hadn't had such a cold, calculating, stingy, snobbish, heartless father! Cause: you! Effect: the death of your daughter!'

Jomier puts down the *Observer*. He can see Judith's shaking shoulders. He can hear her sobs. Should he cross the room to comfort her? Or should he turn on his heel, leave the house and return to Hammersmith? Turning on his heel and leaving the house is not really an option because he is still wearing pyjamas and a dressing gown. His clothes are upstairs in Judith's bedroom; his shaving kit and toothbrush are in Judith's bathroom. If he had dressed before breakfast, he could have written off his pyjamas and shaving kit: with what he would save on the Indians and Viagra, he could buy new silk pyjamas, a gold-plated razor and an ivory-handled pure badger-bristle shaving brush. Jomier thinks these thoughts but he does not act on them. He is not a cold, calculating, stingy, snobbish, heartless brute. Louisa did not go to live in Argentina to get away from her father but because she fell in love with Jimmy. Nor does Louisa have mad cow disease. She is not dying. Jomier is so confident of all this that he is able to stand and cross the kitchen to Judith — embrace her, comfort her, trade apologies, make up.

## 25

LOUISA IS DYING. It is clear to Jomier when he sees his daughter appear through the arrivals portal at Heathrow's Terminal 3. She is in a wheelchair pushed by an employee of the British Airports Authority while Jimmy follows with their luggage on a trolley. There is no flesh on her face. The skin is sallow and loose; the eyes huge. She sees her father and gives a tired smile. Jomier steps forward. They embrace. Two skeletal arms come up to enfold him. Jomier scents decay. He stands and greets Jimmy: a bear hug but no clap on the back. Jimmy says: 'Here we are.' He glances obliquely at Jomier. Jomier avoids meeting his eyes. He does not want Jimmy to see reflected in his expression his shock at Louisa's pitiful condition.

Jomier takes control of the wheelchair from the British Airports Authority employee and leads the way towards the lifts that will take them out of arrivals to the Terminal 3 car park. The first lift takes them to a sloping Bridge of Sighs. Those in the contraflow glance at Louisa and then look away. Jomier wishes his load were heavier. They reach Level 1 where Jomier waits behind excited new arrivals from the Indian subcontinent to pay the car-park charge at the machine. Louisa waits with Jimmy. Jomier reaches the head of the queue. He puts in the ticket, then his debit card, punches in his PIN, then retrieves his now magnetically validated ticket and, after pushing the requisite button, a receipt. They then take a second lift to Level 2 and cross the concrete to the Golf. Jimmy wants to put Louisa in the front of the car but she insists on sitting in the back beside the stacked suitcases; the collapsed wheelchair takes up most of the space in the boot.

They drive into London. 'It so good to see you, Dad. I just wish the circumstances weren't so . . . tiresome.'

Jomier asks after his grandchildren.

'Oh, they're fine.' Louisa begins to give some detail but the effort appears to exhaust her. Her voice tails off. Jimmy finishes for her – a brief résumé of academic progress and sporting achievements. Then: 'Do you know this Professor Adams?'

Jomier shakes his head.

'You must google him,' says Jimmy. 'He's supposed to be the best.'

'He's at St Chad's,' says Louisa quietly. 'Professor Cochella, the specialist in Argentina, studied under him. He says that if anyone can find out what's wrong with me, it's him.'

'He takes private patients?' asks Jomier.

'A few. He's still friendly with Cochella. And it seems that I'm a challenge.'

They reach the Hampton Clinic. Louisa checks in. Jomier and Jimmy accompany her to her room. The nurses are smiling and polite. They ask Jomier and Jimmy if they would like a cup of tea while they wait for Louisa to change and settle into her bed. Both accept the offer. Tea and biscuits are brought on a tray. Jimmy takes this treatment for granted: he is used to travelling club class. Jomier, used to Ryanair and the National Health, feels a grumbling disgust. Why does courtesy and politeness only come with the upgrade?

How would these selfsame nurses treat them if they were poor?

Jomier and Jimmy are readmitted to Louisa's room. Her pretty blue nightdress reveals more of her wasted body. Jomier dares not meet her eyes for fear that she will see the anguish in his eyes. They sit and chat. 'I hear you've got a girlfriend?' says Louisa: 'I hope you'll introduce me.'

Jomier does not want to think of Judith. 'Not really,' he says.

'Not really – you won't introduce me? Or not really a girlfriend?'

Jomier is happy to be teased. He looks into his daughter's laughing eyes. 'I'll certainly introduce you when you're better.'

'You think meeting her might finish me off?'

Jomier smiles. 'Henry and Sandra survived it.'

'They say she's very nice.'

Jomier prepares to leave: Jimmy will stay. Jomier will deliver Jimmy's luggage to the Stafford Hotel. He will come and see Louisa again the next morning. He leans over to kiss his daughter, embracing her lightly for fear of breaking her bones. 'I'll see you tomorrow.'

'Yes. And, Dad . . .'

He turns, holding the open door.

'Pray for me, will you?'

'Of course.'

Jomier returns to his house in Hammersmith. It is growing dark but he does not close the curtains in his living room or switch on the lights. He sits in an armchair in the gloom, staring out of the bay window into the street. A car passes. The click-clack of a woman's high heels on the pavement. The clunk of scaffolding being loaded onto a lorry. The sounds made by people with something to do. Jomier has nothing to do. Or nothing he feels like doing. His journal? Copy out the past? Enter the present? 'Met Jimmy and Louisa at Heathrow. Louisa looks like death.' Would words detach Jomier from his anguish? Would they distance him from his suffering? Is that what keeping a journal has always been about – keeping his feelings at arm's length by writing as if they were felt by someone else? Is that the function of all writing – processing the raw material of human agony into digestible entertainment for airline passengers and reading groups?

Jomier looks with loathing at the carefully catalogued books on his shelves. There is not one that has prepared him for the sight of his dying daughter. He looks at his stacks of CDs. What music could he play that would not disgust him with its manipulation of his emotions – soothing what cannot be soothed, calming what cannot be calmed, healing what cannot be healed? And there, facing him in the gloom, is the black rectangular screen of his television – the open window that has let in all the sham, pretence, denial, distraction and falsity of the world.

Jomier falls asleep. When he wakes only the orange light from the street lamps illuminates the room. He stands, switches on the lights, closes the curtains. He goes to the kitchen. He looks in his fridge to see what he might cook for his supper. There is some lean mince. A bolognese sauce. He goes up the stairs to his study. The red light blinks on his answering machine. Jomier listens to the first and only message. It is from Judith. Her voice is gentle, appeasing. Jomier listens with a cold, clenched heart. How can you forgive someone for delivering so triumphantly your daughter's sentence of death?

Jomier switches on his computer. He checks his emails. The ads for Viagra and Cialis skip into his spam folder. The only message is from Judith. 'i am sorry for what i said about louisa it was cruel i love you xxx judith'. Jomier deletes the message. He goes to Google and types in 'rare blood diseases'. He studies the websites. The possibilities seem infinite. No wonder Professor Cochella threw in the sponge and passed the buck to his mentor, Professor Adams of St Chad's. But is it too late? 'Patients with any blood cancer,' he reads, 'that occurs relatively infrequently may have difficulty finding information about where and from whom to obtain the best treatment. All patients with cancer should seek care from a physician or team experienced in treating his or her disease, and this is especially important for patients with rare blood cancers, because these diseases may be difficult to diagnose – but are sometimes easily treated if diagnosed correctly.' This from the Memorial Sloan-Kettering Cancer Center in New York. *Easily treated if diagnosed correctly.* Why is not Louisa in the US where competition and financial incentives keep doctors on their toes? Why has she come from chaotic, incompetent Argentinian health care to chaotic, incompetent British health care? Why has she been referred by the posturing macho hairy-chested nurse-bonking Professor Cochella to the self-important time-serving golf-playing Professor Adams?

Is it because it is cheaper? Has the credit crunch hit the Miller de Ramirez family trusts? Has the price of beef and soya fallen through the floor? Jomier will pay. He will tell Jimmy the next day that he will liquefy his pension funds and pay for Louisa to go to the US where high-powered physicians will be enticed by thoughts of silver-grey Mercedes and condos in Palm Beach to find out what is wrong with Louisa and come up with a cure. He will tell him that he should have no faith in British consultants because they are exempt from the universal law of the stick and the carrot; they are paid their fat salaries by the state whether they cure their patients or not. The smiles at the Hampton Clinic are smiles of derision at the gullible health tourists who are so easily parted from their money.

Jomier goes down to his kitchen. He starts to chop an onion for a bolognese sauce. The tang makes his eyes water; it is as if he is weeping, and all at once he is weeping. He sits on a stool, his shoulders shaking, tears wetting his cheeks. When do grown men cry? The death of a father. The death of a mother. The collapse of a marriage. And now this.

Jomier abandons the bolognese. He eats half a cheese sandwich, then goes through to his living room to watch television. He switches it on and flicks through the channels. Everything is intolerable. He switches it off. He goes upstairs. He takes a shower, changes into his pyjamas and goes to bed. It is not yet ten at night. He cannot sleep. The earlier nap in the armchair has spiked his fatigue: angry thoughts continue to ricochet in his mind. The elation he had felt earlier at the thought of sending Louisa to the US has collapsed. Even doctors enticed by the carrot of silver-grey Mercedes and condos in Palm Beach cannot cure the incurable; they cannot thwart fate.

Can fate ever be thwarted? 'Pray for me.' Louisa believes so. Louisa believes that there is a deity, a He Who Is who talked to Moses from a burning bush and became *Homo sapiens* as Jesus of Nazareth. She believes that he thwarted fate. That he cured lepers, brought Lazarus back to life and himself rose from the dead. She believes that he is God and could, if he so chose, do something for Louisa. But why should he? Why, out of the many millions who are suffering and dying, should he help Louisa? Because she believes in him? Because she is a Catholic? Don't Catholics suffer? Don't Catholics die?

Jomier gets out of bed and goes to his study in his pyjamas. He switches on his computer. He googles God. There are 475 million hits. He googles Jesus. 183 million hits. Better to flick through the Bible that sits among his reference books on the shelf next to his desk – the prize for RE at school, the sourcebook for his arguments with Theo. He reads, looking for the formula that induces God to do humans a good turn. He sees no hope of a favour from the pitiless despot of the Old Testament – the Hebrew Bible. None, certainly, if one is not a Jew. And Jesus – the protagonist of the New Testament? When the Jews turn up their noses at what he has to offer, he is prepared to give it to the Gentile dogs. But he is quite as demanding as his father who spoke to Moses from the burning bush. Repent, or else. Believe, or else. Love, or else. Forgive, or else. Stick up for me and I'll stick up for you. Nothing is for nothing. Even God expects a quid pro quo.

Fair enough. Jomier is a lawyer. He knows about negotiations. He knows how to enter a plea. He can make deals. If God will save Louisa, he will have his quid pro quo. Jomier will love, believe, repent and forgive. He will forgive the civil servants in the Lord Chancellor's office who turned down his application to become a QC. He will forgive Judith for what she said about Louisa. He will forgive Max for stealing Tilly. He will forgive Tilly for going off with Max.

# 26

JOMIER GOES TO bed at four in the morning. He sleeps through the alarm set for eight and is woken by the telephone at ten past nine. It is Jimmy. Louisa is being moved to Chad's later that morning. Perhaps Jomier would be able to visit her that afternoon?

Jomier gets dressed and goes down to the kitchen. He is hungry after eating so little the night before. He eats his usual weekday breakfast of orange juice, coffee, muesli, wholemeal toast. He reads *The Times*. He has recovered his appetite. He has recovered his interest in the outside world. He ascribes this to the deal he struck in the early hours of the morning. He now sees that there is some point to prayer. Whether or not one believes in a God, let alone a God who intervenes in the lives of human beings, praying is a way of doing something when nothing else can be done. He is also pleased that, should Louisa ask whether he has prayed for her as she requested, he will be able to tell the truth. Not only has he prayed to God, he has negotiated with him – like Abraham at Sodom, or a character in a novel by G. K. Chesterton or Graham Greene.

Step one in the quid pro quo. He goes to his study and calls Judith. He would prefer to send her an email but feels that voice-to-voice contact is necessary if forgiveness is to be 100 per cent. Jesus of Nazareth makes it quite clear: formulaic forgiveness is not enough. There can be no conditions or caveats or restrictive clauses. Must I forgive my brother seven times? asks Peter. No, replies Jesus. Seventy-seven times. And it has to be 'from the heart'.

Judith answers with a little cry – of joy or surprise or relief. Jomier apologises for not ringing before. He tells Judith that Louisa is gravely ill and possibly dying, but not from Creutzfeldt–Jakob's disease. She has a rare blood disorder that has flummoxed the doctors in Buenos Aires. She is now in the hands of a Professor Adams at Chad's.

Jomier can hear sniffing: Judith is sobbing. 'I am so sorry for what I said. I really . . . it just came out.'

'Please don't feel sorry. I said some beastly things about Ophelia. We were both on edge because of our daughters.' Jomier is delighted with the sincerity and warmth in his tone of voice.

'Do you still love me?' she sniffs.

'Of course I still love you,' he says. No need to pause to ask himself whether Jomier means what he says: loving everyone is part of the deal.

Jomier's satnav guides him across London to Chad's Hospital. It takes twenty minutes to find somewhere to park. He goes to reception and is directed to the private wing. A melancholy black woman with a bottom larger than Ruth's cleans the linoleum floors of the corridors with slow token swipes of her mop. Louisa has a room in a gloomy 1960s block. Jimmy is with her. She looks better.

'You look better,' says Jomier as he kisses her.

'I've had a blood transfusion,' says Louisa. 'It won't last.'

Jimmy offers Jomier the one chair and sits on the end of Louisa's bed.

'I brought you some chocolate,' says Jomier. He hands her a small box of Bendicks Bittermints.

Louisa takes it and places it on her bedside table next to a flamboyant bunch of lilies and cellophane sackful of Maison Blanc chocolate truffles. 'I love Bittermints,' she says to Jomier and then, following his glance to the bunch of flowers: 'They're from Mum. A little over the top, don't you think?'

Jimmy takes advantage of Jomier's presence to run some errands. 'Poor Jimmy,' says Louisa. 'He's always been so protective. He finds it hard now that there's nothing more he can do.'

'But pray.'

Louisa laughs. 'Did you say pay or pray?'

'Pray.'

'He subcontracts that to his mother and the children. They've been praying novenas to Our Lady of Guadalupe for months.'

'And it hasn't worked?'

'Not yet.'

'Perhaps Doña Adelina's prayers aren't sincere.'

'I think they are. She's very family-minded.'

'Well, I prayed too,' says Jomier.

'Thanks. It can't have been easy.'

'Because I don't believe?'

'Do you?'

'No. But you can pray hypothetically. What if, outside the space–time continuum, there is a God? What if he hears prayers? What if he sometimes answers prayers?'

'I'm sure a hypothetical prayer is as good as any other,' says Louisa. 'Perhaps better.'

'I was reading the New Testament last night. Jesus says that his yoke is easy and his burden light, but then makes demands that are hard.'

'What kind of demands?'

'Repentance. Faith. Love. Forgiveness. It's hard simply to decide to feel sorry and believe and love and forgive. Either you do or you don't.'

Louisa frowns. 'Surely everyone believes in something, and loves someone and feels sorry for something.'

'Perhaps.'

'Can't one build on that? If you know in your heart that some things are right and others wrong, that means you believe in good and evil. And if you love someone other than yourself . . .'

Jomier takes her hand. 'I love someone much more than myself.'

'There, you see. And you love Henry and Sam and Ned, and my children, and perhaps Sandra up to a point, and your new friend Judith . . .'

'Up to a point.'

'But it means that you know what it is to love.'

'But loving you and Henry and Sam and Ned is instinctive. I love you because you are my children and grandchildren.'

'Would you stop loving us if we weren't?'

'I can't imagine not loving you.'

'There you are.'

She lifts herself up in bed, and leans back on the pillows. 'If you go step by step . . . If you see another little boy like Ned and think how much he is loved by his grandfather, and the little boy's mother, and think how much she is loved by her son and her husband; and there's the young man straightening his tie before going to an interview for his first job and it might be Henry fifteen years ago, or the girl at Heathrow setting off on her gap-year journey round the world which might have been me, then you begin to see how you can love others simply because they are fellow

244

human beings, who love and suffer and get things wrong
. . .' Her voice tails off.

'Like me and your mother?'

'And others. You aren't the only ones.'

Both are silent. Then Louisa says: 'I asked Father Xavier . . .'

'Who is Father Xavier?'

'He's a Jesuit in BA. A nice man, a little pleased with
himself, but nice all the same . . . He was talking about
the different kinds of love in ancient Greece – *eros*, the
sexual love of a man and a woman; *agape*, a general love of
humanity; and *philia*, the love of friends; and how within
a marriage *eros* should develop into *agape* and if possible
*philia*. So I asked him whether the Greeks had a word for
love of parents and children and he said there was but it
was used less which seems strange because when I think
about dying I realise that I've been so lucky to have loved
and been loved by you and Mum and Henry and all the
children, and of course Jimmy; and though I would like to
have lived longer, to see the children grow up, I really can't
complain because the life I've had has been so happy.'

Louisa seems tired. Jomier prepares to leave.

'Come tomorrow, will you?'

'Of course.'

'Mum tends to come in the morning.'

'I'll come in the afternoon.'

'Jimmy's gone to stay with Mum. I hope you don't mind.'

'Of course I don't mind.'

'I couldn't bear to think of him alone in a hotel, and
Mum's got plenty of room.'

Jomier leaves St Chad's troubled by scruples. Did he say he
would come in the afternoon because he wished to avoid

seeing Tilly? Or was it simply to make it more agreeable for Louisa by spreading the visits out over the day? Louisa assumes that he remains on bad terms with her mother. She is afraid that he might mind that Jimmy is staying with Tilly and Max in Phillimore Gardens. She tells him how to avoid running into her at Chad's. This assumption would have been correct the day before but now Jomier is constrained by the terms of his agreement with He Who Might Be. He must forgive.

When he gets home he telephones Tilly. She says: 'It's so awful.' Then: 'What do you think?'

'I think we should all meet.'

'Of course.'

'Can I drop by for a drink?'

'When?'

'This evening.'

'Of course, though Max –'

'Max should be there too. And Henry. I'll call him.'

Henry will visit Louisa in Chad's on his way home from work and then come on to his mother's house in Phillimore Gardens. Jomier drives there from Hammersmith. He climbs the steps and rings the doorbell. It is the first time he has been to the home of his ex-wife. She opens the door. Tilly's face is drawn. Her expression is puzzled. Jomier enters the hall tiled with buffed Carrara marble.

'Come in,' says Tilly. She leads him into the drawing room – beige Wilton carpet, huge Conran sofas, bright halogen downlights, heavy marble mantel, spotlit modern paintings on the wall. 'Max isn't back yet.' She turns with a ready-to-be-annoyed-if-you-think-it's-all-vulgar look on her face.

'Does he have a view about Louisa?' asks Jomier.

'He says Adams is the best man in his field.'

'He doesn't think she should go to America?'

'He hasn't said so.'

'And you?'

'I don't know. I think Jimmy's looked into it all.'

They sit on the sofas. Tilly is dressed in a dark blue skirt and pale grey cashmere cardigan that clings to her breasts – the cantaloupes that were once Jomier's and are now available to be fondled by Max. Her elegant legs are crossed: only the lines on her face and the loose skin on her neck mark the passing of time. She looks younger than her dying daughter.

'Would you like some wine?' Tilly stands and goes to a sideboard where an open bottle stands in a plastic cooler – placed there by a hidden Filipina hand. 'Or something else? There's vodka or rum. You used to like rum and tonic.'

'A glass of wine would be fine.'

Tilly fills a glass and brings it to Jomier together with a small bowl filled with parsnip crisps. She seems uneasy. Uncomfortable. Even afraid. Why is he there? What is he up to? Jomier says: 'It would be good for Louisa if she felt that we are now friends.'

Tilly shrugs as if to say 'you're the one who's been unfriendly' but out comes: 'Of course.'

'And it will be much easier for Jimmy, particularly if he's staying with you.'

'I agree.'

Tilly has fetched herself a glass of wine. She returns to her place on the second of the plush Conran sofas. She looks across at Jomier. 'Do you think she's dying?'

'If they can make the diagnosis,' says Jomier, 'I'm sure they'll come up with a cure.'

Tilly sniffs. 'It's all so awful. I can't bear to look at her. She's wasting away.'

Jomier wants to move to the other sofa and comfort Tilly. He cannot manage it. He cannot bring himself to take hold of her body. Will he have to? Is that what it means to forgive from the heart? 'We mustn't despair,' he says.

'No.' She sobs. 'But it's hard to feel optimistic. I mean, well . . . Max says that what with the Internet and email most medical knowledge is pretty universal so it's unlikely that Adams will come up with something that wasn't thought of by the Argentinian doctors.'

'It's not impossible,' says Jomier. 'We mustn't give up hope.'

Enter Max. Jomier has hardly seen him since the divorce. His hair has receded and what is left is mostly grey. He is not fat but his body has thickened – his neck, his jowls, his girth. Jomier makes as if to stand.

'Don't get up,' says Max. 'Have you got a drink?'

Jomier holds up his glass of wine. Max crosses to fill a glass for himself. A moment later the doorbell rings. Tilly goes from the drawing room into the hall. Jomier is alone in the room with Max. He feels nothing. No anger. No resentment. All passion is spent.

'I am so sorry about Louisa,' says Max.

'It's good of you to have Jimmy,' says Jomier.

Max shrugs. 'It's the least we could do.'

Tilly comes back into the drawing room with Henry and Jimmy. Henry waves to Max, then comes to embrace his father. He has come with Jimmy from the hospital. 'I really hope they know what they are doing. Chad's is such a grim place.' They are given drinks. They discuss the case. Occasionally Jomier intercepts uncertain glances aimed at him. What is going on? Why is he here? What's with this new friendliness with Tilly and Max? Time passes. There is conversational slippage: Max, Henry and Jimmy talk about the credit crunch. Henry says with a forced bravado that in a month he may be out of a job. Max talks to Jimmy about soya futures. Jomier is left with Tilly but can think of nothing to say. He gets to his feet. 'Let's meet at the hospital tomorrow,' he says to Tilly and Jimmy, 'and try to see Professor Adams.' They both agree.

## 27

THE NEXT MORNING Jomier travels to Chad's by public transport: he takes the 94 bus to Holland Park, then the Underground to St Paul's. There is a delay on the Central Line. Tilly and Jimmy are already with Louisa when he arrives. Jomier kisses his daughter. She smiles – a feeble smile: the effects of yesterday's transfusion are beginning to wear off. 'You're very honoured,' she says. 'The great Professor Adams would like to see you. You and Mum.' She rings a bell. A nurse appears. 'My father's here,' says Louisa.

'I'll let them know,' says the nurse.

Tilly sits on the chair; Jimmy leans against the window-sill; Jomier sits on the edge of Louisa's bed. Louisa's huge eyes look from her father to her mother, then her mother to her father: she is content that they are there. Jomier asks if Professor Adams has made any progress.

'He said it's like looking for a needle in a haystack,' says Louisa.

'That's not encouraging,' says Jomier.

'It's a horrible thing to say,' says Tilly.

'Better no bullshit,' says Jimmy.

'Yes,' says Louisa, 'it's better to know where we stand.'

A junior doctor comes to fetch Tilly and Jomier. He escorts them along corridors, up two storeys in a lift, along more corridors, then down some stairs. As they walk he makes some cursory remarks about the rebuilding programme: they hope the refurbishment will be completed by 2011.

They wait in the antechamber to Professor Adams's office. Jomier feels his *odium medicinae* awakening within him: the conceit and complacency of these despotic consultants with their courts of houri nurses and fawning registrars when the chances of a cure from cancer in Britain are the worst in Western Europe. Jomier reins in his resentment: he has undertaken to forgive – even the time-serving incompetence of Britain's NHS. Nor would it be politic to betray feelings to Professor Adams which might distract him from his search for the needle in the haystack.

They are shown in to Professor Adams's office. It dates from the 1960s: one wall is of plate glass giving a view over east London, the others of unplastered brick. Books and papers are stacked on bracket shelving. On the walls – framed certificates, photographs of grinning children, one a girl on a pony, another of Adams playing golf. He is a medium-sized middle-aged Englishman – lean, brisk, fit. He glances at Jomier and Tilly as if assessing their status: should he stand or should he stay seated? He seems to recall that Louisa is a private patient and so gets to his feet. He comes out from behind his desk, shakes them by the hand, then points towards a hard square-armed sofa set against the wall. He himself sits down on a square-armed armchair. 'Would you like some coffee?' Both decline his offer. 'No, quite right. It's from a machine.'

Adams has brought a folder from his desk. He opens it and glances down at the papers. 'As you know, Professor Cochella in Buenos Aires has referred your daughter to me because, while it is clear that she is suffering from a blood disorder, he has been unable to identify the precise type.

The normal process of blood cell growth breaks down – we call this haematopoiesis. Sometimes there is an overproduction of a specific type of blood cell in the bone marrow or they produce abnormal cells that malfunction. There are also uncommon lymphoproliferative disorders, myeloproliferative disorders and other uncommon variations – some of them hereditary. If we can identify the type, then we can come up with a treatment but it isn't straightforward. What I want to confirm with you is that, so far as you know, there is no history on either side of the family of blood disorders of this kind – no hereditary nonspherocytic haemolytic anaemia, or spherocyctic anaemia, no hereditary angioedema, hereditary haemorrhagic telangiectasia ...' He hands an A4 sheet of paper to Jomier and another to Tilly. 'If there have been deaths in the family you may not have been told the cause, but it is worth just looking down the list to see if anything rings a bell.'

Jomier takes up the piece of paper – the haystack in which the needle is hidden – and runs his eye down the list. Aase syndrome, Blackfan Diamond anaemia, Fanconi's anaemia, Frycht's anaemia, haemolytic – warm antibody anaemia, hereditary nonspherocytic haemolytic anaemia, hereditary spherocytic haemolytic anaemia, megaloblastic anaemia, hereditary angioedema, antithrombin III deficiency, cor triatriatum, idiopathic oedema, endocardial fibroelastosis (EFE), factor XIII deficiency, congenital heart block, haemangioma thrombocytopenia syndrome, hereditary haemorrhagic telangiectasia, hypoplastic left heart syndrome, hereditary lymphoedema, Maffucci syndrome, perniosis, acquired pure red cell aplasia, pyruvate kinase deficiency, thalassaemia minor and Waldenstrom's macroglobulinaemia.

'What is Frycht's anaemia?' he asks Professor Adams.

'We've excluded that,' says Adams. 'Your daughter has no Austrian blood. You only find Frycht's anaemia in Austrians – in fact, in one Austrian family, the von Frychts.'

Jomier looks at Tilly. The skin of her cheeks is suddenly flushed. She does not raise her eyes from the piece of paper she holds in her hand.

'Is this wrong?' asks Adams. 'Do either of you have Austrian blood?'

Tilly looks up and glances sideways at Jomier with an expression of terror. 'No . . . no, I don't think so . . . I'm sure I don't.'

Jomier turns back to Adams. 'My grandmother, Elise Jomier, had a long affair with a man called Ferdinand von Frycht. It is quite possible, even likely, that he was the natural father of my father.'

Adams is excited. 'That is certainly something worth pursuing. There have been only two or three cases of Frycht's anaemia this century, but it does crop up every now and sometimes skips several generations.'

'And if it should turn out,' asks Jomier, 'that Louisa *is* suffering from Frycht's anaemia, can anything be done?'

'Five years ago,' says Adams, 'I would have said no, but now, yes. Hasemann in Vienna came up with a cure. It helped win him the Nobel Prize.'

Jomier and Tilly walk down stairs, into lifts and along corridors to the private wing of Chad's Hospital. Tilly is weeping: she chokes and says in a stuttering whisper, 'I . . . I . . . it was just something . . . in a bubble . . . nothing to do with *us*. It just happened . . . I mean, I thought, she *could* have been yours.'

Jomier says nothing. They walk along the corridor in silence. He hides the thoughts going through his head from

Tilly. He hides the thoughts going through his head from himself. All thoughts but one. Finally he says: 'She's going to live.'

'Yes.'

They turn a corner. Another corridor. More silence. Then, without looking at his former wife, Jomier says: 'Did I ever tell you about my grandmother's affair with Ferdy von Frycht?'

Tilly sniffs. 'No. No, I don't think so.'

'A skeleton in the cupboard.'

'Yes.'

'Louisa will be amused,' says Jomier.

'Yes.'

'And Henry? What do you think? A little embarrassed, perhaps, but not ill-pleased. Some blue blood in his veins on his father's side.'

# 28

IT IS AUTUMN. Jomier takes the 94 bus to Shepherd's Bush. The refurbished Underground station is now open – a modernist rectangle of glass and slate. Behind it the new Westfield shopping centre sits like a gigantic spaceship from *E.T.* or *The War of the Worlds*.

Jomier gets off the bus and joins the throng going into the spaceship to trade with the Mammonites from Mars. He is looking for a gift to give to Judith on her birthday. They are no longer lovers. Their affair ended amicably in the summer. Too much baggage. Too set in their ways. But they remain good friends. No more Kama Sutra sex; no more Viagra; but movies, an Indian every now and then, and dinner together on their birthdays.

Jomier goes into Tiffany's and spends £355 on a flower necklace in 14-karat yellow gold. To Jomier it looks like something out of a Christmas cracker but he has taken advice from his daughter-in-law Sandra and she has assured him that it will be appreciated for what it is if it comes gift-wrapped in a Tiffany box.

Jomier leaves Tiffany's and goes deeper into the marble-floored mall to Micro Anvika where he buys a Sony 16 GB memory stick. He returns home with his purchases. He puts the gift-wrapped Tiffany box on his chest of drawers ready for his date with Judith and takes the memory stick into his study. He removes the packaging, then plugs it into the USB hub.

Jomier has completed his task of transcribing his journals on to his hard disk. The past has now caught up with the present. He drags files from different folders from his hard disk C to the new removable disk F. In a couple of minutes his entire archive – his journals, the catalogue of his books, his works of art, his correspondence – are copied and stored. Geoffrey Jomier is now digitalised. With a few strokes on his keyboard he can look back on any period of his life. He does not do so. He does not want to look back. He does not want to remember Tilly returning flushed and sweaty after supposedly playing tennis on a Saturday morning with Marco and Marco's friends. He does not want to ask himself where they had had sex. Or for how long it had gone on.

Jomier might have put these questions to Tilly but he has not. There would be anger in his tone of voice. Anger, rancour, vengeful feelings – all are forbidden under the terms of his contract with God. He lets Tilly believe that he has decided not to make a fuss about the past. To draw a line. To move on. Louisa's paternity is their secret: his grandmother's lover, Ferdy von Frycht, is now part of Jomier family lore. Jomier is affable towards Tilly when he sees her at their grandchildren's birthday parties. He has been to some of Max and Tilly's soirées – the invaluable unattached man. He does not enjoy these encounters. He is angry with Tilly and angry with God. He feels he has been cheated by both. Could he have done a better deal with the Devil? Why had no Mephistopheles come forward with a counter-offer? 'I will cure Louisa if you sell me your soul.' His yoke would surely have been lighter, his burden easier to carry. There would be no need to believe. No need to repent. No need to forgive. No need to love.

If Jomier does not believe, why not renege on the contract? Even if he did believe, could he not argue that God has failed to keep to his side of the bargain? He was to cure Jomier's daughter, not Marco's. Why not go on hating and wallow in rancour? Because, even though he now knows that Louisa is not his daughter, Jomier does not want her to die. Reason may tell him that her cure is not the result of his prayer; that the diagnosis of Frycht's anaemia cannot have had anything whatsoever to do with the intervention of a First Cause from outside the space–time continuum. But Jomier has become superstitious. What if, as Pascal postulated, there are truths inaccessible to reason known only to the heart? Jomier does not yet believe or forgive or repent but he loves. He loves his son, his daughter-in-law and his grandchildren. He loves the daughter who is not his daughter. She is back in Argentina: Skype and emailed photos have shown that she has regained her colour and put on weight. He will go there for Christmas. Professor Adams and Professor Cochella are at one in saying that her cure is 99 per cent assured. But a relapse is not altogether impossible. There remains that 1 per cent. Jomier dares not take the risk of double-crossing God.

It is growing dark. Jomier has three hours before leaving to meet Judith at the Café Anglais. He goes down to his kitchen, makes a mug of tea, carries it through to his living room, and sits down on the sofa to watch *Farewell, My Lovely* which he recorded the night before.

A NOTE ON THE TYPE

Linotype Garamond Three – based on seventeenth-century copies of Claude Garamond's types, cut by Jean Jannon. This version was designed for American Type Founders in 1917, by Morris Fuller Benton and Thomas Maitland Cleland and adapted for mechanical composition by Linotype in 1936.